WZMB

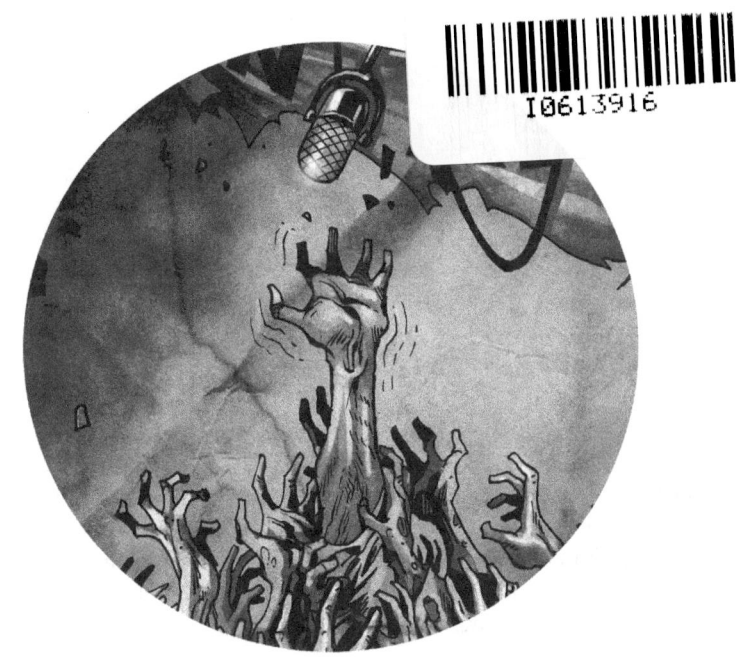

Andre Duza

deadite
press

deadite press

DEADITE PRESS
P.O. BOX 10065
PORTLAND, OR 97296
www.DEADITEPRESS.com

AN ERASERHEAD PRESS COMPANY
www.ERASERHEADPRESS.com

ISBN: 1-62105-172-2

All stories copyright © 2014 Andre Duza

Cover art copyright © 2014 Rudolf Montemayor

Printed in the USA.

To Howard, Robin, Gary, Fred, Ronnie,
Artie, Jackie, Richard & Sal,
the Wack Pack (RIP Eric the Actor),
the guests, the callers...

FEMA

Property of U.S. Department of Homeland Security—Mount Weather Emergency Operations Facility

The following video-clips of the Martin Stone Show have been compiled to serve as a record of the events leading up to the ongoing development of the experimental vaccine known as Lazarus. The clips are presented to MWEOF Personnel in their original format, unedited and uncut. Viewer discretion is advised.

THE MARTIN STONE SHOW

Satellite radio show hosted by controversial American "Shock Jock" Martin Stone. The show features topical news discussion, celebrity gossip, skits, prank phone calls, and game-show style bits usually involving porn stars or members of the show's stable of social misfits known as "The Freaks," along with unusually candid celebrity interviews that have become a staple of the show. Other cast members include: Co-host and news anchor Raven Cordelia Tremble, writer Ted Morrison, producer Larry Del Rossi, and Donnie "The Bodyguard" Lindberg. Originally broadcasted from WXTU in Philadelphia, the drive-time show gained prominence in the late 90s before moving to satellite radio in 2006 as a response to numerous fines for "indecency" by the FCC. The show is filmed for television as of 2001.

WZMB

FRIDAY, SEPTEMBER 6th, 2014
8:47am

THUNDERSTRUCK by AC/DC plays over a black screen…

Male voice (deep and rich with a laid-back demeanor): Yeah! Thun-DAH! YEAH!

FADE IN…

WXTU STUDIOS, BALA CYNWYD, PA

The lighting is dim in Studio A. The color scheme is mostly indigo with hints of red. Soundproof walls emblazoned with the Martin Stone Show Logo. Another logo broadcast from a large, flatscreen mounted on the wall.

Seated in a raised, crescent-shaped booth in the back, Martin Stone (Caucasian, 49) thrashes his air guitar to the music on the tail end of a commercial break. A flat screen monitor and several consoles populate the countertop that wraps around him. A phallic microphone attached to a long, jointed arm reaching off into the unknown, floats in front of his face.

Raven Tremble (African American, 41) and Ted Morrison (Caucasian, 45) occupy two smaller booths on either side of Martin's. Ted nods his head to the music. Raven reviews her notes. A cozy seating area built like the VIP section of a high-end nightclub at the booths' feet. A young professional (Zach Wyatt, Caucasian 32) lounges confidently on the couch waiting for the interview to resume.

Raven shakes her head and smirks at Martin's over-the-top performance.

Raven (an air of pretention in her tone): You should see how ridiculous you look.

Martin: I'm feeling the music, Raven. We need to get these guys back in here.

Donnie Lindberg (Caucasian, 50) enters the room in a hurry.

Donnie (surly, aggressive, breathing heavily): You guys gotta hear this!

Martin: I thought you left.

Donnie: I did. But now I'm back. What's the big deal?

Martin: Shit. Are we back from commercial?

Larry Del Rossi (Caucasian, 42) interrupts via an intercom from his office down the hall.

Larry (nasally, via intercom): Yeah…I told you.

Martin: Well, I didn't hear you.

The music cuts off.

Raven: Me either.

Martin: Thanks to Donnie.

Donnie: What'd I do now?

Martin: You storm out in the middle of a segment. Then you come back in. What's it gonna be; in or out?

Donnie: I'm here aren't I? Besides, I didn't storm out. I got a call on my cell, so I left the studio to answer it.

Raven bursts into laughter.

Raven (laughing): That's even worse.

Martin: No shit, it's worse! You answer your phone in the middle of the show?! Are you fucking mental?! It better've been the fucking President.

Donnie: It was my friend, Loren.

Martin: The crazy burnout?!

Donnie: I feel bad for the guy. He's one of those dudes who's too smart for his own good. He told me he started doing drugs just to quiet all the noise in his head. Anyway, he hasn't been doing so good lately. I'm trying to keep him in line.

Martin (exhales): Mother-*fucker*...Now I'm gonna look like a dick if I keep yelling at you.

Ted (soft-spoken): That's how Donnie gets you.

Martin: Look at that. You woke up Ted.

Donnie: Oh, shut up, Ted.

Ted laughs.

Larry (via intercom): It's always something dire with him. Then you feel bad for being mad at him.

Ted: Right.

Donnie: Oh, Fuck you guys! Larry...with your fuckin' bug eyes, like Igor...

Soundbyte (From *YOUNG FRANKENSTEIN*, Marty Feldman as Igor): Yessss Mah-stah.

Laughter.

Raven: Well, how did you know he called, Donnie? I didn't hear a phone ring.

Donnie: He was in pretty bad shape when we talked this morning. I told him to call me if he needed anything. And my phone was in my pocket...*on vibrate*. It's still in there. See?

Donnie pulls a cell phone from his pocket and shows it to Raven.

Martin: I thought I said no cell phones in the studio?

Larry (via intercom): You did. Numerous times.

As Donnie slides the phone back into his pocket...

Donnie: Why're you trying to instigate things, Larry?

Larry (via intercom): I'm just stating the facts.

Donnie: You're such a fucking brown-noser, Larry.

Larry (via intercom): And you've got the emotional range of a 13-year-old. So, I guess we're even.

Laughter.

Donnie: I bet you thought that was clever.

Larry (via intercom): Actually, I did.

Donnie: Ok brown-noser. How does Martin's ass taste?

Ted (instigates): Ooooo!

Martin: Down boys.

Donnie takes a deep breath and puts on an air of forced calm.

Donnie: My buddy was in trouble, so I was being a good friend by trying to be there for him. I'm sorry I broke the rules. It won't happen again.

Martin: Damn right it won't. I mean...if you knew he might call while you were in here, then why not give your phone to Larry or the guys in the back office until after? Have one-a-*them* take the call if it was an emergency.

Raven: Or he could've just told us. Then he coulda taken the call on the show.

Martin: Good point.

Donnie: Everybody's busy gettin' ready for the Vegas Show. I didn't think you'd want me to bother 'em...or *you* for that matter.

Martin (frustrated): Oh my *GODDD*! Why are you such a pain in my *ASSSS*?!

Raven: So, what did your friend, Loren want?

Donnie: Who, the hell, knows? He was wasted off his ass, as usual. It's impossible to understand him when he's all shit-canned like that.

Martin: Well, what did he say?

Donnie: It didn't make any sense.

Raven: Why don't you let *US* be the judge of that?

Donnie: He's got this stick up his ass about the Illuminati, whatever the fuck that is?

Martin: The Illuminati?

Donnie: Exactly. Like I said, who knows what, the fuck, is going on in that head-a-hiz? He was basically just rambling on and on about how he just witnessed proof of the Illuminati's plan to wipe out the 99-percent. Something about a guy in a suit trying to eat people, and then the bike messenger, and the pretty lady was trying to eat people too, and how the suit and the bike messenger were grown in a lab by the Illuminati because nobody could take as many bullets as they took and keep on coming.

Martin: You're right. It doesn't make sense.

Raven: Wow! He's really far gone, huh?

Donnie: Yeah. It's kinda sad.

Larry (via intercom): That's cool that Donnie's looking out for the guy and all…But don't you think this is really all about turning attention away from his iWingman results? You saw how mad he got just before he stormed out.

Martin: I think you might be right.

Donnie: *WRONG!* You're so stupid, Larry! Why the hell would I come back in here, if that was the case?!

Larry (via intercom): I'm just saying what everybody else is thinking.

Martin: You came back in here because you knew we were gonna pick up where we left off before the break and you meant to sabotage it.

Donnie: That's not true!

Raven: That *does* fit your M.O., Donnie.

Donnie: Oh, shut up, Raven! You were too chicken-shit to do the damn thing. So, you can't talk.

Raven: No. I simply had the sense to know that I'd probably disagree with the results. And I don't feel like wasting the time and energy defending myself against something that I'm not sure I believe in the first place.

Donnie: Whatever! I guess I'm not as smart as you.

Raven: I guess not.

Zach Wyatt: I assure you that the science behind the app is real, Raven.

Raven: Whatever you say.

Martin: I'm sorry, Zach. For those of you just tuning in, we're joined today by Zach Wyatt, inventor of the iWingman Personality Screener App for the iPhone, iPad, and iPad

Mini. The app, which according to Zach, was developed from technology used by FBI Profilers, works by extrapolating a brief personality summary from 30 seconds of recorded video.

Zach: At least 30 seconds…And yes, the technology was used by the FBI. You can check it.

Martin: We'll take your word for it, Zach. So, were you shocked when the app took off as a dating tool? What is it; something like a couple million downloads as of this morning?

Larry (via intercom): I think it's five million.

Zach: That sounds about right.

Martin: Holy shit, man! You must be rolling in dough.

Zach: I'm doing all right.

Martin: That wasn't your original plan though, right? To make it a dating tool?

Zach: We initially developed the app for police officers— which we're still pursuing, by the way. We also had some early interest from Morgan Brand…

Martin: The billionaire weapons developer. Nice…He's from Philly, you know?

Zach: I know. The deal with him eventually fell through, though.

Martin: What, the hell, happened?

Zach: We weren't ready, to be honest. We were in waaay over our heads and he called us on it. Gave us some great advice, though. The fact of the matter is, I might've had some reservations about this whole dating tool thing at first, but a couple hundred-thousand in your pocket has a way of making you come around.

Martin (laughs): I bet it does. So help me understand something. The fact that the conversation has to be recorded without the subject's knowledge in order to get the best results would seem to open the app up to possible lawsuits. No?

Zach: Like I was saying, we do emphasize that you get a person's consent before recording them.

Martin: Well, wouldn't that alter the read-out if the person's aware that they're being recorded?

Zach: There are people who'll give an honest reading even if they're aware, but for the most part people put on an act when they know they're being watched or recorded. Sometimes it's subtle things that you might not pick up on, but the iWingman will, and the resulting reading won't be accurate. The way you do it is, when you get their consent, you give them a timeframe. Say…anytime within the next 24 hours. Then you can record them whenever you want within that timeframe and they don't even need to know.

Martin: Oh. I see.

Zach: With you guys, we just took samples from the show once we knew we were booked to appear.

Martin: Speaking of which…Myself, Larry, Ted, and of course, Donnie have all done the screening. Raven has declined for her own personal reasons.

Raven laughs.

Ted (mocks in stuffy British accent): I…won't…do-it!

Raven (laughing): Screw you, Ted.

Martin: Larry and Ted came out pretty much unscathed…

Larry (via intercom): It said I was a predictable bore.

Ted: Well, mine said I was socially awkward, and an introvert.

Larry (via intercom): Yeah, but that sounds about right?

Laughter...

Ted (defensive): So does yours.

Martin: Yours both sound about right.

Raven: You could listen to the show all day and not know who Ted is. I think that says something for being introverted right there.

Ted: Fuck off.

Martin: She's right. You hardly ever say anything, dude, and only the fans know it's you behind the soundbytes and stuff. In your case, Larry, I would think boring is a good thing for a guy with a wife and kid.

Zach: I agree.

Larry (via intercom): I still disagree with the assessment.

Zach: Can't please everyone, I guess.

Martin: Nobody can please Donnie. Just so you know.

Laughter...

Donnie (annoyed): Whatever...

Martin: I like how my results started off sounding good, but then took a turn for the worse: A born leader. Loyal and trustworthy to a fault. Extremely results oriented. Strong-willed, yet emotionally immature. Known to lash out at those closest to him to allay his own feelings of inadequacy. Borderline obsessive-compulsive narcissist with delusions of grandeur. Mah-rone! Give it to me straight, why don't you.

Laughter...

Zach: Do you disagree with the results, Martin?

Martin: Wellll…

Laughter…

Raven (laughing): I think it's pretty on the money.

Larry (via intercom): Oooo! That's cold.

Ted laughs.

Raven: You guys know it's true.

Martin: Don't *you* start, Raven. I'll make you do the stupid screening. See what it says about you.

Raven: Oh, no you won't.

Zach: So, let's talk about your results, Martin. What do you agree or disagree with?

Martin: I think I'd much rather make fun of Donnie's results some more.

Donnie: C'mon dude! That's not fair. I had to deal with it.

Martin: You had to deal with it? You stormed out. I can't storm out. It's *MY* show.

Donnie: I say let's take a vote. Who wants to make fun of my results some more, say aye?

Martin: Aye.

Ted: Aye.

Donnie: Okay. Who wants to make fun of Martin's results, say aye?

Donnie: AYE!

Raven: Aye.

Larry (Via intercom): Aye. Sorry Martin.

Zach: Aye.

Martin: You guys are all fired.

Laughter...

Zach: You can't fire me.

Martin: Okay then. Get outta my studio!

Laughter...

Martin: Let's go to the phones. See what the callers think. Eddie from Northeast Philly...You're on the air.

Caller: Eddie from Northeast Philly (28)

Eddie: Yo! That story Donnie was talkin' about with the guys biting people. I just drove past the crime scene. It's right on the corner of 20th and Market in Center City. There's blood everywhere. They got police tape up and everything.

Martin: You're fucking kidding me? You mean that was real?

Eddie: Yeah, man. I didn't see what happened. I guess they were attacking random people. Supposedly the cops shot the guys like 20 times or something.

Martin: Twenty times?!

Raven: That can't be right.

Eddie: That's what the guy said when I stopped to ask what happened. By the way...That shit with Donnie's results had me dying. I thought I was gonna piss myself. But, I think it's only fair that Raven does the screening.

Raven: Nope. Not doin' it.

Eddie: See. That's not right.

Raven: Maybe not, but—

Eddie: Holy shit! Are they…are they naked?

Martin: Naked? Eddie? What's going on out there?

Eddie: Looks like some kinda protest or something up ahead. SonofaBITCH!

Eddie pounds on his horn.

Eddie (to naked protestors): SOME OF US HAVE JOBS, YOU KNOW!

Martin: Describe what you see, Eddie.

Over the phone we hear a cacophony of blaring horns and angry voices.

Martin: Eddie!

Eddie (to Martin): It's a bunch-ah naked people. Like 20 or 30 of 'em. Looks like they got some kinda special effects make up on or something.

Eddie pounds his horn again.

Eddie (to naked protestors): GO PROTEST SOMEWHERE ELSE YA GODDAMN FREA—! Holy shit!

Martin: What?!

Eddie (to Martin): They just attacked a guy! Oh sh…They're attacking people! What the FUCK! (to other drivers): GET BACK IN YOUR CARS! LADY! GET BACK IN YOUR—

Dialtone…

End call

A silent pause…

Martin: That wasn't for real, right?

Zach: I was going to ask *you*…

Ted: Sounded real to me.

Raven: Me too.

Larry (via intercom): Sorry for interrupting, Martin, but you should check your email.

Martin: What the FUCK! Now *you're* interrupting the show?!

Larry (via intercom): Just check it. I just forwarded you a cell phone video. You *HAVE TO* watch it.

Martin: Has everybody gone fucking mad around here?!

Larry (via intercom): Just watch the video, Martin. Trust me.

Dead air……

Martin: Wait a minute…Listen.

Somewhere outside the studio…the sound of sirens passing at high speed. It sounds like several vehicles—police and fire department.

Ted: That coming from outside the studio?

Martin: Well, where else would it be coming from?

Zach: Musta been some kind of accident.

Raven: Hope no one was hurt.

Martin: My apologies, Zach.

Zach: No apology necessary. It's an honor just being here.

Martin: As it should be.

Laughter…

Martin: This video better be good, Lar.

Larry (via intercom): I wouldn't have interrupted you if it wasn't.

Martin: All right. I'm gonna put it up on the flatscreen.

ON FLATSCREEN

VIDEO
The scene shakes to clarity...

Morning rush in the big city. The hustle and bustle of nine-to-fivers hurrying to work. A woman's scream in the distance briefly disturbs the busy flow. In the street, traffic crawls along like any given day. Horns blaring. Colorful exchanges between angry drivers. The unseen woman screams again. Her voice is louder this time. Suddenly, the crowd of nine-to-fivers separates and a middle-aged woman runs screaming out of a subway entrance at the end of the block.

A tall, thin man, dressed like an executive, stumbles from the subway entrance in awkward pursuit.

Martin (re: executive): Look at thiz guy. Tha fuck's his problem?

Raven: Looks like he's on something.

VIDEO (CONT'D)
Something off about the executive's appearance; the venous, ashen hue, the sunken eyes rife with hunger, the hang-jawed expression or all of the above. He stops when he notices the crowd of spectators.

The middle-aged woman runs out into the street screaming and rubbernecking back to the subway entrance. She doesn't see the taxi traveling toward her at a high rate of speed. A muted THUD scores the impact as the taxi hits the woman. Her body wraps around the front end of the vehicle...

Raven gasps.

An audible wince from Ted.

Martin: OH my God!

Zach: Oh *NO*!

Larry (via intercom): Just keep watching.

VIDEO (CONT'D)
The middle-aged woman is thrown 20 feet into the gridlocked morning traffic. Screams. Brakes squeal as the taxi skids to rest. Several people run toward the woman. The rest stay put, staring in awe at the sickly executive, who stands there, staring back at them.

The executive lunges at the nearest person, a man, who gets away. He goes after the next closest, and the next, constantly adjusting his focus as each intended victim evades him.

Martin: What the fuck?!

VIDEO (CONT'D)
A bike messenger whips around the corner unaware of the scene unfolding. He swerves and attempts to go around the executive. Seizing the opportunity, the executive reaches out and yanks the boy from his expensive-looking bike. He falls on top of the bike messenger and immediately takes a bite out of the boy's exposed throat. The boy cries out. More screams from the spectators. A man with an umbrella runs up and whacks the executive on the head as he proceeds to devour the thrashing bike messenger.

Martin (awestruck): This is some seriously fucked up shit right here.

Donnie: You got that right.

Larry (via intercom): Just wait. It gets worse.

VIDEO (CONT'D)
A scream from down the block. The camera shakes.

[Image indecipherable]

The camera zooms in on a blurred image. As the frame clears we see the middle-aged woman who was hit by the taxi. She is covered in blood, her body horribly disfigured by the taxi's front end, yet she is on her feet, tussling with a man down the street, trying to bite him.

Zach: Z'that the woman that just got hit by the cab?

Martin: Looks like it.

Zach: There's no way she's alive...After the way that cab hit her...

VIDEO (CONT'D)
The scene shifts back to the executive as he flashes his snarling, bloody maw at the man with the umbrella. The camera's iris takes a moment to focus. In that time, the executive gets up and goes after the man.

The bike messenger writhes on the ground, coughing and choking on his own blood. His hands are clamped over his neck. Blood pours through his fingers and quickly pools beneath him. A woman hurries over and kneels beside the boy. He dies in her arms.

People run away screaming as the executive goes after this person and that one, his focus ever shifting. In the background, the bike messenger sits up in a robotic fashion. His normal pigment has been replaced by a venous, ashen hue, sunken eyes and an expression of hang-jawed bewilderment. He turns his head and lunges at the woman kneeling next to him. He tackles her, tearing at her face with his hands and stuffing the warm, loose flesh into his mouth. Several men run up and pull the bike messenger off of the woman. He takes a bite out of one of their arms in the process.

The executive has caught another victim, a pregnant woman. The woman screams as he clamps his teeth down on her shoulder. She pulls away and runs leaving the executive standing there chewing on her flesh. A look of mystified satisfaction on his face.

Authoritative Male Voices (in unison): FREEZE!

The camera whips left and reveals four cops standing with their guns trained on the executive. They open fire. The camera shakes.

[Image undecipherable]

Bullets find purchase in the executive's chest, abdomen, and thighs, shoving him backward. He is still standing when the shooting stops, swaying drunkenly. Bloody vomitus pushes through his lips. He lets out a confused grunt. His eyes roll back. He sways one last time, and then falls backward.

A few feet away, several men are tussling with the bike messenger. One of the cops yells at them.

Cop #1: Get away from him!

The men move away. One of them nurses a bite-wound on his forearm. The bike messenger turns his focus onto the cops, his mouth painted with bloody drool.

Cop 1#: Get down!

Cop #2: Get on the ground! Now!

The bike messenger keeps coming. The cops open fire. The messenger lurches backward but doesn't go down.

Anonymous voice: Look out!

The camera whips around...The executive lumbers toward the cops, his off-the-rack suit peppered with bullet holes. They open fire on the man. A headshot finally takes him down.

Here comes the bike messenger...The cops open fire on him again. He staggers, but keeps coming.

Anonymous voice: Shoot him in the head!

A single headshot, and the bike messenger goes down hard. The camera whips around toward the woman who was kneeling next to the bike messenger. She has just sat up and locked a sunken-eyed stare at the person standing closest to her. Screams in the background...

STATIC...

END VIDEO

The room is silent while Martin, Raven, Ted, and Zach Wyatt attempt to digest what they've just witnessed.

Martin (worried): I don't even know what to say to that. I mean...are you fucking kidding me?!

Zach's expression turns cynical.

Zach: Nice try guys.

Larry (via intercom): That was just emailed to me by the guy who filmed it.

Martin: I swear-ta-God we had nothing to do with it, Zach.

Zach: *Riiight.*

Raven gasps. It startles Martin.

Martin: What?!

Raven (shocked): I'm looking at my computer screen. I'm gonna read these off to you. They're all within the last half hour…

—Kensington man, thought dead, attacks staff at local funeral home.

—In Center City:

Cops shoot 2 dead following "biting spree"

Naked mob causes gridlock

Deranged woman attacks commuters on Subway

—Bizarre string of "biting" attacks sweeps nation.

—Biting attacks reported in London, Cardiff, Tokyo, Zimbabwe.

Zach laughs.

Zach: You guys really do go all out.

Martin: It's not us! I swear! Wait, Raven…This was on the News?

Raven: It's on Philly dot com.

Martin (scared): What the fuck's going on, man?!

Raven (scared): Maybe we should be thinking about getting out of here?

Martin: Good idea.

Donnie: Nah. We'd be stuck in that traffic just like everybody else.

Ted: I agree with Donnie.

Zach: Me too.

Martin starts to panic.

Martin: Shit! Shit! Shit!

Larry runs into the room unexpected and startles everyone.

Raven: Jeeezus Christ, Larry! You scared the hell outta me!

Martin: No shit, dude!

Larry (exasperated): Turn on the News! Cnn! Fox! Whatever! Just turn it on!

Martin (scared): Okay! Okay! Hang on.

ON FLATSCREEN

VIDEO
A confused Anchorman sits behind a desk. A newsroom in chaos behind him. People hurry back and forth. We catch the Anchorman in mid-sentence…

ANCHORMAN:…several theories to try and explain the sudden outbreak of random violence. The attacks seem to follow a similar pattern with the assailant or assailants attempting to bite, and even eat their victims.

Raven gasps.

Martin (disbelief): No way!

Larry leaves the room as hurriedly as he entered.

VIDEO (CONT'D)
ANCHORMAN (CONT'D) Reports of the bizarre attacks began coming in just over 30 minutes ago. These reports seem to place hospitals at the epicenter of the outbreak, which has led some to speculate a contaminant or possibly even a virus of some sort as a cause.

Martin: I *knew* it! I fucking *knew* it! Didn't I tell ya if anything got us, it was going to be a fucking disease?! Moth-ther *FUCKERS*!!!

Raven: Shhhhh! Quiet Martin! I'm trying to listen!

VIDEO (CONT'D)

ANCHORMAN (CONT'D): *In every case thus far, it has been necessary for police, and in some cases, civilians to use deadly force against the extremely aggressive attackers, who appear almost impervious to pain. Many point to this heightened aggression and pain tolerance as a sign of possible drug intoxication. You'll recall the incident last month in Miami when a man, thought to be high on the drug known as 'bath salts,' was shot multiple times and killed by police while attempting to devour another man's face.*

Martin: I remember that.

Zach: Me, too. I was actually in Miami at the time.

Raven: Shhhhh!

VIDEO (CONT'D)
ANCHORMAN (CONT'D): *Similar reports from Europe, Asia and Africa, seem to suggest that we have a bonafide global phenomenon on our hands. As I sit here at a loss for words, I can't help wondering—*
…I'm being told that we're going to go to some video that has just come in. I must warn you. Much of the footage is of an extremely graphic nature.

BALTIMORE, MD
An angry mob clings to the sides, back, and roof of a mini van, pounding on, and clawing at the windows, as it travels at a high rate of speed around the top level of a multi-level parking garage. The driver swerves and crashes into parked vehicles attempting to throw the people off. The mini-van accelerates and misses a turn, crashing through the concrete barrier, and plummeting 100 feet to the street below. Traffic swerves to avoid being crushed. People run screaming from their vehicles. Wriggling bodies and pulverized concrete rain down in the mini-van's wake. Some of the bodies get up and attack the horrified spectators.

NEW YORK, NY
A shaky image of a hospital hallway. People screaming and running away from something.

Male voice: They're coming up from the morgue!

The camera whirls around and reveals a shaky stampede of upright corpses lurching toward us.

Larry (via intercom, scared): The guys in the back office are leaving. I'm thinking about doing the same. I'm sorry, but I've gotta get home to my family.

Martin: Fuck this! I'm right behind you, Lar!

Raven: Waaait a minute, Martin!

Donnie: How the hell you gonna get there?!

VIDEO (CONT'D)
LOS ANGELES
A wall of riot cops march forward hiding behind a barrier of clear, Plexiglas shields. They are preparing to engage a staggering, lurching mob of deceased commuters who climb from of an ugly pileup of smoldering vehicles that clog a freeway off-ramp.

Donnie (re: television): You see how it is out there! I mean, look at that shit!

Martin: You don't understand! I've gotta get to my wife! You still there, Lar?!

No answer…

VIDEO (CONT'D)
Quick cuts of chaos in the streets. New York. London. Tokyo. The scenes are virtually interchangeable. Gridlocked traffic. Cars left unattended. Staggering fiends dressed like regular folk chasing people down and eating their flesh. People being shot, and run down by panicking motorists.

Martin (to Ted): What're you gonna do?!

Ted: I just talked to Alicia. She's on her way home right now with Tara. I've gotta go be with them. I'm sorry, Martin.

Martin: Fuck it, man! I'm going too!

Donnie: It's better to wait it out in here, guys!

Martin (panicking): I don't even know where Karen is, Donnie! Wait. Wait…I'll try her cell.

Donnie: Calm Down, Martin!

Martin (panicking): DON'T FUCKING TELL ME TO CALM DOWN!

VIDEO (CONT'D)
ANCHORMAN
The confused Anchorman sits behind a desk. The newsroom in chaos over his shoulder. Many people have left.

ANCHORMAN: *We stress that you stay in your homes and await further instructions. If you find yourself in the presence of one or more of the attackers, use what you can to defend yourself, but in no way, shape, or form, should you attempt to take on or apprehend them. The National Guard has been deployed to several cities to help deal with the rash of violence. In the meantime, keep your televisions tuned to CSN News for the latest updates as new information comes in.*

The Anchorman touches his earpiece and makes a "listening" face.

ANCHORMAN: *We're going to go to CSN Contributor, Carlos Arroyo in Delaware County. Carlos…You okay out there?*

CARLOS ARROYO
Carlos faces the camera with microphone in hand awaiting his cue to start speaking. Behind him we see a crowd of people gathered outside an iron fence that surrounds a vast cemetery. They are looking through the fence at something inside.

CARLOS: So far so good. I'm standing outside the Fernrock Cemetery where people have stopped and gotten out of their cars to witness a…I suppose we've used up our lifetime allowance of the word 'bizarre,' but there really is no other way to describe what's been going on all over the world this morning. Rather than try to explain it, I'm going to let you hear it for yourselves.

Martin (panicking): Karen's not answering. FUCK! I gotta go!

Martin fumbles with the console.

Raven (welling up): Please stop, Martin?

Zach: I think you should reconsider, Martin. You don't wanna be sitting out there in traffic with those people running around like that.

Donnie: He's right, Martin.

Martin: I DON'T WANNA RECONSIDER, GODDAMMIT! I JUST WANNA BE WITH MY WIFE! FUCK! FUUUCCCK! I DON'T KNOW WHAT TO DO! I DON'T KNOW WHAT TO FUCKING DO!

VIDEO (CONT'D)

CARLOS ARROYO
Reporter, Carlos Arroyo walks up to the fence, sticks the microphone through the iron bars, and points it at the field of headstones and mausoleums. The camera begins a slow zoom toward the headstones/mausoleums.

Over the voices of the crowd that has gathered at the fence, we hear a fractured chorus of muffled screaming, anguished growls, and pounding. The noise appears to be coming from beneath the ground.

THE MARTIN STONE SHOW

MONDAY, MARCH 26th, 2015
6 months since the dead rose...

The crackle of a live microphone...The *CALL TO THE COWS* section of Rossini's *WILLIAM TELL OVERTURE* kicks in over a black screen.

Martin Stone: (whispering over the music): Listen to it, folks...The birds are chirping. The sun is peeking over the horizon waiting for its cue to come out and make the new day official, and the streets...the streets are ("Call to the Cows" is replaced by an aggressive guitar riff) OVERRUN WITH THE ROTTEN, STINKIN' CORPSES OF YOUR NEIGHBORS AND FRIENDS AND RELATIVES AND LOVED ONES! THEY'RE OUT THERE, FOLKS! THEY'RE HUNGRY! AND THEY'RE LOOKING FOR WARM FLESH TO EAT! THAT WOULD BE YOU AND ME, FOLKS! SO WAKE UP! SHAKE OFF THAT DREAM OF THE WAY THINGS WERE! SHAKE IT OFF! KEEP YOUR WEAPONS CLOSE AND BE VIGILANT, FOLKS! YOU'VE LIVED TO SEE ANOTHER DAY! AND THAT'S A GOOD THING!

The aggressive guitars are replaced by a more radio-friendly riff, the theme to a popular morning show.

FADE IN...

Brand Compound – Reef Tower
(Formerly Waterfront Luxury Apartments)
Philadelphia, Pa

A studio hastily built in the living room of Apartment 3216. A circular pit lined with a plush, leather couch in the middle of the room. A microphone, perched atop a slender stand, pointed at the couch.

A spiral staircase leads to the loft area, where Martin, Raven, and Ted's booths look down on the circular pit. A large, flatscreen monitor mounted on the wall across from the loft area, where it can be viewed by everyone in the room.

Dark-colored sound attenuation blankets cover the walls and the floor-to-ceiling windows that look out at an identical building (The Regatta Tower) 100-feet away. The Martin Stone Show Logo emblazoned on the blankets. Colored lighting mimics the indigo and red atmosphere of their former studio at WXTU.

Martin: That's right, folks. Broadcasting on Brand 96 on the Brand Satellite Channel and Brand 103 for those of you with access to video…It's that time again, time for your favorite un-undead purveyor of wisdom, The King of All Airwaves, Martin Stone, comin' at you *LIVE* from high atop the Reef Tower at the Brand Compound on the Philadelphia waterfront.

Soundbyte: Canned applause.

Martin: And sitting to my right is the lovely, Raven.

Soundbyte: Cat calls. Canned applause.

Raven: Good morning.

Martin: The intro you just heard goes out to a caller from Friday's show named Joyce. In case you missed it, Joyce was lamenting about a reoccurring dream in which the dead had never risen. Apparently this dream is so vivid that when she wakes up to reality it triggers a massive panic attack every single time.

Raven (annoyed): *PAH-leeze!* Who hasn't had that dream?

Martin: We've got a big show for you today, folks. We've got more undead celebrity sightings. We've got…

Larry interrupts, via intercom, from his office in one of the apartment's two bedrooms.

34

Larry (via intercom): It's a no-go on the celebrity sightings. At least for today.

Martin (annoyed): You wait 'til we're on the air to tell me that? (to audience): Our producer, Larry, ladies and gentlemen...

Soundbyte (From *YOUNG FRANKENSTEIN*, Marty Feldman as Igor): Yessss Mah-stah.

Soundbyte: Canned laughter.

Larry (via intercom): Ted was supposed to tell you.

Ted: Yeah...He *did* ask me, but I forgot. Sorry about that.

Martin: That's not Ted's job, Lar. That's *your* job.

Larry (via intercom): I'm busy trying to put the show together, Martin.

Martin: Well, you're not trying hard enough.

Larry (via intercom): So, what? You'd rather me sacrifice the entire show to—

Martin: It woulda taken you two seconds, for Christ Sakes!

Larry (via intercom): Well, I guess it's all my fault, then. Once again.

Martin: That's right it's your fault. Now crawl back into your cave and do your job like you're supposed to! (venting to himself) Can't rely on him for anything.

Larry (via intercom): Yeah. Because I do such a horrible job running this show...

Martin: That's right! Now GET OFF MY AIRWAVES!

Raven: Excuses. Excuses.

Larry (via intercom): Shut the fuck up, Raven!

Martin: Don't you tell her to shut up!

Raven (playfully instigates): Oh my! So ungrateful.

Martin: As I was saying, before I was so rudely interrupted, we've got a great show for you today, folks. We'll be speaking with an inventor who claims to have developed something that will help solve the problem of the dead eating the living.

Raven: Another one?

Martin: Yeah. But this guy's a doctor...And from what I hear, he's actually onto something.

Raven (scoffs): Oooo, a doctor...As usual, I'll believe it when I see it.

Martin: Must be from a decent-sized settlement, thiz-guy. Did'ju see the size of that helicopter he came in?

Raven: I thought all the big settlements were done?

Martin: They are.

Raven: Apparently not.

Ted: Those military copters require a shitload of fuel, too. So they must be doing all right.

Martin: Yeah...Strange. We'll ask him about it when he comes in. (pause) So, Raven...I heard you had breakfast in the cafeteria this morning.

Raven: I did.

Martin (upset): Well, what the hell'd you do that for?! I thought we discussed—

Raven: Relax...I was just meeting with a friend. She's really

36

been having a hard time lately and needed someone to talk to.

Martin: You didn't eat anything, did you?

Raven: No. I wouldn't do that.

Martin: Whew. (to audience): Let me just state, for the record, folks, that there's nothing wrong with the cafeteria food here at the Brand Compound. My obsession with preparing my own meals stems from my own paranoia.

Raven: Which you managed to suck all of us into...as is usually the case.

Martin: It's not that bad. So, you miss out on proper meals, but I just feel like it's one less thing to worry about.

Raven: I don't miss it as much as I thought I would.

Ted: Me, either.

Larry (via intercom): Same here.

Raven: Plus, I'm the thinnest I've been in years.

Martin: The canned food diet. I should market that.

Soundbyte: Canned laughter.

Martin: Seriously though...I would hold on to your supply. There seem to be fewer and fewer people showin' up to barter lately.

Larry (via intercom): Speaking of the cafeteria...Was there some kind of incident between you and the guards this morning, Raven?

Raven: I thought I was gonna have to defend myself at one point.

Martin: Come on. They're good guys.

Raven: Most of 'em are. I'll give you that. But there're a few who make it uncomfortable, especially for the women in the compound. I won't name names, but you know exactly who I'm talking about. It's gotten to the point where I go out of my way to make sure I'm not in the cafeteria or the gym at the same time they are. That's a lot of work, you know.

Martin: Yeah. I guess they *have* been getting a lot of complaints about those two.

Raven: Well. I'm officially registering another one—*on the air*—so the board can't give me that, "we were never informed," bullshit.

Martin: Those guys put their lives on the line every day, though. I just feel weird saying anything bad about them.

Raven: Like I said…I'm not talking about security as a whole. And nobody's suggesting that they kick those two out of the compound. Maybe just revoke their access to the common areas. The cafeteria. The fitness center. The lounges. Have the one leave his radio, though. I actually like the playlists he puts on in the gym.

Martin (scolds playfully): Hey guys! Stop harassing Raven! (to Raven): There. You happy?

Raven (chuckles): It's not just me.

Martin: Okay. (playfully scolds) Stop harassing…whoever you're harassing.

Soundbyte: Canned laughter.

Raven (sarcastic): Yeah. That should do it.

Martin: Well, I don't know what else you want me to do.

Raven: You *know* the board is listening.

Martin: That doesn't mean they're gonna do anything about it. They all hate me.

Raven: So what. Half the people in this compound hate you…

Ted: They hate all of us…

Larry (via intercom): Ted took the words right outta my mouth.

Raven: Right. But they all know that Martin's in tight with the old man, so it doesn't matter what they think.

Larry (via intercom): That just makes 'em hate us more.

Dead air…

Martin (to Raven): Not to be a dick or anything…But, it just makes me a little uncomfortable when you put it out there like that. You know how I am.

Raven: I'm sorry. I didn't mean to…

Martin: I know you didn't. I just don't want the audience to think that I'm the kind of guy who would use his influence—

Raven: Audience? What audience?

Martin points a scolding finger at Raven.

Martin: We're supposed to act like there're still millions of people out there, Raven. It instills hope in the listeners.

Raven: Is that what the old man told you?

Martin: You know me so well, Raven.

Raven laughs.

Raven: Well, that's what happens in a marriage.

Martin: Is that what this is? Don't tell my wife.

Raven laughs.

Soundbyte: Canned laughter…

Raven: Do you realize that we've been together for 20 years?

Martin: I know. I was just talking about that with Karen the other day.

Raven: Remember, when we started back at WMMR?

Martin: How could I forget? I thought we had finally made it. Now look at us; sitting on top of a world filled with dead people who won't stay dead. The old man's got a point, though. Maybe most of the larger settlements are gone, but as long as we keep getting calls, you've gotta assume that there's still a good amount of people out there.

Ted: They seem to be more spread out now, in small pockets.

Martin: Yep.

Dead air…

Martin: All right folks…A lot to get to today…We've got Part Two of our popular new segment; Stone Show Closest Calls. Today's entry is from our beloved writer, soundman extraordinaire, Ted Morrison.

Soundbyte: Canned applause.

Martin: We'll hear from our good friend, Dave Straussman, aka Dave from Security, about what's doin' beyond the walls.

Larry (via intercom): Dave's actually holding on line one right now.

Martin (confused): I thought we weren't doing that 'til later?

Larry (via intercom): He says it's the only time he can call in today.

Martin: You there Dave?

Caller: Dave from Security (32)

Dave: I'm here.

Martin: Where're you stationed today?

Dave: I'm right above you guys workin' the roof turrets on the Reef Tower.

Martin: How's it looking down in the streets?

Dave: Things are pretty quiet outside the compound, but deeper in the city...I see dead people. Lots and lots of dead people.

Soundbyte: Canned laughter.

Martin (to Raven): You know, we'll be featuring Dave's episode of Closest Calls on Wednesday's show.

Raven: Oh really?

Martin: You know it's gonna be good, too. Dave's a real man's man.

Dave: I don't know about all that, Martin. But thanks.

Martin: Anytime. All right, Dave. As usual...

Dave: Got it. Anything happens out here and you'll be the first to know.

Raven (laughing): Well, maybe we shouldn't be the first.

Dave laughs.

Dave: Okay. You'll be the second.

Martin: Oh. And Dave...

Dave: Yeah?

Martin: Sorry if any of you guys took offense to our little discussion about Raven's incident with the guards this morning.

Dave: None taken. And if it'll make you feel any better, Raven, I'll talk to those two myself.

Raven: I don't want to cause any trouble.

Dave: No trouble at all. Talk to you later, guys.

Martin: See ya, Dave.

Raven: Thanks, Dave. Stay safe.

Ted: Take care.

End call

Martin: I feel safer knowing that real men like Dave are watching over us.

Raven: Me too.

Martin: We've gotta get a camera on him, though. Like a helmet cam or something. Hey, Lar...

Larry (via intercom): We already discussed this, Martin. Head Office has a problem with us using the footage for entertainment purposes.

Raven: What don't they have a problem with when it comes to the show?

Martin: Entertainment purposes? I want to give people a first-hand account of what it's like out there. We *ARE* a News show, too. Ya know? The old man brought us here because, like the mayor, he, as a fan, is aware of my unique ability to connect with the public on a personal level. Part of accomplishing that is being able to find humor in otherwise tragic situations. I mean…whaddo they want; solemn music and constant boo-hooing about how bad we have it. Where's that gonna get us?

Larry (via intercom): You're preaching to the choir, Martin.

Martin: I CAN'T HELP IT! IT PISSES ME OFF!

Dead air…

Martin leans away from his microphone and takes a deep, calming breath. He chuckles at his outburst, and then leans forward.

Martin: Okay. What's next, Raven? You wanna hear the top five songs in the world?

Raven: Do we have to?

Martin: Positive thinking, Raven. Remember?

Raven: Okay, Mr. Brand.

Soundbyte: Canned laughter.

Martin: Just for that, I'm gonna play 'em.

Raven laughs.

Raven: Like you weren't going to anyway.

Martin: Here they are, folks; your top five songs…Number five

Soundbyte: A wayward zombie wails in a dry rasp.

Martin and Ted laugh throughout the countdown.

Martin: Number four…

Soundbyte: Two zombies wailing.

Martin: Number three…

Soundbyte: Three zombies wailing…

Martin: Number two…

Soundbyte: A small crowd of zombies growling aggressively.

Martin: And the number one song in the world…

Soundbyte: Hundreds of zombies worked into a frenzy.

Soundbyte: Canned laughter.

Raven (laughing): So stupid…

Martin: Hey! Whatever happened with the mayor's address? Wasn't he supposed to go on last night?

Raven: They're saying he's sick.

Martin: Really? I hope it's nothing serious.

Raven: They say it's just a cold.

Martin: A cold can kill you these days.

Raven: I didn't get the impression that he was in dire straights or anything.

Martin: Yeah…He'll be all right. They're pretty well stocked over at City Hall from what I remember. All right. Let's get on with the show. Oh! Look, Raven. We've got a caller.

Soundbyte: Celebratory game show music.

Soundbyte: Canned applause.

Martin: Hello caller. You're on the air.

Caller: Alex from Maple Shade (24)

The call is plagued by static.

Alex: Is this Martin?

Raven (re: static): Oh my God! Listen to that.

Martin: Who is this?!

Alex: Alex.

Martin: I can barely hear you, Alex!

Alex: We passed one of your cell towers layin' in the road on the way here. Probably got somethin' to do with the reception.

Martin throws his hands up in disgust.

Martin (to audience): Goddammit, people! Our guys risked their lives putting these towers up so that we can have a line of communication with each other during this thing. And this is how you repay them? I tell you what...How bout we have the guys in the control room stop operating the damn satellite and we can all watch it fall from the sky like the hundreds of other ones did. (pause) Where're you calling from, Alex?!

Alex: I'm in an old stable house in Bucks County, but I'm originally from Maple Shade, New Jersey.

Raven (to Alex): You said "We" passed one of the cell towers. Are you with a group?

Alex: It's just me and my mom. She's sick.

Raven: I'm sorry to hear that! What happened?!

Alex: She got bit. We managed to get away from the deadfucks and hide in here. There's a portable generator, but it's empty. All the cars in the area've had their tanks cleaned out. I need your help. I need to get in touch with the alternative fuel guy.

Martin: The Grease Man? I'm not sure he's still around. (to Raven): See. This is what I mean about keeping old ads in the rotation.

The call begins to break up.

Alex: I need…get…some…light…here…before nightfall.

Martin: Alex! You're breaking up!

Alex: Martin! Ca…Yo…hear me?! MARTIN!

Martin: Listen, Alex…I'm gonna put you through to Mr. Hoffman at the guard station! He'll be able to—

Dialtone…

End Call

Martin: ALEX! Shit! We lost him.

Dead air…

Martin: Wait! I think he's calling back. Hang on…Alex? That you?

Caller: Maggie from Lancaster (60s)

Maggie: This is Maggie, from Lancaster.

Martin (disappointed): I'm sorry, Maggie. We were just talking to—

Maggie: You people ought to be ashamed of yourselves.

Martin: What did we do this time?

Maggie: You know what you did, what you do…Makin' light of the dead for entertainment value. They were people once, you know?

Raven: Here we go.

Martin (fired up): Exactly my point, Maggie. And now they're dead. As long as we hold on to these sentimental feelings toward what we assume are still our friends and family members, those of us who remain won't move forward as a society. And to that end, maybe we can use this most unfortunate circumstance that we've found ourselves in to learn something about the way we treat each other as a species.

Maggie: Let's assume that I agree with you. So your idea of progress is to provide a platform for all the sinful things people do to the dead? Using them for sex...or...or target practice. Making slaves of them. Hunting them like animals. Making them fight. What exactly are we supposed to learn from that?

Martin: You're missing the point, Maggie. My job is to expose what's going on out there. To shine a light on what's become of humanity no matter how ugly or off-putting it may be.

Maggie: No. You're encouraging irresponsible behavior is what you're doing. That's why Clay Edelman kicked you out.

Martin: First of all, the mayor didn't kick us out. We left City Hall of our own volition. (to Raven): Or is it 'of our own accord?'

Raven: Either one is fine I think.

Martin: So, get your facts straight, *Maggie*!

Maggie: You ever stop to consider the cost of what you're doing? Because, if you did—

Martin (interrupts): Oh for Christ Sakes! GET OFF MY PHONE LINE! YA CRAZY BITCH! NEXT TIME CHECK YOUR FACTS BEFORE YOU PASS JUDGEMENT ON ME! Raven...Where's that paper with the stats?

Raven shuffles through a pile of paper on the counter and quickly finds the one she's looking for. She slides on a pair of glasses and holds the paper up to her face...and then hands it to Martin.

Raven: Here.

Martin takes the paper...

Martin: Thanks.

...and looks over the stats.

Martin: Still there, Maggie?

Maggie: Unfortunately.

Raven: No one is forcing you to stay on the line, Maggie.

Martin: No. I want her to hear this. Now, Maggie, I'm holding in my hand a list of stats compiled by the Emergency Broadcast System. Because of me...Suicide. DOWN! Homicide rate. DOWN! People are less stressed and report having a generally more positive outlook. ALL BECAUSE-A-ME! YOU HEAR THAT, MAGGIE?! YOU KNOW WHY?! BECAUSE I PROVIDE A FORUM FOR PEOPLE TO VENT THEIR FRUSTRATIONS!

Raven: People used to call that therapy.

Martin: That's right, Raven. Maybe I should start charging.

Maggie: You might have something if that report wasn't two months old.

Martin: Oh! So, you're a listener! Only a listener would know that. I was just testing you.

Maggie: And to your statement about charging a fee; the only payment you deserve is from your maker for all the filth you spread.

Raven: I figured that was coming.

Martin:…and a religious listener at that. I find myself fascinated by the religious…with everything that's happened.

Maggie: And when Our Lord and Savior comes down from the sky on his flaming chariot, I, and the faithful, will be waiting to be taken to the kingdom of Heaven where we will enjoy eternal life. Where will you be?

Raven: You can't win this argument, Martin.

Martin: But don't you think God or whoever would look favorably upon me considering the service I'm providing here in the meantime.

Maggie: God does not reward sin or those who spread it. The only service I can see is distracting people from the only true path.

Raven: Which is?

Maggie: Which is accepting Christ, Our Lord and Savior, into your heart.

Raven: Of course. Since he's done so much for them up to this point.

Maggie: How dare you!

Raven: How dare *YOU*!

Martin: Raven!

Soundbyte: Cats fighting.

Laughter in the studio…

Maggie: Everybody that you people lure away from the word of God with your perversion and your misplaced faith in science and technology is doomed to be left behind to suffer through the Great Tribulation.

Martin: Ohhh...The Great Tribulation...How could I forget? I guess we should just give up then? We shouldn't even try to salvage what we, as a species, have worked so hard for, for centuries, and sacrificed so much to establish. Right? I mean...don't we, at the very least, owe the surviving children a fighting chance at rebuilding? Not that I have any of my own, but...

Maggie: The only path to salvation is through God.

Martin: You said that already.

Maggie: That's all that needs to be said.

Martin: You know what? I'm officially tired of you, Maggie. More power to you with God's plan and all, but this is where I get off this ride.

Maggie: You and your listeners will wish you listened to me when you're burning for eternity in the fires of—

Martin: You're a listener...So, I guess you'll be right there with us burning for eternity, huh?

Dialtone.

End call

Martin: I think I touched a nerve.

Raven: I told you it was a waste of time.

Martin: Yeah...Sorry about that, folks. I just find it so interesting the way people cling to religion despite so much evidence to the contrary.

Raven: The dead aren't really evidence of anything...to play Devil's advocate. So far science hasn't been able to offer up an explanation. And to the Bible's credit, it did mention the dead coming back to life as part of how the world would end.

Martin: Yeah, but you can't honestly think that God would be behind all the shit that's gone down. Men, women, and children being eaten alive…raped. Innocent people killed for supplies.

Raven: I'm not saying I believe it.

Martin: Whew! You had me scared for a second there.

Raven laughs.

Raven: Thought you were losing me to the Jesus-freaks, huh?

Martin: In a strange way, though, I envy their unwavering faith. Sometimes, it makes you wonder. You know? Like… what if they're right?

Raven: You mean sometimes it makes *YOU* wonder.

Martin: I can never fully commit to the thought, though. You know. Like I'm embarrassed or ashamed to even be considering it or something. But every once and awhile, it slips in there.

Larry (via intercom): I've been there.

Ted: Yeah. Me too.

Raven: You're all nuts.

Laughter…

Martin: I wonder if the doctor's ready. Hey Lar…

Larry (via intercom): He's still downstairs with security, Martin.

Raven: Really?

Martin: Hmm. I wonder what that's all about. All right. (to Raven): You wanna do Closest Calls?

Raven: Why not? I'm curious to hear Ted's story.

Larry (via intercom): Me too.

Martin: Fifty bucks says it'll be as boring as Ted, himself.

Ted: Fuck off!

Martin (to Ted): Is this a long story?

Ted: I'd say it's on the longer side of short.

Martin: It couldn't just be a simple answer with you, huh?

Raven: Is it ever with Ted?

Ted (defensive): I said 'the longer side of short.' What's not simple about that?

Raven: It was just a very "Ted" answer, is all.

Ted (annoyed): Oh please…

Martin: All right, then folks. Here we go…

ON FLATSCREEN

VIDEO:
STONE SHOW CLOSEST CALLS #2
Ted Morrison – Writer/Sound-effects

A medium shot of Ted Morrison, from the waist up, seated against a black background.

Ted: It was a week after the shit hit the fan. I was holed up in the house with my wife Alicia, and my daughter Tara watching the broadcasts from the Emergency Broadcast System. They were getting pretty sporadic at that point. I had this neighbor, Frank Rockwell, who'd been patrolling the area along with a group of guys from the neighborhood. For a while they seemed to have things under control as far as taking out the deadfucks in the area. We lived out in Mount Airy. Upscale neighborhood. Quiet. The houses are pretty spread out. Frank tried to recruit me, but I didn't want to leave my family. Tara, especially, was having a real tough time with everything. We were hearing gunshots every second. People screaming. Car accidents in the distance. The EBS's reporting on the same shit going on all over the world. It was awful.

Frank's going up and down the neighborhood like Paul Revere, shouting occasional updates. He says that the looters are headed this way. I get a knock at my door shortly after. It was Frank and the crew asking for my help with the looters. We had all heard the horror stories about them on the EBS. We'd seen the footage. People committing outright murder in broad daylight. Rape. I remember being shocked that we had sunken so low, so quickly. Frank assured me that my family would be safe. They had all the women and children together in one house that they all took turns guarding. So, I agreed to help.

The looters…Man, they came in like a tidal wave. Almost like an organized mob. And they brought the deadfucks with them. Not intentionally, of course. They weren't exactly concerned with keeping a low profile, is what I'm saying. It was the first time I had ever been in a gun-fight. First time I ever fired a gun at another person. It's not something that you think you'll ever do.

They took out a couple of our guys and we took out a couple of theirs. We're both puttin' down deadfucks at the same time. It got to the point where there were too many of them and the looters pulled out.

So, now the looters are gone, but we got all these deadfucks. We got separated while trying to lure them away from the neighborhood. I was pinned down in a Gas-Station Mini Mart a few blocks from my house. The place was fucking surrounded. I'm in there with this punk kid. Probably around seventeen. He's running around all balls-out, taunting the deadfucks through the windows, getting them all riled up. I kept trying to tell him to stay out of sight and they'd eventually *go away, but he wouldn't listen.*

In hindsight, I think the kid was in shock.

The land-line wasn't working, so I wasn't able to call my wife. We stayed close to the radio—this little piece-a-shit static box from the 80s'. At some point the EBS reported on an explosion that killed everyone at a shelter set up at the Please Touch Museum. "Poor bastards," I remember thinking. I spent a whole day in there before I was able to get out.

I make it back to my neighborhood, but everybody's gone. I see handwritten signs everywhere that say, "Go to Please Touch Museum." My heart dropped. Man…There are no words to describe how utterly alone I felt at that moment. I considered just ending it, putting a gun in my mouth and… POW! Lights out.

I eventually hooked up with a group sheltered in a church in Bryn Mawr. There's this chick there that I made out with in college. Sheila was her name. She had lost her family, too—a husband and two kids. She's already sorta linked up with another guy there—a real asshole. I mean, everybody there had a problem with this guy. One of those types. And you could tell that he felt threatened by my arrival. I was in no condition to even think about stealing his girl, and I assured him of that.

But as time goes on, Sheila and I start to get closer. She becomes my shoulder to cry on and I hers. The asshole didn't like that too much. Sheila confided in me that she had been trying to distance herself from the guy, but he wasn't having it. So, I stepped in, and told him to back off.

We become really close after that. Both of us had been holding off from doing anything out of respect for our mutual spouses—I guess that was a real sticking point when she was with the asshole. But she didn't even kiss him. We finally decided that we would take it to the next step. We planned a big night. Candle light dinner in her room. Drinks. Earlier that day, I caught the asshole skulking around outside Sheila's room. I warned him to stay away, and he left. Here's me feeling all triumphant while I watch him walk away.

So, we're getting drunk later when I get called downstairs to help subdue the asshole. I guess he had tried to steal medicine from the little stash that we had. Sheila says she's not feeling well anyway, and could use the time to take a quick nap. So, I go help out. By the time I get back Sheila is asleep. I climbed into bed with her, drunk off my ass. We're lying there spooning naked when things just sorta happen. I roll her over and start to get on top when I see that her face looks…different. Then I realize how cold she is. A second later, she lunges up at me and tries to take a bite outta my face. I jump off of her and run out of the room naked.

Long story short, the asshole had managed to taint Sheila's insulin with saliva he'd collected from a deadhead—Sheila was diabetic, by the way. I was so drunk that I didn't even notice she had turned.

END VIDEO

Martin: Holy Shit, man!

Raven: Now *that* was some story.

Martin (to Ted): Who the fuck *are you*, dude?!

Ted: What?

Martin: No offense. But, I would never have thought you'd be capable of the shit you mentioned in your piece.

Ted: Me either, to be honest. But you do what you've gotta do.

Martin: So, you actually stuck your cock in her?

Ted (embarrassed): Yeah.

Simultaneous groans from Martin, Raven, and Larry (via intercom).

Martin: So, you fucked a zombie.

Ted: I knew you were gonna give me shit about that. I thought she was alive, you dipshit!

Martin: Calm down. I'm just bustin' your balls.

Raven: What happened to the kid in the Mini Mart?

Martin: Oh yeah…

Ted (hesitates): No comment.

Raven gasps.

Martin: No shit. I guess you had to do it, huh? I mean, you had Alicia and Tara to think about. And the way the kid was acting…he probably would've gotten you killed.

Ted: I'd rather not talk about it.

Martin: Fair enough. I guess, in some way, you're lucky. I mean, you found out that Alicia and Tara survived the explosion at the Please Touch. And since Sheila was dead when you fucked her, it doesn't really count as cheating. I mean it's basically the same as fucking a Real Doll or something.

Soundbyte: Canned laughter.

Raven: Yeah. But the Real Doll doesn't move and make noise.

Martin (to Ted): Was she…it…responding to what you were doing?

Ted: No comment on that either.

Martin: Awe, come on!

Ted: Nope.

Raven: Leave him alone.

Martin: What about the asshole? The one who poisoned Sheila?

Ted: Take a wild guess.

Raven: They killed him?

Ted: Yeah. And for once, I was okay with it. I was originally for banishing him from the group, mind you, but we were out voted 11 to 7.

Martin: Fuck that. After what he did, I'da killed him myself.

Raven: Somehow I doubt that.

Martin: What? You saying I'm a pussy?

Raven: Wellllll….

Martin: Don't answer that.

Soundbyte: Canned laughter.

Martin (annoyed): Oh my God with this fucking canned laughter!

Raven: I know.

Ted: Talk to the old man. It's his idea.

Raven: Positive thinking, Martin. Remember?

Martin: Maybe I'll mention it the next time we talk.

Raven: How's he doing by the way?

Martin: I don't know. They don't let me speak to him unless I have a scheduled appointment. I'm supposed to meet with him next week, though.

Raven: He sure likes his privacy.

Ted: Back to what you were saying, Martin, about how you'd kill the person yourself if they'd done what that asshole did...

Martin: Yeah...

Ted: I was going to say that you've never been in the position of having to decide somebody's fate. It's not as easy as you think. Even when it's a low-life, shit-bag.

Martin: All right...Well. There you have it, folks. Ted Morrison with a surprisingly gripping story. Well done, Ted.

Soundbyte: Canned applause.

Ted: My pleasure.

Larry (via intercom): The doctor just got off the elevator, Martin.

Raven: Oh. Good. I've been looking forward to this.

Martin: Ok. Let's take a short break and we'll bring him in when we come back.

Guitars build into the Martin Stone Show theme. The theme rambles on and then gradually fades out...

AUDIO

Announcements & Ads

BSN Announcer: The following announcements and ads are provided as service of the Brand Satellite Network and the Emergency Broadcast System. The BSN and EBS accept no responsibility for any loss or damage arising in any way out of the use of, or inability to use the products or services mentioned herein.

Announcement 116
The following is an important message from Mayor Clay Edelman...

Mayor Edelman: On behalf of the people of Philadelphia, I want to thank the thousands of volunteers that have helped to police our streets, clear debris, and distribute food, water, and medical assistance to their friends and neighborhoods and strangers alike since the beginning of this greatest of tragedies through our organization, the Consortium of Able Bodied Volunteers. Your compassion toward your fellow man and woman, and your bravery in the face of nearly insurmountable odds stands as the pinnacle that we must all strive to achieve if we are to successfully begin anew. Many have lost their lives in the process, as will many more as we struggle to rebuild. But their contribution will not be forgotten, nor will the ideals from which their actions drew inspiration. This is why we must continue to rebuild. Yes, we are significantly fewer than we were. Yes, we are weaker. But we must not be deterred. I beg of you to help us continue to fight the fight.

In closing, please be on the lookout for the following member and family members of my staff who have recently gone missing. Any information on their whereabouts should be forwarded to the main guard station at City Hall.

BSN Announcer: Donald Allencamp 46—reported missing on

the 6ᵗʰ of March. Donald was last seen in the Art Museum Area of the city where he'd gone to look for his wife Donna, who disappeared in the area some time ago and was never found. Mr. Allencamp, who suffers from dementia, was under the impression that his wife was waiting to meet him at the location, according to the last person to see him.

Brother and sister, Lindsey and Kurt Danvers, 17 and 13, respectively, were reported missing on March 13th. They were last seen hiding in their family's disabled SUV on Cobbs Creek Parkway, where they were instructed to wait while their mother Jessica Danvers searched for help. Jessica Danvers' partially devoured remains were found the next day, floating in Cobb's Creek.

Announcement 117:
The Martin Stone Show Theme creeps up from dead silence…
It continues to play in the background as Martin speaks.

Martin: Hey guys. It's been brought to my attention that people have been advertising 'listening parties' at several settlements with access to the show. As a result people are risking injury or death to travel to some of these settlements. While we, here at the Martin Stone Show, appreciate your dedication, we ask that you stop this extremely dangerous activity at once. Please take down your signs and do your best to discourage anyone from attempting to reach your settlement for this purpose. The show is aired several times throughout the day and can easily be recorded and distributed in a safe fashion using the barter and trade rules and regulations of your individual settlements. Let's do what we can to keep each other safe.

Ad 126: CONSORTIUM OF ABLE-BODIED VOLUNTEERS
Solemn Male Voice: The Consortium of Able-Bodied Volunteers provides a variety of services for those in need. From construction to medical assistance, to security, to waste disposal, to general labor, our team of dedicated men and women are waiting to help you with whatever you need.

Ad 127: HAGER PORTABLE SHELTERS

Male Voice: America, once a symbol of freedom and independence seen round the world...Now, a decaying landscape of empty buildings and abandoned vehicles. Danger lurks at every turn from the living and the living dead. With settlements falling by the day, the need for temporary shelter is imperative as you attempt to safely navigate what's left of the world in search of decent folk to link up with. My Hager portable shelters are just the answer. Constructed of Teflon-coated Owens Corning Fiberglass, and built in the shape of a looted, burnt-out vehicle shell, my shelters provide protection from the environment, while acting as a decoy to lure away any unwanted guests looking to rob or eat you alive. Deadheads and scavengers alike will think you're just another abandoned vehicle and move on to a more appealing target. Remember...Hager Portable Shelters.

CONTACT INFO
BSN Announcer: To inquire about any of the products or services mentioned herein, or to request having a cell tower erected near your settlement, or to obtain information on constructing your own satellite dish, please contact Mr. Hoffman, who will connect you with the appropriate parties. Those without access to a phone may send an unarmed representative to inquire at the Brand Compound Guard Station at the former Waterfront Luxury Apartments at 901 Penn Street between the hours of 10am and 1pm. Payment in Barter only. Weapons, Food, and Medical Supplies preferred. Please be clear and concise when presenting your inquiry to the guards. Any attempts at intimidation, or threats leveled at the guards or at any designated member of the Brand Compound will be viewed as an act of violence and handled as such. Thank you.

END AUDIO

THE MARTIN STONE SHOW

MONDAY, MARCH 26th, 2015 (CONT'D)

BRING THE PAIN (INSTRUMENTAL), by Method Man plays over a black screen…

FADE IN…

Brand Compound – Reef Tower
(Formerly Waterfront Luxury Apartments)
Philadelphia, Pa

The studio (aka Apt. 3216). Martin and Raven sit in their booths nodding their heads to the music. Ted comes hurrying out of a downstairs bathroom. He runs up the staircase and into his booth.

The music fades into the background…

Martin: Annnd we're back. (to Raven): You know…I can probably recite the Mayor's announcement verbatim, at this point.

Raven: Why is the old man so adamant about keeping these outdated announcements and ads in rotation?

Martin: He just wants to make sure that people have access to—

Raven: Hello! Everybody's dead! Didn't he get the memo?!

Martin: Calm down, Raven. He means well.

Soundbyte (Martin's June 6th, meltdown): DON'T FUCKING TELL ME TO CALM DOWN!

Soundbyte: Canned laughter.

Martin (embarrassed): You guys are never gonna let me live that down, huh?

Raven: You wouldn't if it was one of us.

Martin: You're right. I wouldn't. Hey…What about that PSA we did about the listening parties? How old's that thing?

Raven: At least a couple months, right?

Ted: Somethin' like that.

Larry (via intercom): We first heard about it back in January, so that's two months.

Martin: Seems silly to keep running it, but hey…whaddo I know. Maybe there's still people out there holding parties. I don't know…

Raven: I seriously doubt it.

Larry (via intercom): The doctor's ready when you are, Martin.

Martin: Ok. Great. Send him in.

"BAD CASE OF LOVING YOU (DOCTOR, DOCTOR)," by Robert Palmer plays as Dr. Franklin Hammond (Caucasian, 56) enters the studio looking haggard and sleep-deprived, yet flashing a warm smile.

Martin: There he is. Where's the thing; your invention?

Dr. Hammond walks down the short staircase, into the circular sitting area, and sits down behind the microphone.

Dr. Hammond: You'll see in the video I brought.

Larry (via intercom): It's actually pretty cool, Martin.

Martin (to Larry): So, you're doing reviews now? Who, the hell, told you to watch the video?!

Larry (via intercom): After the last inventor, I wanted to make sure he wasn't just wasting our time. Lest you think I'm not doing my job.

Raven: You're still on that?

Larry (via intercom): Nobody's talking to you, Raven.

Martin: And nobody told you to watch the damn video either! (pause) Raising your voice at poor Raven like that.

Raven (coy): How *dare* he!

Larry (via intercom): She likes to stick her nose where it doesn't belong.

Raven: I do no such thing.

Martin: That's not important right now.

Larry (via intercom): It is to me.

Martin: No. No. What's most important to you is that you remember this one thing...You ready?

Larry (via intercom): Okay. I'll add it to the list.

Martin: Don't do anything unless I tell you. You got that! I say jump. You say, "How high...boss?!" And what's with this *our* time? It's *my* time! MY TIME! GET THAT THROUGH YOUR THICK SKULL!

Larry (via intercom): Okay. Now you're just being a dick for the sake of the show. (to audience): Don't believe the hype, people. He's not like this off the—

Larry's microphone is cut off suddenly.

Martin: I shut off his microphone. Stupid idiot. With those "Igor" eyes of his. Makes you just wanna punch him, doesn't it?

64

Soundbyte (From *YOUNG FRANKENSTEIN*, Marty Feldman as Igor): Yessss Mah-stah.

Raven: Well, I wouldn't go that far.

Dr. Hammond: I like Larry.

Martin: Of course, I'm only teasing. Larry knows that. He's a great producer. I'd be lost without him. He's just a little annoying. Here, I'll turn his mic back on.

Raven: He's fun to mess with, too. He takes it so personally.

Larry (via intercom): I love you guys, too. Assholes.

Laughter.

Martin: What was the hold up with security, doc?

Dr. Hammond: No hold up. I was speaking with Mr. Brand. He came down to the security depot to welcome us.

Martin: How do *YOU* get to see the old man?

Dr. Hammond: We worked together in the past; before 9/6. I was complimenting him on these solar cell towers that your people have been putting up.

Martin: Yeah. They're great. Aren't they? We lost a few good guys in the process, though. It was just our dumb luck that the damn things were just sitting there in a warehouse waiting to be shipped to Afghanistan when the shit hit the fan.

Raven (to Dr. Hammond): So, you're with the military?

Dr. Hammond: No. Mr. Brand's people contacted me about my research. He was interested in possibly applying it to the treatment of wounded soldiers.

Martin: I see.

Dr. Hammond: This place is quite the fortress.

Martin: Yeah…The old man spared no expense. All that money he contributed to military weapons development really paid off in the end, I guess.

Dr. Hammond: In spades, it would seem. All things considered. (pause) Each building's like a self-contained city, I presume?

Martin: Pretty much. You got Head Office, the security depot, and the building's control room on the ground floor. The next five floors are common areas; cafeteria, gym, infirmary, offices, ballrooms. (pause) When are we gonna stop with that, by the way?

Raven: What's that?

Martin: Calling them ballrooms…Conference Hall, maybe… Auditorium…Event space, even. But Ballroom? What? Is this the roaring 20s? There're no balls going on in there.

Raven (to Dr. Hammond): Welcome to our world.

Dr. Hammond laughs.

Martin (to Dr. Hammond): I'm an extremely irritable guy, doc.

Dr. Hammond: Yes. I've heard you mention that in the past.

Martin: What? Like every day?

Soundbyte: Canned laughter.

Martin: Anyway…The rest of the building, between the eighth and 31st floors is residential. Then there's our studio up here on 32, which is the only difference between the two buildings, by the way. All powered by the sun, and alternative fuel.

Dr. Hammond: Impressive…

Martin: Yeah…And to think, I used to bitch about all the security cameras that the city started putting up a few years ago. Here you can't go five feet without a camera—*with sound*—up your ass. And you know what? I ACTUALLY PREFER IT THAT WAY!

Soundbyte: Canned laughter.

Martin (to audience): All right, folks...Our guest today is, Dr. Franklin Hammond. (to Hammond): Medical doctor?

Dr. Hammond: Yes. I'm a Neurologist with a specialty in Biomedical Prostheses.

Martin: That's a mouthful. What exactly does *biomedical prostheses* mean, in English?

The doctor leans forward and becomes more animated.

Dr. Hammond: I'm in the study of stimulating "broken" or dysfunctional areas of the brain through the use of implanted microchips.

Raven (excited): I've read about this. Real cutting edge stuff.

Martin: Microchips? Implanted into the brain?

Dr. Hammond: That's right.

Martin (skeptical): So like, mind control?

Dr. Hammond: Well...in a manner of speaking. However, we've only had limited success...stimulating simple motor response in paralyzed patients, rudimentary brain-to-computer interface and such...until now. What, with the sudden surplus of test subjects.

Raven: I bet. Especially since things like ethics have gone out the window.

Dr. Hammond: Well. We still like to follow a code of ethics, but yes, in the face of such dire circumstances we have certainly pushed the boundaries of what would have been deemed ethical before 9/6.

Martin: I don't think anybody's gonna complain. So, what are you here to show us, doctor?

Dr. Hammond: Okay. We've developed a chip—and by we, I mean myself, along with a team of scientists and physicians—that, upon being implanted into the brains of the reanimated deceased or the living dead, zombies, shamblers, deadheads, deadfucks...whatever you want to call them, will allow us to, in a sense, tame them.

Martin snickers.

Martin (dismissive): Sounds a bit far-fetched if you ask me, doc.

Raven: I don't know, Martin. Like I said, I remember reading about this kind of research a few years ago. And they were doing some pretty remarkable stuff back then.

Martin: Even still. I don't want to keep their rotten, smelly asses as a fucking pet. I want them gone.

Raven: Now, I'm with you on that.

Dr. Hammond: You're both thinking small. *Taming* the dead would be a means to an end; that end being complete eradication of the problem so that we can get on as a species. Rebuild and repopulate. With that as the end goal, think of all the ways in which the dead can be useful with our device. You could, let's say...program them not to crave human flesh...to crave each other instead. We've accomplished this in the lab, several times. Consider this; it's widely known that the dead will adopt a herd mentality in large groups. Right? One gets excited and the others follow...

Martin: Yeah...

Raven: Sure.

68

Dr. Hammond: Why not use the implanted subject as a decoy? The subject lures the herd to a specified location…*away* from populated areas…or to clear an area that you might want to search for resources or to use as shelter or storage…or you can lead them to a destination to be disposed of in large numbers, without risking lives. The possibilities are almost limitless.

Martin (to Dr. Hammond): Look at you. I bet you've got a hard-on right now.

Dr. Hammond: Let's just watch the video, shall we.

Martin: You wanna watch it, Raven?

Raven: Sure. This could be a big deal if it works like the doctor says.

Dr. Hammond: It does.

Martin works the console.

Martin: We'll see.

ON FLATSCREEN

VIDEO:
Clip #1
We are in a large freezer-room in an old meat processing plant. Rows of nude bodies in various stages of decay, suspended from meat hooks. Some are moving. A few reach aggressively at a lab-tech wearing a heavy winter coat over a bloodstained lab coat. He is standing next to one of the motionless bodies taking notes on a clipboard.

Living dead voices growl in hunger or protest. The perpetual rumble of a generator. High ceilings and bad acoustics. It's hard to hear anything.

Raven bristles at the images on the screen.

Raven: Oh my goodness!

Martin: What is that…a meat freezer?

Dr. Hammond: We're headquartered out of an old Meat Processing Plant in Downingtown.

VIDEO (CONT'D)
In the front of the room, a dark-skinned man, dead, but living, cut in half at the waist, is suspended from a meat hook. Wires protrude from his exposed brain. A look of utter confusion on his face. He hangs before a long table and a towering rack on wheels stacked with complicated monitoring equipment. Wire dreadlocks snake down the living dead torso's back, travel along the floor, and up to where they connect at the backs of the complicated monitoring equipment.

Martin: Looks like a medieval dungeon in there. And how, the hell, can you hear anything?

Dr. Hammond: You get used to it. (re: dark skinned zombie) This here is one of our early test subjects. We called him Bob Marley.

Groans and laughter. Dr. Hammond remains stone-faced, unaffected.

Martin: A piece of advice, doctor…Leave the comedy to the professionals.

Raven: I was gonna say earlier…I don't know if I'd be so forthcoming with my location, doctor.

Martin: That's a good point.

Raven: The heat you're gonna get at even the slightest whiff of a cure…And they aren't gonna ask nicely.

Dr. Hammond: It's not a cure…

Raven: That's right. It's a means to an end. But even still...

70

VIDEO (CONT'D)
Another lab-tech, similarly clothed, sits at the long table typing on a laptop. Dr. Hammond is standing over him. Two more doctors—a man, and a woman—standing behind Dr. Hammond all dressed in outerwear over lab coats. An unruly quaff of graying, 70s-heartthrob hair hangs to Hammond's shoulders in the back, a facemask of graying stubble beneath eyes left opened for days. The other doctors share the same sleep-deprived look.

Dr. Hammond: I appreciate the concern, but our security force is equipped to handle any threat they may arise. Much like yourself, we've been lucky enough to have assembled a dedicated team of ex-military soldiers and officers who share in our vision.

Martin: Our security guys work for the old man. Not me.

Dr. Hammond: I think you hold more influence over them than you realize.

Martin: Why? They say something to you?

Dr. Hammond: No. It's just a hunch.

VIDEO (CONT'D)
Dr. Hammond converses briefly with the other doctors and then leans forward and says something to the lab-tech. The lab-tech types. The zombie torso lifts, and then lowers its right arm. It does the same with its left arm.

Martin: Mah-rone! Would you look at that?

Raven: I told you.

Martin (to Hammond): You're like Dr. Frankenstein or something…Dr. Hammond-stein.

Laughter.

Soundbyte (from *FRANKENSTEIN,* 1931, Colin Clive as Dr.

71

Frankenstein): It's alive! It's alive! It's alive!

Soundbyte: Canned laughter.

Dr. Hammond: This was a significant break-through for us. Yes. There had been great strides made in research into neurochip implantation and brain-to-computer interface over the last 10 years leading up to 9/6, however, as I mentioned earlier, this amounted to say, re-establishing communication between damaged areas of the brain. Or, in the case of brain- to-computer interface, the progress had been mostly in controlling a cursor via brainwaves or manipulating a character onscreen, much like a video game played with the mind. Being able to control specific physical actions robustly and succinctly, as you see here, ran a close second to understanding the "soul" as a major hurdle for us.

Martin: I've gotta say, I'm impressed, doc.

Raven (to Hammond): Just imagine if you had come up with this before 9/6? You'd probably be up for the Nobel Prize.

Dr. Hammond: And that's the irony of it. But we're confident that our research can still be put to good use.

VIDEO (CONT'D)
The lab-tech reaches across the table and offers the zombie a legal pad clamped between the robot-like fingers of an arm extender that the lab-tech controls with a trigger. The zombie looks over the pad, confused, hungry. It looks past the pad, at the people behind the long table and begins to salivate.

Martin (imitating zombie): Fuck this. I'm hungry.

Laughter.

Soundbyte: Canned laughter.

Dr. Hammond appears annoyed.

Dr. Hammond: Just watch.

VIDEO (CONT'D)

The lab-tech shoves the legal pad forward into the zombie's chest. He repeats this action until the zombie takes the pad. A few seconds later…a pen, clamped between robot fingers hovers in front of the zombie's face. Confusion…The lab-tech shoves the pen forward until the zombie eventually takes it.

The zombie looks at the lab-tech as if awaiting instruction. The lab-tech types something into his computer and then he mimics writing on a pad.

Martin (re: zombie): I say he takes a bite outta the pad.

Raven: Shhhh!

VIDEO (CONT'D)

The zombie begins to awkwardly scribble on the pad. The doctors clap. The lab-tech types, and then he mimics turning the pad around and holding it up. The zombie trepidatiously obeys. We can barely decipher a word, "Hello."

Raven: What's that say? Zat…hello?

Dr. Hammond (prideful): Mm hmm.

VIDEO
Clip #2
A small, windowless room. White walls. Zombies shambling about without ambition. One zombie in particular stands out from the rest; a youngish man, recently deceased. Flesh missing from his neck, most likely where he was bitten. The wound has festered into a gaping hole with flayed edges and a border of purple with lightening vein tentacles reaching in every direction. He is shirtless, a huge fist with the middle finger extended tattooed on his chest.

We hear a door open off-camera. Jangling sounds. Tiny, hooved footfalls. A goat bays nervously as it is shoved into the frame. Ambition enlivens the zombies' wayward disposition. They react with aggression, sudden determination in their listless, clouded eyes.

73

Martin (re: goat): Awe…really? I can't watch this.

Martin puts his hands over his eyes.

Martin: Tell me when it's over.

Raven: Are you serious?

Martin: You know how I am about animals.

Raven: But you can watch people get eaten with no problem?

Dr. Hammond: Which speaks to a larger issue that has hastened the rapid decline of our species…

Martin (sarcastic): Don't tell me, doc…you're a psychiatrist in your spare time?

Dr. Hammond: Hardly. (pause) Had we a more…*humane* method of testing our research, I assure you that we would've explored it.

Martin: No need to explain yourself, doc. I understand. I just don't wanna see it.

VIDEO (CONT'D)
The goat bays in protest to the hostile environment and starts to run. It weaves between the zombies' legs, dodging reaching arms and fingers curled into claws. One of them grabs hold of the goat's hind leg. The goat kicks and bays. More zombies swarm around it, fighting each other for a prime spot in the feeding frenzy. The goat shrieks in terror as the ambush of cold hands and teeth clamping down tear away its flesh in sloppy chunks.

Martin (re: the goat's cries): Or hear it. Jesus!

VIDEO (CONT'D)
An aggressive tug of war breaks out over the goat. We can see that the animal is still barely alive as it is ripped in four directions. Blood everywhere. The walls. The floor. A zombie

74

slips in the blood. Then another.

The image cuts to…

The same, windowless room. Blood-spatter on the white walls, but the floor has been cleaned. The same zombies shambling about without ambition, wearing facemasks, and shirts, and gloves made of goat's blood.

Raven (to Martin): Okay. You can look now.

Martin: Really? You're not fucking with me, are you?

Dr. Hammond: She's telling the truth.

Martin slowly lowers his hands. His eyes are squeezed shut. He opens them, one at a time, and grimaces at all the blood.

Martin: Look at all that blood. Poor thing...

VIDEO (CONT'D)
A lab-tech seated in a folding chair in the middle of the crowded room thumbs through a book as if he is at home on his couch. The zombies are aware of the lab-tech however they appear utterly disinterested. They brush against his legs and bump into him as they pass. Although the lab-tech appears relaxed, upon closer inspection we see his eyes darting nervously to all of the potential threats.

Martin: This guy's got some serious balls. I don't give a fuck what the research says.

Raven: They're not even paying attention to him.

Dr. Hammond: Exactly. And I assure you that he's perfectly safe.

Raven (mystified): And those are the same deadheads from earlier?

Dr. Hammond: Same ones. What this means is that we're

now able to essentially turn off their appetite for human flesh.

VIDEO (CONT'D)
The shirtless zombie seems to sense that something is wrong as he stares at the lab-tech with eyes trying to remember, "Shouldn't I feel some way about you?" The lab-tech has the shirtless zombie in his peripheral vision. Shirtless eventually gives up. As he lurches away, he pounds his fist against the side of his head in frustration.

Martin (re: shirtless zombie): That one knows something's off.

Dr. Hammond: It would appear that way. It's to be expected that some are going to be more or less susceptible than others.

Raven (to Dr. Hammond): You do realize how huge this is?

Dr. Hammond: I do. We all do. That's why I'm here. Everyone listens to your show, Martin. Your voice has become a symbol of hope in a hopeless time. We need that kind of exposure in order for this to be successful.

VIDEO
Clip #3
A large open space. Dormant machinery in the dark background. A freezer door a few feet back on the right. Lane markers painted on the floor. The camera pans left to right.

Lane 1: A zombie lurches forward dragging a weighted sled with two 45lb plates sitting on top. The sled is connected by rope that criss-crosses the zombie's chest. A lab-tech walks alongside the sled carrying additional weighted plates.

In the immediate background, we see two lab-techs carrying a corpse to the freezer. They set it down and one opens the freezer door.

Martin: Raven's right, doc. I don't know if you're ready for the heat this is gonna bring?

76

Dr. Hammond: If you're referring to the Government; what's left of *them* is—as you know—hiding out in an underground bunker in Mount Weather without a military at their disposal, scrambling to figure out their next move.

Martin: I'd just be worried that they'd try something sneaky, considering some of the shit that went down after 9/6. If they could get control of this thing, then they'd hold all the cards. And I'm not sure that's such a bad idea.

Dr. Hammond: We *do* have a plan in place to present to the Government when the time is right.

Raven (re: video, astonished): Look at that...

VIDEO (CONT'D)
Lane 2: Two tables set up 10-feet apart. A zombie awkwardly transfers objects (stacked boxes, tools, a tray full of dishes) from one table to another.

We can see into the freezer as the lab-techs carry the corpse inside and place it onto a pile of bodies that have worn out their usefulness. We see that one of those bodies belongs to the troubled, shirtless zombie from Clip #2.

Martin (re: shirtless zombie): What'd that one keep giving you trouble?

Dr. Hammond: Huh? Oh. His...resistance made him a safety concern. We're currently studying his brain, in fact.

VIDEO (CONT'D)
Lane 3: A zombie standing at attention faces the camera. Something familiar about this one, but we can't put our finger on it. Music jumps out of the ether, "THRILLER" by Michael Jackson. The zombie comes to life and begins to dance like Michael Jackson.

Raven (re: dancing zombie): What the..!

Martin: No way that's real!

All eyes are on Dr. Hammond as he tries hard to maintain his unaffected gaze. A smile eventually breaks through.

Dr. Hammond: No. That's John, one of our lab-techs, under the make up.

VIDEO (CONT'D)
The music plays. The zombie continues to perform a medley of popular zombie-dance moves from the "THRILLER" music video.

END VIDEO

Laughter...

Dr. Hammond (re: dancing zombie): Just a little something we put together for your show.

Raven (laughing): He was actually pretty good.

Martin (laughing): Now *that* was funny. You've officially redeemed yourself for the Bob Marley joke.

Raven: I have a question.

Dr. Hammond: Sure.

Raven: This is great and all...I mean, really next level stuff, but it's going to take implanting a lot of dead people to make any real difference. How exactly do you plan on doing that?

Dr. Hammond: The plan is to start small. We target the areas where they're most densely populated. We send out our implanted zombies with instructions to find those areas and lead the dead to a predetermined place, somewhere large enough to contain a sizable amount of them. Convention Centers. Concert venues. Town halls. Once inside we bring the buildings down.

Martin laughs.

Martin: I'm sorry, doc. I'm not laughing at your plan. I guess I just expected something a little more…complex than (imitating a surly, dumbed-down version of Dr. Hammond) "We gonna put 'em all in that building over there and then blow it up real good."

Soundbyte: Canned laughter…

Dr. Hammond: It *is* rather brutish, I must admit. And I didn't come up with it, by the way. In fact, I was resistant to it in the beginning.

Raven: I noticed that most, if not all, of the subjects we saw in the footage appeared to be recently deceased? Does that have any bearing on your implant's effectiveness?

Dr. Hammond: Actually, yes. The chip works best with newly reanimated subjects. The waves degrade as the subject decomposes. Anything over a few days is generally unusable.

Martin (disappointed): That really narrows it down, then.

Raven (disappointed): It sure does.

Dr. Hammond: Do you have any idea how many people die everyday, in this country alone? The death rate was something like 6-to-7,000 people before 9/6. And that was back when people had access to adequate healthcare. Imagine what that rate is today. (pause) Finding subjects is just a matter of getting the word out to the remaining settlements and setting up some method of acquiring their recently deceased.

Raven: What remaining settlements? The time to do this was months ago.

Dr. Hammond: We're still hopeful that we can make it work.

Martin: How'd you guys manage all this, doc? We were all under the impression that there weren't really any big settlements left.

Dr. Hammond: There aren't, really. We're actually not that big.

Martin: You seem like you've got your shit together, though.

Dr. Hammond (laughs): That, we do. Thankfully. It's been a hard road, though.

Martin: Can you elaborate a little on that?

Dr. Hammond: Sure. Maybe a week after this all started, I got a call on my cell phone from Dr. Charles Thoreau out of Children's Hospital here in the city. I knew of Dr. Thoreau quite well as he's one of the leading Neurosurgeons in the world. Apparently, he had heard of me, too. He said the military was putting together a team of physicians and scientists with the goal of finding a cure, or at least a way to deal with the dead. They had a private medical facility in the Pocono Mountains. At the time I was barricaded in the attic of my neighbor's house in Harrisburg.

Raven: What happened there?

Dr. Hammond appears uncomfortable.

Dr. Hammond (reluctant): It's a long story…

Martin: Uh oh…I sense a sore spot. It's cool if you don't wanna talk about it?

Dr. Hammond: No. It's fine.

The doctor takes a deep breath.

Dr. Hammond: I had…suspected that my wife was having an affair for some time.

Martin: With the neighbor?

Dr. Hammond: That's right.

Martin: Awe man. I'm sorry. So, what'd you go over to confront the guy?

Dr. Hammond: Yes. Except it wasn't a guy.

Martin: Whoa! Now you're talkin'. No offense, doc. So, what happened?

Dr. Hammond: Yours is the typical reaction to that story. However, in reality, it doesn't sting any less when the object of your spouse's affection is of the same gender.

Martin: Was she good looking, at least? The neighbor, I mean.

Dr. Hammond (hesitant): Yes.

Martin: I don't know, doc. I'm thinking I'd have more of a problem with some guy shoving his big, fat cock into my wife's vagina, than a hot chick licking it. Hell, I'd probably watch that.

The doctor smirks, mild annoyance hiding underneath.

Raven: Would you just let him finish!

Martin: I'm sorry. Gahead, doc.

Dr. Hammond: I had to run home that morning to pick up a file. My wife wasn't home, which, in itself, wouldn't have been all that unusual, except that her car was still in the driveway. I walked over to the neighbor's house and started to ring the doorbell when I noticed that the front door had been left ajar.

Soundbyte: Ominous music

Dr. Hammond: I walked inside, fearing—

Dr. Hammond stops speaking and tosses a glare at Ted.

Dr. Hammond: Is that music really necessary?

Ted throws his hands up in playful surrender.

Ted (to Dr. Hammond): Just doin' my job.

Martin: Just go with it, doc. You *have* listened to the show before. Correct?

Dr. Hammond: And I quite liked it. It's just a little different when you're the one in the hot seat.

Martin: It's nothing personal, doc.

The doctor sits back and adopts a relaxed posture.

Dr. Hammond: So, anyway…back to the story.

Martin: Yes. Please, doctor.

Dr. Hammond: I go over to the neighbor's house and I see that the front door is ajar. I go inside afraid of what I might find. I hear noises coming from the kitchen.

Martin: What kinds of noises?

Dr. Hammond pauses to shudder at the painful memory.

Dr. Hammond: Grunting and heavy breathing. An occasional slapping sound.

Martin: Uh oh…So, you found 'em goin' at it on the kitchen floor?

Dr. Hammond: If by "going at it," you mean my neighbor was eating my wife. Literally.

Raven gasps.

Raven: Oh no…She was a deadhead?

Martin: Fuck me! (to Dr. Hammond): So, then what'd you do?

Dr. Hammond: I shoved the woman off of my wife, at which point she turned her attention onto me. I ran and hid in the attic.

Martin: No shame in that, doc. I probably would've got eaten.

Raven: So, you never found out for sure about the affair?

Dr. Hammond: Oh. But I did. Apparently my wife had gone over to the neighbor's house wearing one of my old lab coats with lingerie underneath. I can't remember the last time she wore anything like that for me.

Martin: Awe-haw-haw, man...I feel for you, doc.

Dr. Hammond: Took a while to wipe the image out of my head. That's for sure.

Awkward silence...

Raven: Sooo...you eventually found your way to the Poconos?

Dr. Hammond: Yes. They flew us out in a MH-60S Knighthawk Helicopter.

Martin: The same one you came in today?

Dr. Hammond: Same one. They flew us out to the Poconos. Gave us our own military regimen. Things were going pretty well. The soldiers...they underestimated how strong the dead can be in numbers. The facility was overrun. We lost a lot of people, but we managed to escape. We searched for a place with its own generator, and that's how we came to the Meat Processing Plant.

Martin: That's cool that the soldiers stayed with you.

Dr. Hammond: Most of them did, anyway. Their superiors tried to pit us against each other in order to do their bidding. When that didn't work, they ordered the soldiers to take control and force us. But we had all bonded by that point. We were a family. And the soldiers saw what we were trying to do. The ones who stayed had either lost their families or had none to begin with.

Martin: Well, I think what you're doing is incredible, doc, and I wish you the best of luck. There just seems to be too many variables for this to work the way you envision, in my opinion. But hey...more power to you.

Dr. Hammond: Thank you, Martin.

Raven: Before you go...We've heard all the theories regarding a cause for the dead rising; some kind of contaminant or chemical spill, a virus, the wrath of God, I think they were even talking about a passing comet at some point...

Martin: You want crazy theories...try aliens, or...technology run amuck was another...

Larry (via intercom): My favorite is a Native American curse against the white man.

Martin: The white man? What about everyone else?

Larry (via intercom): Exactly.

Ted: Can't forget about the Illuminati. You're with them, right, doc?

Laughter...

Martin (laughs): The Illuminati? I tell ya. Ted has got the best memory.

Dr. Hammond: The Bavarian Illuminati?

Martin: What was that?

Ted: That's what it was originally called.

Martin: What the hell is it?

Dr. Hammond: Well, the Illuminati was originally founded back in 1776 by a group of people who considered themselves freethinkers. But it has since become a term for some imagined conspiratorial organization that supposedly controls the world. Good job they've done, huh?

Laughter...

Dr. Hammond: Your friend claims to be a part of it?

Martin: More like a friend of a friend who's no longer with us. He claimed that an early attack on 9/6 was part of an Illuminati Conspiracy.

Larry (via intercom): Remember when Donnie left the studio to take his call?

Martin: Man, was I pissed. We all thought his buddy was crazy...Well, he *was* crazy, but it turned out he was telling the truth about the attack. (pause) That it happened, not that it was an Illuminati Conspiracy. Just to clarify.

Laughter...

Raven: That was the day you had your meltdown on the air.

Martin (embarrassed): I was *so* scared, man.

Raven: We all were.

Martin: Poor Donnie, huh?

Raven: Yeah. I miss him, too.

Larry (via intercom): Speaking of Donnie...We've gotten a few requests about replaying your Closest Calls segment, Martin.

Dr. Hammond: I'd like to hear it.

Martin: No way, man...It was hard enough reliving that nightmare once.

Ted: For all the arguments, and the attitude, and the

combativeness, Donnie really was a great guy.

Raven: Did you ever think he would risk his life for you like he did?

Martin: Actually, no. But I'm forever in his dept because of it.

Martin wipes his eyes with the back of his hand.

Martin (welling up): All right, so now you got me all choked up.

Ted: Raven was asking the doc about the cause of the outbreak...I was going to say that global warming was another theory that was thrown around; like the Earth's trying to get rid of us.

Dr. Hammond: I wouldn't be so quick to dismiss that last theory.

Martin: What? The Earth trying to get rid of us?

Dr. Hammond: There's no proof to substantiate it, of course, but one popular theory—even amongst some of my colleagues—is that a plant-based toxin is the cause.

Raven: What do *you* think?

Dr. Hammond: I'm convinced that the answer lies in the brain—a switch, if you will, maybe located in the hypothalamus that doesn't completely shut off upon death.

Martin: Makes sense to me.

Dr. Hammond: I've yet to prove it, however. And believe me, I've tried. The truth is...we just don't know. We may never know. However, I think it's safe to say that it's not the wrath of God, to reference your earlier conversation on the subject.

Martin: How can you be so sure?

Dr. Hammond: You're right. We can't actually disprove that

either. Let's just say I wouldn't bank on it.

Larry (via intercom): Sorry to interrupt, but "I love my wife" is on line 2.

Martin rolls his eyes.

Martin: Greeeaat...

Raven: That guy gives me the creeps.

Martin (to Raven): You wanna talk to 'em?

Raven: Not particularly.

Martin (to Hammond): We're just about finished here, right?

Dr. Hammond: Ahhh. Well. I'd like to speak with you a bit more in private about the announcements.

Martin: Okay. Just sit tight, doc. We'll talk to the guys in the control room about getting you on. I'm gonna put the caller through. Maybe you can help us with this one.

Dr. Hammond: What's wrong with him?

Martin: Just listen.

Raven: You're wasting your time...again.

Martin (to caller): You're on the air.

Caller: ILoveMyWife (60s)

ILoveMyWife: (regretful, almost in tears): I love my wife.

Raven: How did I know he was gonna say that?

Martin: Indeed. Now look, dude. I put you through—against the advisement of my beloved Raven, I might add—because I think there's more to your story. So, let's not waste each other's time, okay? I think it's abundantly clear to everybody listening that you love your wife. Did something happen to her?

ILoveMyWife: I love my wife.

Raven: See. I told it was a waste of time.

ILoveMyWife: I love my wife…

Martin: You're killin' me, dude.

Dr. Hammond: Where's he from?

Martin: We tried asking him that on Friday's show. He just kept saying that he loves his wife.

ILoveMyWife: I love my wife…

Raven: Just hang up.

Dr. Hammond (to ILMW): Sir. You sound like you might be in some kind of duress. In the interest of getting you some assistance, be it medical or security, or whatever, if that's, in fact, what you need, you're going to have to tell us—

ILoveMyWife: I love my wife.

Martin: See what I mean?

Raven: Well, what'd you think was gonna happen?

Martin: Aren't you the least bit curious to see what this guy's deal is?

ILoveMyWife: I love my wife.

Raven: No! There's just something about him. I get the feeling that we'd regret asking if we ever did find out what's going on with him.

Heavy static.

Martin: All the more reason to get to the bottom of it—. (re: static) Shit! You hear that?

Raven: I hear it.

The static becomes more intense, occasionally washing out their voices.

ILoveMyWife: I love my wife.

Dr. Hammond (re: static): What's happening?

Martin: We're at the mercy of the satellite, unfortunately. Sometimes the signal—

END BROADCAST

THE MARTIN STONE SHOW

WEDNESDAY, MARCH 28th, 2015

The crackle of a live microphone against a black screen…A rooster call turns ugly, bestial. Aggressive guitars play a familiar theme.

FADE IN…

Brand Compound – Reef Tower
(Formerly Waterfront Luxury Apartments)
Philadelphia, Pa

The studio (aka Apt. 3216). Martin, Raven, and Ted seated in their booths. Martin leans into the microphone as the theme music fades out.

Martin: Goooood morning, everybody. Good morning. That's right, folks. You've lived to see another day. Whether that's a good or a bad thing, that's yet to be determined.

Raven: I vote for good.

Martin: The lovely Raven making sense, as usual.

Soundbyte: Cat calls. Canned applause.

Raven laughs.

Martin: Broadcasting on Brand 96 on the Brand Satellite Channel and Brand 103 for those of you with access to video…It's that time again, time for your favorite un-undead purveyor of wisdom, The King of All Airwaves, Martin Stone, comin' at you *LIVE* from high atop the Reef Tower at the Brand Compound on the Philadelphia waterfront.

Soundbyte: A large crowd boos.

Raven (re: booing): Now. Now.

Martin: Can you believe that even now, with the rotten, stinking, bodies of their friends and loved ones walking around eating people, trying to eat *them*...Even in the face of all that, I'm somehow still the scum-of-the-Earth to some people in the compound. Me! The guy who provides a forum to vent all the pent-up frustration, and fear, and depression that we're all feeling. I thought I was doing a good thing.

Raven: You *are* doing a good thing. Why do you let those people get to you?

Martin: It probably has something to do with my childish need to be loved by everyone.

Raven: You need to get past that.

Martin: It's not easy, Raven.

Raven: Sure it is.

Martin: Nah. You didn't grow up with my mother.

Raven: She always seemed like a sweet woman to me.

Martin: That was her talent. It's like a goddamn super power.

Raven: She's like an X-man.

Martin chuckles.

Martin: Yeah. The Passive Emasculator.

Soundbyte: Canned laughter.

Martin: As usual, I apologize for our abrupt departure on Monday. I'm sure that, by now, most of you know that we are at the mercy of the satellite. (pause) Hey! Didju guys hear that they found two girls in the subway concourse last night?

Andre Duza

Raven: Yeah! I didn't get the details except that they were really young.

Martin: I think one's 17, and the other is 12.

Raven: They're just kids! Were the guys on a scouting run or something?

Martin: I'm not sure. I wonder what their story is, though... how they survived down there by themselves.

Raven: Dave might know. Or Jimmy Tran, the driver. He always knows the inside scoop.

Martin: Either of them around? Hey Lar?

Larry (via Intercom): Gimme a sec...

Soundbyte: Theme from *JEOPARDY*.

Larry (via intercom): Jimmy's down in the main office with the rest of the guys who went out last night. And Dave...Oh, wait...He's calling in right now. Line 1.

Martin: Dave...You there?

Caller: Dave from Security

Dave: I'm here, Martin.

Martin: So what happened last night? Were you with them?

Dave: Nah...That was Team 2. I was on Gate Duty here at the compound. You guys remember Erich Ganz?

Silence...

Dave: You know. The guy we kept catching trying to sneak out of the compound about a month ago?

Raven: Yeah...yeah...

92

Martin: The guy with the fucked up teeth...

Dave: That's the one. Well, he tried to bribe one of our guys to let him out this time. But the guard ratted him out. Get this… Apparently, Ganz was part of some string of major pharmacy heists before 9/6. The last one was like a week before, even.

Raven (fascinated): Really?

Dave: His job was to sit on the drugs until the heat died down. He split the stuff into two separate duffel bags and stashed one in his gym locker at the Bally's Gym in the subway concourse. That's why our guys were down there.

Martin: What about the other bag?

Dave: That's classified, Martin. Sorry. You never know who's listening.

Martin: Understood.

Dave: Speaking of which…It probably wasn't a good idea to go into such detail regarding the layout of the compound on Monday's show.

Martin (embarrassed): I know. I wasn't thinking. I got an earful from Head Office about it yesterday.

Dave: I know ya did. And I don't mean to kick you while you're down, but like I said…you never know who's listening.

Martin: Won't happen again. You have my word.

Dead air…

Raven: So, what kinds of drugs are we talking about? Ganz's stash, I mean…

Dave: Steroids, painkillers and antibiotics, mostly. Stuff that we could use. You know how hard-up our infirmary is for medicine. And we're talking like 30-to-50 thousand dollars worth of the stuff.

Martin: Who isn't hard up for medicine? Was he planning on keeping it for himself?

Raven: I would think he was planning to use it as leverage.

Dave: That's exactly right.

Raven: Medicine is money these days.

Dave: Medicine, and food-n-water, and gasoline.

Martin: And weapons.

Dave: Definitely weapons.

Raven: He could've set himself up pretty nicely if he would've played his cards right.

Martin: Shit, man. Goes to show how you never really know people. I've seen that guy in the halls. Seems like a nice enough guy. Then you find out he's involved in some shit like this. And you guys wonder why I stay holed up in my apartment. Well…aside from my wife's magical vagina.

Soundbyte: "Magical" harp chords.

Soundbyte: Canned laughter.

Raven: They're a lot of good people in the compound, Martin.

Dave: I've gotta agree with Raven.

Larry (via intercom): A lot of good people at City Hall, too, when we were there.

Raven: Yup.

Martin (to Larry): Traitor.

Soundbyte: Canned Laughter.

Raven: Compared to the nut-jobs out there? Forget about the dead. You've got criminals, rapists, murderers. All the people who couldn't figure out how to make it work back when things were normal.

Martin: I think some of them prefer the chaos.

Dave: I think so, too.

Raven: Probably so. The settlements didn't want these people. So, they're just out there doing all sorts of despicable things in the name of survival.

Martin: I think you'd be hard pressed to find anybody who hasn't done something despicable in the name of survival.

Raven: You're right. But you know what I mean.

Martin: You've always been on that "people are essentially good" kick. Not me, man. People are mean, and selfish, and conniving, and they'll smile in your face, then stab you in the back in a second to take what you've got.

Raven: I'm still holding out hope.

Dave: You've never really been out in the shit, Martin. I know you've seen tons of footage and heard all the horror stories, but it's not the same as experiencing it firsthand. Raven's absolutely right about how bad it is. Being in here is a world of difference.

Martin: YOU'RE ALL WRONG AND I'M RIGHT!

Raven: Here we go.

Martin: I'M ALWAYS RIGHT…(echoed, bad Romanian accent) for I am the great Martin Stone, ruler of all that I survey. And my word is sacred.

Soundbyte: Canned laughter.

Dead air......

Martin (echoed, bad Romanian accent): You may proceed with your tale of woe, young David.

Raven: Tale of woe?

Martin: I don't know. It sounded like the right thing to say. Hey, where're you stationed today Dave, that you can stay on so long?

Dave: I'm walking the floors today. Thankfully, there's not much action going on in the halls.

Martin: Both buildings?

Dave: Plus the gym and the garden.

Martin (scoffs): The garden...

Dave: I was laughing my ass off at your rant the other day about eating food from the garden.

Martin (laughs): I can't help thinking that it used to be a parking garage.

Raven (to Dave): It's silly, right?

Dave: Yeah...Kinda. Sorry, Martin.

Martin: Look. I said, I know how stupid it sounds. Oh fuck you guys!

Laughter.

Martin: So, back to what happened last night, Dave...I was joking when I yelled at you, by the way. Lest you think I was serious. I wouldn't want a guy like you mad at me.

Dave (laughing): You're a funny dude, Martin. So, anyway, Team 2 went out to retrieve the pharmaceuticals from Ganz's gym locker in the concourse. I guess the girls musta been living in one of the old stores down there. Apparently the older girl came outta nowhere and attacked one of our guys with a machete. Hacked 'em up pretty good, too.

Raven gasps.

Raven: Who was it?

Dave: Les. You know…. The bald, biracial guy?

Martin: I know who you're talking about.

Raven: Oh yeah…I like him.

Dave: They were forced to shoot the girl to get her off him— just in the leg, though. Both girls are recovering in the infirmary as we speak.

Martin: Shit! What are you gonna do, though? I probably woulda shot her, too in that scenario.

Raven: Sounds like they had no choice. Poor thing. She probably mistook them for scavengers.

Dave: From what the guys told me, they were both pretty far gone, mentally.

Raven: So, the older one got Les pretty bad, huh?

Dave: They're saying he might lose his left arm.

Raven: Oh no!

Martin: Sheesh!

Dave: I know. Right? Les is a good guy, too. Trustworthy. That's hard to come by anymore.

Martin: If you're listening Les, we wish you a swift recovery.

Raven: Yes. And thank you for putting your life on the line in order to get that medicine. You never know. It could be one of us in need of it one of these days.

Martin: Yeah. Thanks to all the guys. You, too, Dave. Your service is greatly appreciated.

Dave: Thanks, Martin. I gotta go.

Martin: Okay, Dave. Keep listening, though. We're gonna play your close calls in a bit.

Dave: Will do.

Raven: Bye Dave.

Dave: See ya guys.

Dialtone......

End call

Martin: Okay. That was Dave from Security with the lowdown on last night's drama. (pause) So, everybody's going nuts about Dr. Hammond's microchip.

Raven: It's the talk of the compound.

Martin: Yeah. A lot of people talking about volunteering to help out.

Larry (via intercom): They're thinking about sending a group out to his place this weekend.

Raven: Maybe this is the start of something big.

Martin: Could you imagine? Me, the most hated man in the world, playing a major part in saving it.

Raven: Well, it's already been established how important the show is to people out there.

Martin: That's right, Raven. (pause) So, I relistened to the doctor's interview last night. There's a part where he makes a passing mention of all the euphemisms we've come up with for the Z-word—living dead, shamblers, deadheads, deadfucks, pus-bags, pus-buckets.

Larry (via intercom): Like doody or poop for taking-a-shit.

Raven: Or the litany of euphemisms for sex.

Martin: Exactly.

Raven: But are names like deadfucks and pus-bags really euphemisms? A euphemism is used to *lighten* or *defang* an offensive word or phrase.

Martin: In that they're meant to ridicule or demean, I'd say they qualify.

Raven: I see what you're saying. I just call 'em deadheads, though. It somehow seems more…respectful, to me. Considering that they were people like you and me once.

Ted: I like deadfucks.

Larry (via intercom): Me, too, Ted. Sometimes deadheads.

Martin: I go back and forth between deadfucks and zombies. But I think I'm going to make an effort to call them zombies from now on. My point of all this was how all these names came out of our reluctance to accept what was happening in the beginning. Remember when nobody wanted to say zombie? Like people were afraid that they were gonna turn into one if they did.

Ted laughs.

Martin: By the time we did come around to accepting them for what they were, all these other names had become part our vocabulary.

Larry (via intercom): Deadfuck just fits them so well, in my opinion. Zombie sounds so…

Ted: Silly? Like something that should only exist in horror novels and movies?

Larry (via intercom): Exactly.

Raven: Some people would say that's exactly what the world has become—like a horror film.

Martin: Regardless, I'm still going to make an effort to say it more often.

Raven: Well, good for you.

Martin (to Raven, sarcastic): I knew I could count on you to appreciate where I'm coming from.

Raven laughs.

Martin: Moving on…Not everyone was pleased with the doctor's interview, Raven.

Raven: Oh, really.

Martin: Yep. Take this voicemail here for example…

Raven: Oh no. Who's it from?

Martin: You'll see.

Voicemail: Maggie from Lancaster

Maggie: You think you know everything with your doctors and scientists. There is no SOLVING the problem. Don't you know that this is all Gods plan as prophesied in Matthew 24:21-22: "For then there will be great tribulation, such as has not been from the beginning of the world until now, no, and never will be. And if those days had not been cut short, no human being would be saved. But for the sake of the elect those days will be cut short."

End Voicemail

Raven: I shoulda known.

Martin: You know my theory on people like Maggie. Happy people don't have time to obsess over stupid shit like this. Having religion is one thing…And look. It might not be my cup of tea, but if believing in God helps you get through the day-to-day with everything that's going on, then more power to you. But people like Maggie are a whole different story.

Raven: It's called crazy, Martin.

Martin: To say the least. Speaking of religious kooks, Larry turned me on to this completely fucked up video. It's from some church out there…

Raven: Do I even want to see this?

Martin: You'll want to see it. Trust me.

Raven: I don't know.

Martin: Trust me. Hey Lar…Where's that video you showed me this morning?

Larry (via intercom): Cued up on Track 23 under "Larry's Vids."

Martin: Got it. All right, folks. You think Maggie's crazy? Well, feast your eyes on this shit.

VIDEO
An ambush of church music. Many voices singing in unison. A blur of solid colors as the camera whips around, and then settles on an image.

Martin: Keep watching

Raven: I'm watching. I'm watching.

VIDEO (CONT'D)
We are at waist-level in a crowd of people facing one direction and singing from Hymnals. It appears that the camera-person is trying to conceal the camera. We can see hints of the place (a church), via the spaces between singing parishioners standing shoulder-to-shoulder. Quick glimpses of activity on the altar, but we can't quite make it out due to the motion blur as the camera-person attempts to find the best angle. Deep within the rows of singers, we see a single file line of people inching forward every 20 seconds or so.

Martin: Just wait...

VIDEO (CONT'D)
The camera tilts upward at the backs of peoples' heads, and the ceiling.

The camera suddenly straightens and begins to slowly ascend until we can see the altar up front...

Raven gasps, horrified.

Raven: Anht unh! You've gotta be kidding me. I mean, you have *GOT* to be kidding me!

Martin: Crazy, right? Still think people are essentially good?

VIDEO (CONT'D)
People sing as they approach the altar in single file. A man crucified to a 10-foot wooden cross at the center of the altar. He is gaunt, his abdomen painfully concaved, his skin powder-white. Long, stringy blond hair. He is dead...but alive. His arms are outstretched and impaled at the wrists by large wood nails. His ankles are tied to the post. He is clothed only in a loincloth and a crown of thorns fashioned from barbed wire. Trails of blackened blood stream from his wrists and hairline as he writhes and growls, jutting his head forward and down, and stretching his neck as far as his decomposing muscles will allow. His mouth is open wide, longing to taste the warm, living flesh of the parishioners who file past and kiss his feet. A robed priest stands at the foot of the cross,

waving people forward and wiping the living dead man's feet with a damp towel after each kiss.

END VIDEO

Raven: I might just have to change my stance on that after seeing this. Although, it does also prove my point about what's out there beyond the compound gates.

Martin: I just can't wrap my mind around how they could not know that what they're doing is crazy. All right. Moving on…

Dead air…

Martin: That's your cue, Ted.

Ted: Oh…Sorry.

Soundbyte: Somber piano music.

Martin: There's something I've been wanting to talk about for awhile now, but I just wasn't sure if I should do it on the air. (pause) You know what? I need a minute. Let's do Dave's Closest Call first.

Raven: Wait a second! You can't just throw something like that out there, and then leave us in suspense.

Martin: No. Really. I need a minute.

The piano music stops.

Ted: You all right, man?

Martin (welling up): That fucking music. I didn't realize it would get to me like it did.

Larry (via intercom): Hey, Martin…This have anything to do with Karen?

Martin (hesitates): Yeah…

Raven: Oh my God. She's not sick, is she?

Martin: No…Nothing like that. Not physically anyway. Let's just do Closest Calls, then I'll tell you guys afterward. (to audience): All right folks, as we promised, here is Episode Number #3 of Stone Show's Closest Calls, featuring Dave from Security.

ON FLATSCREEN

VIDEO
STONE SHOW CLOSEST CALLS #3
Dave Straussman (aka Dave from Security) – Brand Compound Security

A medium shot of Dave Straussman, from the waist up, seated against a black background.

Dave: I was running with this group out in Jersey, bunch of intellectual types who thought they had it all figured out. They were convinced that the government would have a handle on this thing soon. All we had to do was sit tight and wait it out. They had signs up and everything in case any survivors happened by.

So, me and this other guy, Jake, kept trying to tell 'em that it ain't just the deadfucks we gotta worry about. Sometimes the living are worse. This was back when looters were going house-to-house scavenging for supplies…and pussy, which is what we tried to make the intellectual-types understand. But they're all, "You should learn to have faith in humanity." Meanwhile, we're in this big-ass estate right off of the Jersey Turnpike. You could literally see the place from the highway. We were like sitting ducks.

Me and Jake…we would take down the signs as quickly as they put 'em up. Or we would paint over them. Then they would put 'em right back up again. And we would take 'em right back down. Caused a looootta problems. We lasted about a month before the place was overrun with deadfucks. The looters came in right after. It was awful, man. Musta been about 20 or 30 of 'em—looters, I mean.

First they dragged the leader outside—older guy named Bruno. Real nice guy, but way too trusting. They roughed him up pretty good, then they knee-capped him and left him right inside the front door as bait for the deadfucks.

The rest of us were hiding in the basement, but we could hear the whole thing. And he didn't go right away; Bruno. Shit still gives me nightmares. I don't know what was worse, listening to him being eaten alive or listening to the kids in the group fucking lose it right in front of me. I had my hand over this 8-year-old boy's mouth, trying to keep him from giving away our position.

Dumbass Bruno had gone up there thinking he could reason with 'em. Everybody panicked when we heard what happened to him. Jake figured making a break for the back door was our best option. I tried to tell 'em it was a trap; that the looters were out there waiting. And surely enough…

They shot all the men, execution-style, including Jake, and they took the women and children prisoner.

So, now the place is crawling with deadfucks. I hid in this huge walk-in freezer in the basement. I must've stayed in there for hours. I could hear the bastards shuffling around on the other side of the freezer door. They were everywhere from the sound of it. Problem was, it was cold as balls inside that freezer. I was starting to come down with hypothermia. All I wanted to do was lie down and go to sleep, but I knew if I did that I'd either never wake up again, or I'd wake up as one of them.

I knew that the looters were long gone, so I decided to take my chances with the deadfucks. It was a miracle I got outta there alive. They had me down twice. They're all clawing and reaching and snapping teeth at me. There were so many that they sort of got in each other's way. That's how I was able to get away from them. So, I finally make it out the front door. I run as fast as I can into the woods on the east side of the estate. I finally stop after about a quarter-mile. I'm standing there trying to catch my breath when I look down.

105

There's a severed arm hanging from the hip pocket of my jeans and another one grabbin' hold of my shirt.

END VIDEO

Martin: Mah-Rone! Dave from Security with another great installment of Stone Show's Closest Calls.

Soundbyte: Canned applause.

Raven: Wow…I think I'd rather be eaten.

Martin: Not me.

Raven (to Martin): So you'd rather be passed around between 30 guys, raped in every way imaginable on a daily basis for the rest of your life? At least if you're eaten it's over with in a matter of minutes.

Martin: I see your point.

Raven: Either way is horrible.

Martin (exhales): Okay. I promised Karen I wouldn't talk about this on the air, but I have to get it off my chest before I go completely nuts. (pause) So, any longtime fan of the show knows how passionate my wife, Karen has always been about animal rights, and philanthropy, in general. I call her my little angel. I make jokes. I mock her naïveté here and there—which, I'm sure some shrink would say is out of jealousy, or because I feel that I don't measure up…Who knows? Maybe, to some degree, they're right.

Raven: That's not true.

Martin: Karen…She wants to help this one. She wants to help that one. If it were up to her, we'd be out there in the shit, using our resources to help in a more aggressive way. "But I AM helping. We ARE helping," I say to her. I go on and on about the impact of the show, blah, blah, blah. She says she knows that my heart is in the right place, but calls the show vulgar. The stupid stunts…People risking their lives for entertainment…Mayor Edelman throwing us out…Those were her words, by the way. Once again…We were not *thrown out* of City Hall.

Larry (via intercom): I still get people asking me about that.

Martin: Needless to say, it's always been a point of contention for us. In the past it was more about my paranoia over who she was associating herself with. As soon as people would find out who she's married to…

Raven: If they didn't already know.

Martin: Right. They'd immediately start scheming about how they can get to me through her. And if you think my paranoia was unwarranted, I assure you that it's happened on more than one occasion.

Raven: I think we can all vouch for you on that one.

Martin: But like I said…it's different now. Now it's literally about keeping her alive. Maybe I've become overprotective. So what. There's fucking dead people walking around out there waiting to eat your ass. Ya understand? They don't give a shit that you're a good person. You're nothing but food to them. You might as well wear a fucking cheeseburger costume.

Laughter.

Raven: Like in the old cartoons.

Martin: She says she feels overwhelmed with guilt that we live so comfortably in here, while there are people out there struggling to survive. She says she can't pretend everything is normal anymore. I'm like. "Hello. I do a show where 90% of the subject matter is topical. How is that pretending that everything is normal? People call us WZMB, for Christ sakes." I do wish they would stop with that, by the way.

Larry (via intercom): I think it's here to stay, unfortunately.

Martin: It was just a sketch people. I appreciate the love. I do. But, stop it. It's called the Martin Stone Show. THE MARTIN STONE SHOW!

Soundbyte: Angry dog growling

Martin (dismissive): WZMB…Sounds like some shitty podcast or something.

Raven (laughing): It does.

Martin: But seriously. I just don't know what to do about Karen at this point. She's actually mentioned running away a few times.

Raven (shocked): By herself?!

Martin: Yeah!

Larry (via intercom): Where the hell does she expect to go?

Martin: She doesn't know. Anywhere but here. That's what she said.

Raven: Oh, Martin. This is bad.

Martin: It's been getting worse and worse, man.

Larry (via intercom): Have her talk to Dave. Or what about Jimmy Tran? They'll set her straight about what it's like out there.

Martin: It won't do any good.

Larry (via intercom): How do you know unless you—

Martin: Cause I tried it already! *That's* how I know!

Larry (via intercom): Who'd she talk to?

Martin: The big guy in the kitchen, the one with all the stories.

What's his name?

Larry (via intercom): You mean Big Ron? I forgot about him. Yeah, he's definitely got some stories.

Martin: Lotta good that did, though. I think with Karen, her claustrophobia has a lot to do with it. Growing up in Montana and everything, she prefers wide open spaces. You know? She's always hated living here, but now it's warped into something unbearable…to the point where she feels trapped.

Raven: Trapped?

Larry (via intercom): That's what I was gonna say.

Martin: It doesn't help that these Yentas downstairs in the women's groups keep filling her head with those ridiculous rumors about some supposed "Shangri-La" settlement in Virginia or Ohio, where life is like a Norman Rockwell painting.

Larry (via intercom): Awe, dude. Those chicks are the worst. They complain about everything.

Raven: I don't understand the mentality there. It's like, if you hate it here so much, then go somewhere else.

Larry (via intercom): Right. Go start your own settlement. That rumor's been going around for months, by the way. The version I heard put it in upstate New York.

Martin: We've been arguing daily; me and Karen. I made an appointment for Karen this morning to see one of the shrinks. She promised she wouldn't do anything rash until she, at least, talks to someone. Fucking Yentas had it out for me from the start. You remember when we first came here, how they were screaming bloody murder?

Larry (via intercom): I remember.

Raven: How could we forget?

Martin: Poisoning Karen's mind every chance they get. They think they're rescuing her from me. Worthless hags. I hope they're listening.

Raven: Of course they are.

Larry (via intercom): They'd never admit it, though.

Martin: Nope. So, I had Larry put together a little video for them.

Raven: What kind of video?

Martin: Just a little something to show them some alternatives for Karen to being with such a monster like me. We should probably take a break first, though. (to audience): All right, folks. We're gonna take a short break for announcements and ads. See ya on the other side…

Guitars build into the Martin Stone Show theme. The theme rambles on and then gradually fades out…

Announcements & Ads

BSN Announcer: The following announcements and ads are provided as service of the Brand Satellite Network and the Emergency Broadcast System. The BSN and EBS accept no responsibility for any loss or damage arising in any way out of the use of, or inability to use the products or services mentioned herein.

Announcement 118
BSN Announcer: The Shelter Report, Philadelphia has been updated as of 12/20/2014...

-The following shelters are still accepting survivors: St. Thomas Episcopal Church, Girard College, The Christian Street YMCA, The Southwest Community Center.

-The following shelters are filled to capacity: The Philadelphia Convention Center, Lincoln Financial Field, Citizens Bank Park, Wells Fargo Center, The First Unitarian Church of Philadelphia, The Tenth Presbyterian Church, Independence Charter School.

-The following shelters are no longer in service: The Lansdowne YMCA, West Philadelphia High School, Penn Wood High School, Upper Darby High School, Community College of Philadelphia, The Kimmel Center, The Gallery, Springfield Mall, Granite Run Mall, The Franklin Institute, The Academy of Natural Sciences, The Philadelphia Art Museum, The Maritime Museum.

Ad 128: BOBCAT COBURN'S 'SURVIVING HELL ON EARTH'

Hi. I'm Bob "Bobcat" Coburn. You may remember me from my old cable reality show, Surviving the Collapse. While I may have been way off on the cause of society's ultimate collapse, the fact is that we find ourselves in a world not unlike that which was portrayed in countless scenarios on my show. If you've watched the show then you know that the name of the game is remaining calm and devising a plan.

First and foremost is acceptance. The dead have risen with the single-minded purpose of eating the flesh of the living. That means you and me. Don't waste time, trying to understand it. It is what it is. If you're going to survive, then you must arm yourself and prepare to use deadly force to defend your life and the lives of your loved ones.

Next, you must find adequate shelter and establish a food and water supply. These two things are the most important factors in ensuring your prolonged survival. Published three years before the collapse, my book, *Last Man Standing* is filled with useful information that will give you the knowledge and the tools to help you succeed.

From discussing various edible berries and plants to self-defense tips, to instructions on building your own improvised shelters, and animal traps, let *Last Man Standing* be your guide to survival.

Ad 129: ZOM-B-GONE

Rustling sounds. Heavy breathing. In the distance a crowd of zombies groan and wail.

Actor #1 (tired, scared): We've been crouched behind this rock for hours. I think I'm gonna pass out if I don't eat something.

Actor #2 (scared): But there's too many of them between here and the shelter. Radio's dead, so there's no way to reach anybody inside for help.

Actor #1 (scared): Shit! We're doomed!

Actor #3 (Calm and cool): Not so fast boys.

Actor #1: What's that?

Actor #3: It's…

Product Spokesman (rapid-fire, TV-pitchman delivery):… ZOM-B-GONE STICKY BOMB PERSONAL EXPLOSIVE DEVICE! ZOM-B-GONE STICKY BOMB PERSONAL EXPLOSIVE DEVICE! ZOM-B-GONE STICKY BOMB PERSONAL EXPLOSIVE DEVICE!

Actor #2 (exaggerated curiosity): What does it do?

Product Spokesman: The Zom-B-Gone Sticky Bomb Personal Explosive Device is a tennis ball-sized, hand-held explosive that resembles a pin-cushion. Upon being thrown at a soft object, the Zom-B-Gone Sticky Bomb Personal Explosive Device adheres to said object via sharpened, steel spikes that cover the entire circumference of the device, which can then be detonated from a safe distance. The rubber outer shell houses an explosive charge with a blast radius of 15-to-45 feet. So, whether you're talking about five zombies or 50, the Zom-B-Gone Sticky Bomb Personal Explosive Device is just what you need to survive in today's world.

Actor #3 (to #1 and #2): Cover your ears guys.

A few seconds pass… We hear an explosion. The background voices have been silenced.

Actor #1: Whoo hoo!

Actor #2: Looks like you got 'em all!

Actor #3: That's right boys. Zombies go to pieces over the Zom-B-Gone Sticky Bomb Personal Explosive Device. Now, who's hungry?

CONTACT INFO
BSN Announcer: To inquire about any of the products or services mentioned herein, or to request having a cell tower erected near your settlement, or to obtain information on constructing your own satellite dish, please contact Mr. Hoffman, who will connect you with the appropriate parties.

Those without access to a phone may send an unarmed representative to inquire at the Brand Compound Guard Station at the former Waterfront Luxury Apartments at 901 Penn Street between the hours of 10am and 1pm. Payment in Barter only. Weapons, Food, and Medical Supplies preferred. Please be clear and concise when presenting your inquiry to the guards. Any attempts at intimidation, or threats leveled at the guards or at any designated member of the Brand Compound will be viewed as an act of violence and handled as such. Thank you.

END AUDIO

THE MARTIN STONE SHOW

WEDNESDAY, MARCH 28th, 2015 (CONT'D)

BLACK HOLE SUN, by SOUNDGARDEN plays over a black screen...

FADE IN...

Brand Compound – Reef Tower
(Formerly Waterfront Luxury Apartments)
Philadelphia, Pa

The studio (aka Apt. 3216). Martin, Raven, and Ted seated in their booths. Martin rocking to the music, as usual. He leans toward the microphone as the music fades...

Martin: Annnd we're back...Before we get back into it, I wanted to stress that the listeners please disregard the outdated Shelter Report in today's announcements...Most of those shelters have been out of service for months.

Raven: I was going to say...

Martin: Keeping the old ads in rotation is one thing, but running an outdated shelter report is dangerous. Hey Lar... Can you talk to the guys in the control room about doing away with those shelter reports? I'm worried that people are going to try and make it to one of those shelters.

Larry (via intercom): I'm on it.

Martin: While you're at it, tell them to fix Elevator A. (to Raven): Did you hear that somebody else got stuck in that thing yesterday?

Raven: I did.

Martin: It's just a matter of time before somebody gets hurt.

Ted: Not to change the subject, but anybody else got the theme from that fuckin' Zom-B-Gone ad stuck in their head?

Soundbyte: (Zom-B-Gone Spokesman): ZOM-B-GONE STICKYBOMB PERSONAL EXPLOSIVE DEVICE! ZOM-B-GONE STICKYBOMB PERSONAL EXPLOSIVE DEVICE! ZOM-B-GONE STICKY BOMB PERSONAL EXPLOSIVE DEVICE!

Soundbyte: Canned laughter…

Martin (laughing): Yeah. That's a good one. They've unloaded a shit-load of those things, too.

Ted: It's that commercial.

Raven: It stays in your head.

Larry (via intercom): Martin…

Martin: Yeah…

Larry (via intercom): I just talked to the guys in control. They're going to run a retraction with the next round of ads.

Martin: Good. Thanks, Lar.

Larry (via intercom): Speaking of Zom-B-Gone…You ever try saying that shit really fast, like the guy from the ad?

Martin (imitating Zom-B-Gone Spokeman): Zom-B-GonePersonalStick…Ahhh shit! Zom-B-Bomb…God-dammit!

Laughter.

Larry (via intercom): It's impossible, right?

Martin: I give up. (to audience): All right folks, so…about that video I mentioned before the break.

116

Raven: Ugh…I was hoping you forgot.

Martin: I never forget, Raven. I'm like an elephant. Especially when it comes to a bunch of know-it-all Yentas trying to interfere with my marriage…

Larry (via intercom): It's pretty bad, Raven. Martin hand-picked the clips.

Martin: Damn right, I did.

Raven (half-joking): I'm scared.

Martin (playfully ominous): Be afraid, Raven. Be very afraid. (pause) This one goes out to all the Yentas in the compound. You know who you are…

VIDEO
"PEOPLE" by Barbra Streisand plays over a montage of amateur video, surveillance camera, and News footage.

—A middle-aged woman runs with a limp down a dead-end street. Hastily abandoned vehicles, and bodies, and looted storefronts populate the scene. The woman is on the run from four men brandishing improvised weapons. They corner her against the driver-side door of an abandoned car. They force her to the ground. One of the men straddles her and rips her shirt, revealing her bra. Something in the woman's right hand—a screwdriver. She strikes with an upward motion and hits the man in the throat. The man grabs his throat and falls to the side. Blood seeps through his fingers and out of his mouth. The woman attempts to get up, but the other men run over and stomp, and kick, and beat her with their weapons. The wounded man writhes and kicks on the ground, his hands wrapped around his throat. A puddle of blood forms beneath him.

—An SUV barrels through a limitless swarm of zombies. They smother the vehicle with their bulk, pounding and clawing at the windows, causing the SUV to list violently. They clamber onto the hood and press their faces against the windshield.

The vehicle eventually becomes stuck. The windows finally give. Desperate arms reach inside and pull out an entire family. The family members kick and scream as the zombies dismember, and eat them alive.

—Two small factions of survivors trade gunfire with one another inside a looted grocery store.

—A man is chased through a looted shopping mall by a unisex mob of ordinary folks. A laundry-bag, filled to capacity, slung over the man's shoulder. Weighted down by the laundry-bag, the man quickly tires. The mob catches up. One of them grabs the bag as the others punch and kick the man. They knock him to the ground and began stomping and kicking him. He curls into a fetal position and refuses to let go of the bag even as canned goods spill out of it. One of the pursuers pulls a gun and orders the others to back off. They back away and began snatching up the fallen canned goods. The armed pursuer aims the gun at the man on the ground. Out of nowhere, the armed pursuer is shot in the head by an unseen gunman. The other pursuers are picked off one-by-one as they try to flee the scene.

—Suburban neighborhood. A few cars hastily abandoned, but otherwise rather peaceful looking. A car swerves into the frame and crashes, head-on, into a tree. We see the female driver's head slam into the windshield and crack it. A large bloodstain where her head hit the windshield. Smoke rising from the hood. A teenaged girl in the passenger-seat, unconscious. Zombies coming out of the wood work. They slowly converge on the crashed vehicle. Through the windshield, we see the teenaged girl slowly regain consciousness. She unlatches her seat belt and cries out in pain as she reaches toward the driver. After several attempts to revive the driver, the girl opens the passenger-side door and falls out into the street. Zombies approaching. They quicken their steps when they see her. The girl tries, but cannot stand. She crawls forward on her belly attempting to get away, but the zombies eventually surround her in a frenzy of tearing hands and teeth clamping shut. A separate faction of zombies pull the driver from the vehicle and begin to devour her. The first bite wakes the

woman from near death, but she can do nothing, but scream and thrash.

Larry (via intercom): Sorry to interrupt, but I've got Dave on line one. He's saying it's urgent.

Martin: They probably asked him to reprimand me about the video.

VIDEO (CONT'D)
—*A gang rape in progress inside an abandoned auto repair garage.*

Martin: They're gonna say I'm inciting fear.

Larry (via intercom): I don't think so.

Martin (nervous): Really? Okay. Put 'em through.

VIDEO (CONT'D)
—*Quick shots of:*

The dead being used as target practice.

A group of drunken men laughing as they kick around a zombie's decapitated head like a soccer ball.

A pot-bellied man dances, in his underwear, around a female zombie clothed in lingerie and chained, by the neck, to a wall. His full erection pushes against the fabric of his tightie-whities. Make up crudely slathered on the female zombie's once beautiful face. Long blond hair matted with blood on one side. The man dances into and out of the zombie's reach as she tries to grab him.

A car barrels down a road purposely slamming into zombies. We see the driver cheer with each hit.

END VIDEO

Martin: You're on the air, Dave.

Caller: Dave from Security

Dave: You might wanna take this in private, Martin.

Martin (worried): Why? What is it?

Dave: It's your wife. We got a call from the infirmary stating that she didn't show up for her appointment with Dr. Milton.

Martin: Goddammit! She promised.

Dave: There's more...The doctor sent one of his staff upstairs to check on her and found that your door had been left open.

Martin: What?!

Dave: The woman called out to Karen, but didn't receive an answer, so she called us.

Raven gasps.

Martin springs from his chair.

Martin: Oh my God! Is she all right?!

Dave: Upon checking your residence, our officer failed to determine Karen's whereabouts. He did, however, state that it looked like someone had left in a hurry.

Martin: What?!

Raven: Oh no!

An alarm sounds. The unexpected noise startles Martin, Raven, and Ted.

Raven: Oh! That scared me.

Martin: What, the hell, is going on?! Where's Karen now?!

No answer.

Martin: Dave?!

Dave: There's activity at the west gate!

Martin leans over the console and yells into the microphone.

Martin: Will someone please tell me where my—

Dave: It's Karen! She's trying to climb over the fence!

Martin snatches off his headphones and hurries out of the booth.

Raven: Martin! Wait!

Martin hurries down the stairs and toward the front door of Apartment 3216. Larry comes running out of his office, just as Martin blows past him and out the door.

END BROADCAST

THE MARTIN STONE SHOW

MONDAY, APRIL 2nd, 2015

The hiss of white noise over a black screen...Sobbing...A familiar voice...

Voicemail: ILoveMyWife

ILoveMyWife (sobbing): I love my wife...I love her. I do...But I can't let her go on like this. She wasn't always this way. Please forgive me for what I must do. I love her so...I love her...I love my wife...

End voicemail

The crackle of a live microphone cuts in...A rooster call turns ugly, bestial. Aggressive guitars play the Martin Stone Show Theme.

FADE IN...

Brand Compound – Reef Tower (Formerly Waterfront Luxury Apartments) Philadelphia, Pa

The studio (aka Apt. 3216). Martin, Raven, and Ted seated in their booths. As the music begins to fade...Martin leans forward and prepares to speak.

Martin: Gooooood morning, everybody. Good morning. That's right, folks. You've lived to see another day. And that's a good thing. A lot has happened since we last spoke. As you know, my wife, Karen had somewhat of a breakdown last Wednesday. I'm not gonna lie. It's been rough. I think I spent the whole time since then in that damn infirmary. I am happy to report, however, that Karen is back home and doing well. And I have a big announcement that's directly related to Karen's recovery that we'll get to later in the show.

Soundbyte: Canned applause

Ted: Glad to hear that Karen's doing okay.

Raven: Yes. We were all worried. S'pecially since you weren't answering your phone.

Martin: I was a complete mess. You wouldn't have wanted to talk to me...

Raven: Well, an update would've been nice...considering the shape you were in the last time we spoke on Wednesday.

Martin: What did I say? I was so fucked in the head over Karen's trying to run that I don't even remember.

Raven: You were talking about giving up. (imitating Martin) I'm such a shitty husband. Maybe Karen would be better off without me. All I do is bring her down. Maybe I should stop doing the show and just disappear. Who are we even broadcasting to anymore? Everybody knows there's nobody left.

Martin (embarrassed): Wow. I said all that, huh?

Raven: And then some...

Martin: Yeah...Like I said; I was a mess.

Raven: You still feel that way?

Martin: About being a shitty husband to Karen?

Raven: About all of it.

Martin (dismissive): Nah. Come on. I had just found out about Karen at the time. Whadda you expect?

Larry (via intercom): You shoulda seen Raven, Martin. I mean...worried is an understatement.

Martin becomes agitated.

Martin: Okay! I'm sorry! But I *did* kinda have my hands full, ya know. It's not like I was just sitting around on my ass.

Raven: No. *I'M* sorry. (wells up) It's just that I care about you so much. All of you guys.

Soundbyte: Somber piano music.

Raven shakes her head at the piano music, while trying not to smile.

Raven: Oh…Fuck you, Ted!

Laughter.

Martin: I hear what you're saying, Raven. And I think I speak for everyone when I say that the feeling is mutual.

Soundbyte: A chorus of female voices: Awwwweeeee…

Raven (under breath): If the feeling was mutual you would've answered your phone.

Martin (to Raven): Would you knock it off!

Raven laughs…

Martin (to audience): This morning's intro comes courtesy of regular caller, I Love My Wife, who left the voicemail you heard…What was it; Friday Lar?

Larry (via intercom): Yep. Friday morning, when we would've been on the air.

Martin: It certainly gives us a little more insight into the guy.

Raven: He was much more talkative this time. I've gotta say, I sorta feel sorry for him now.

Larry (via intercom): I'm thinkin' he's got the wife chained up in the attic or something.

Martin: Yeah…Normally, when I hear that sort of thing, it's like; "Just put her out of her misery, dude." But I found myself thinking about that damn voicemail all weekend. What would I do, if, God forbid, Karen turned? Could I do it…or would I be like ILoveMyWife?

Raven: I could.

Larry (via intercom): But you've never been married, Raven.

Raven (defiant): So.

Martin: He's right.

Raven: That's ridiculous. If I loved someone enough to want to spend the rest of my life with them, I would think that I'd want to spare them the horror of walking around like a friggin' deadhead. I'm of the belief that the dead must be aware of what's happening to them on some rudimentary level. Can you imagine how awful that would be? Not only are you dead and rotting, but you're walking around killing and eating people… your friends, family members…You've got a front row seat to their pain and terror as you eat them alive…And there's *nothing* you can do about it. Why would I want to subject the person I love to that?

Ted: But pulling the trigger…or swinging the bat, whatever, would be much harder than you think, Raven. And *when* do you do it? As soon as they're bitten, to spare them the pain of turning? Do you hold off and let them savor every last excruciating bit of life that they have left? What's it take, about two- to-three days from the point you're bitten or otherwise infected?

Larry (via intercom): Most people go in two if they don't die right away from the initial bite.

Ted: Right…Or do you wait until your loved one wakes up, in

the off chance that they'll recognize you, which, we all know ain't gonna happen.

Raven: That's a hard one. I think it would depend on what *they* wanted. But I would still do it.

Ted: Could you kill one of us, Raven—if it came to that?

Raven (thinking): Hmmm...

Martin: I don't think I could.

Larry (via intercom): If my family's safety was in jeopardy...I think that's the only way I could do it.

Ted: Yeah. Me, too.

Larry (via intercom): I'm still waiting for Raven's answer?

Raven: I'm thinking...

Martin: Speaking of watching friends turn...I'm assuming everyone saw the Mayor's address to the city. What a travesty that was, huh? I know I'm gonna catch hell for this, but whose bright idea was it to let him do that?

Larry (via intercom): A bunch of the guys were saying that he looks infected.

Martin: Of course he's infected. That's my whole point. There ain't enough make up in the world to hide that fact.

Raven: They sure did try, though. Didn't they?

Martin: The guy looked like the Joker for Christ Sake's.

Laughter.

Raven: So, are you suggesting that the mayor's people advised him to do the address or somehow made him do it under duress?

Martin: Clay's a prideful guy. I'm sure it was his idea to go on like that, however, there comes a point when I think the medical staff needs to step in and deem him unfit. I mean, the guy could barely hold his head up.

Raven:…or keep his eyes open.

Martin: Exactly. Is that any way to honor a guy who's done so much for this city? Here's a man who's been a local icon for the last 20 years; a symbol of strength, and confidence. And you reduce him to a skinny, shivering, slumping, slurring, bobbled-headed scarecrow. And then you make him yell "the sky is falling." That's essentially what they did. (pause) I'm sorry. I get so passionate because I really like the guy. He was always good to us when we were in City Hall.

Raven: It's because of him that we were there in the first place.

Martin: Right. And if it were up to him we'd *still* be there. The fact of the matter is that Clay fought to keep us in City Hall, but he was out-voted. (pause) Let's change the subject. This conversation is bumming me out.

Raven: Agreed.

Martin shuffles through a stack of papers. He comes to one of interest. His face lights up.

Martin: Oh! How could I forget about Dr Hammond! I thought there would've been more volunteers to go out to the doctor's place. I know it hasn't run on the announcements yet—that's today, by the way…But just based on the buzz around here after his interview, I thought people would jump at the chance to participate. What were there; like 8 people that went?

Larry (via intercom): Yep. Eight. I think people aren't completely sold on the doctor's research. They're waiting to see how it goes before they decide to jump on the bandwagon.

Martin: It does seem too…What's the word I'm looking for?

Larry (via intercom): Implausible?

Raven: Complicated?

Martin hums in partial agreement.

Ted: Overly ambitious?

Martin: There you go.

Ted: Requires too many variables in order to be successful?

Martin: Even better…I guess what I'm trying to say is that I was a little disappointed that people weren't more gung ho about it when it actually came down to doing something. I get it, though; why they weren't. (pause) Needless to say, the first group of volunteers arrived safely at Dr. Hammond's compound in Downingtown on Saturday afternoon.

Raven: The meat processing plant?

Martin: That's right, Raven. Stay tuned to the show for updates, and info on any future trips out to the doctor's place.

Martin shuffles through papers.

Larry (via intercom): Hey Raven…

Raven: Yeah?

Larry (via intercom): I love how you dodged Ted's question about whether or not you could kill one of us.

Raven laughs.

Martin: That's a skill, the way she does that.

Raven (coy): I don't know what you're talking about.

Martin: All right, folks…We've got a packed show today. We whip out some old-favorite games. We have a new segment called Getting to Know Your Neighbors, where we'll interview fellow residents here at the Brand Compound. And, last, but not least...Raven catches us up on news and gossip from around the compound.

Soundbyte: Canned Applause.

Raven: I'm still not so sure about the Getting to Know Your Neighbors segment.

Martin: It'll be fine. (to audience): Raven's worried that we're gonna stir up trouble within the compound. (to Raven): Look. You're always complaining about how I isolate myself from everyone like a recluse. Well, this is my attempt to get to know our fellow residents.

Raven: No. It's more like your attempt to find out why these people hate you so much, and to sneakily win them over.

Martin: Well, that, too.

Soundbyte: Canned laughter

Raven: I just feel like, why bother? Remember that survey back in the 90s that found that most people who disapproved of you still listened to the show to see what you were gonna say next. I don't think it's any different now. So, what's the point? Let 'em think you're some kind of degenerate misogynist. Dumbasses!

Ted: Who eats babies...

Laughter.

Martin (laughing): While stomping on puppies.

Soundbyte: Babies Crying. Puppies whimpering

Soundbyte: Canned laughter.

Martin (to audience): Those were Raven's words, by the

way…Lest anyone think I called them a dumbass.

Raven: I'm only referring to the people who criticize you or the show unjustly.

Martin (instigating): Even still…It sound's like you're the one stirring up trouble. How're we suppose to win them over if they feel as if they're coming into a hostile environment?

Raven: None of the people that you're trying to win over are gonna agree to come on the show.

Martin: There's where you're wrong, Raven. In fact, today's guest is currently waiting in the green room. I was gonna wait until after the big announcement to bring her in here, but since we're on the subject…Hey Lar…You wanna send her in?

Dead air…

Martin: Lar…

Larry (via intercom, reluctant): Ah…She actually just left.

Martin: Whaddayou mean, she just left?!

Larry (via intercom): She said she changed her mind.

Martin: What?! Why?!

Larry (via intercom): I'm assuming it's because of you guys' conversation.

Martin: Goddammit, Raven!

Raven: Hey…Don't blame me. I was just voicing my opinion.

Martin: Yeah, but you didn't have to call them dumbasses.

Raven: Oh please! Compared to some of the things they've said about us…about you…If anything, I saved you a lotta hassle.

Martin exhales, defeated.

Martin: What happened exactly, Lar?

Larry (via intercom): She came storming out of the green room and said something like, "This was a mistake."

Martin: Listen guys…I can see how my desire to make peace with these people might seem out of character, but just try to think of Karen. Being cooped up in our apartment is really taking its toll on her. It's not fair that I expect her to be a recluse like me, you know. She's the kind of person who needs social interaction. But no one will talk to her because she's my wife.

Raven: That's ridiculous. I can think of a number of good people who don't care about all that.

Martin: It's different for you, Raven. People see you as the voice of reason on the show. They might look at you and wonder, "How can she stand to work with that degenerate?" But Karen, she's married to the devil himself. They look at her with disgust. And the ones you mentioned are too afraid to jeopardize their standing in the compound, so they avoid her.

Dead air…

Martin: Just do it for me, huh Raven? Call it a favor.

Raven: All right. I won't say another word about it.

Larry (via intercom): Somehow I doubt that.

Soundbyte: Canned laughter.

Raven: Shut up, Larry.

Ted: So, who was it; the guest?

Martin: Her name's Annette Sullivan. She's with the Concerned Mothers group.

Raven laughs.

Raven: The lonely housewives brigade? Good luck with that one.

Martin: C'mon, Raven…

Larry (via intercom, re: Raven's remark): What'd I tell you?

Raven: Shut up, Larry!

Martin: Yeah…Shut up, Larry.

Soundbyte (From *YOUNG FRANKENSTEIN*, Marty Feldman as Igor): Yessss Mah-stah.

Soundbyte: Canned laughter.

Larry (via intercom, to Martin): What're you coming at me for?

Ted: Wasn't she one of the women protesting outside of the building over the weekend?

Martin: Yup. Hey Lar, could you try and reach her for me. See if we can't get her to reconsider.

Larry (via intercom, laughing): Been trying since she left.

Martin: All right. Well, keep trying please?

Larry (via intercom): Will do. Didju see some of the signs the protestors had? I saw one that said "AT LEAST THE DEAD WERE HUMAN ONCE!"

Laughter.

Raven (laughing): That's a good one.

Martin: I don't know whether to laugh or take offense to that.

Ted (to Martin): How, the hell, didju get this chick to agree to

132

an interview?

Martin: For one thing, we told her that she'd have carte blanche to say whatever she wanted about me. Whether or not I agreed with her, we were interested in having an intelligent discussion between two adults. Our goal here is to try and find some common ground, us being neighbors and all.

Raven (laughs): And she bought that?

Martin: Well, we also told her that she could use the show to promote her group.

Ted: That's what did it. Those chicks have been squabbling over who should be their leader since they started the group. This'll give her the advantage.

Martin: I'm only interested in getting to the heart of the problem between us.

Raven (cynical): Sure you are. Like you don't already know…

Martin: I'm actually pretty serious, Raven. I've had a lot of time to think over the past few days and I came to the conclusion that I'm sick of fighting. You know? I feel like I've been fighting my whole career, and for what? So I can have the number one radio show? Somehow it all seems insignificant now. It sorta plays into my big announcement, actually.

Raven: So, let's hear it.

Martin: You really wanna know, huh?

Larry (via intercom): Yes. Please.

Raven (sarcastic): No. We've just been on pins and needles since you mentioned it at the meeting this morning.

Martin: All right. All right. Calm down. Okay. So…You know those two sisters they found in the concourse? Actually,

Andre Duza

they're not really related. They just call themselves sisters. Anyway, they were with us the whole time we in the infirmary. Not in the same room, mind you, but...

Raven: I got it. Go on...

Martin: That guard, Les was in there, too. The one who lost his arm...

Raven: How's he doing?

Martin: Not good, I'm sorry to say. They kept him sedated the entire time we were there. Apparently he's been really struggling with losing that arm.

Raven: Who wouldn't be?

Martin: It got to the point where they were afraid he might try to harm the girls.

Raven: Ohhh... That's terrible.

Martin: I know, right? But you can't really be mad at the girls. It's just bad all the way around.

Raven: I hope he pulls through.

Martin: Yeah... Me, too.

Dead air...

Martin: Back to the girls, though. The younger one, Sara—real sweet girl—she locks herself in the bathroom one night—I think it was Friday—and refuses to come out and take her medication. So, she's in there pitching a fit. The doctors couldn't get her out. The older sister couldn't get her out. The older one's Margo, by the way. So, here comes Karen, still woozy from the meds they had her on. She comes staggering out of her room and talks the girl right out of the bathroom. You shoulda seen it.

Raven: What'd she say?

Martin: I don't remember exactly, but you know how Karen is. You've seen her with animals.

Raven: Yes. She's very maternal.

Martin: Right. Sara was like her shadow from then on. I mean, she followed Karen everywhere.

Raven: What about the other one?

Martin: Margo. She's a different story. She never says a thing. With that haunted expression of hers...I made the mistake of getting too close to her and the look she gave me...

Raven: Well, how old is she; 16 or 17?

Martin: Margo? She's 17. Sara's 12.

Raven: Yeah, 17's a tough age to go through what they did. Sara's still young enough that she probably doesn't completely understand it.

Martin: Margo would watch us like a hawk whenever Sara was around. Gave me the creeps the way she would just pop up outta nowhere. Or sometimes you would see her standing in shadows or something and you'd realize that she'd been standing there all along. And she carries thisss...filthy stuffed animal around with her everywhere. The thing's literally falling apart. S'got this huge hole in the side where it looks like some animal chewed on for awhile. I think it's supposed to be a rabbit. It's hard to tell, the thing's so filthy.

Raven: Sheesh...I'd keep my eye on her.

Martin: Nah...She's all right. I'm more surprised that Sara is as normal as she is. She's such a sweet kid. Margo, too. She's just waaay guarded...

Raven: Well, that's certainly to be expected. But, I'd still keep my eye on her.

Larry (via intercom, to Martin): Can I say something?

Martin: Gahead.

Larry (via intercom): It's funny to hear you gushing over a little girl.

Raven laughs.

Raven: I was thinking the same thing.

Martin: I know, right? But I can't help it.

Larry (via intercom): No. I think it's a good thing. Kids have a way of maturing you.

Ted: Yup.

Martin: So, what're you saying? I was immature?

Larry (via intercom): You know what I mean…

Raven: What happened in your case, Larry?

Soundbyte: Canned laughter.

Larry (via intercom, sarcastic): Ha. Ha. Very funny. You just couldn't resist taking a shot at me, could you, Raven?

Raven laughs.

Raven (to Martin, disappointed): So, that was the big news; that you got Sara to open up? I mean, that's great and all, but…

Martin: No. Be patient.

Raven: I have been patient.

Martin: The big news is…(pause) Can I have a drum roll please, Ted?

Raven: Oh, would you just come out with it.

Soundbyte: Drum roll.

Martin: The big news is that...(pause)...we've officially adopted Sara.

Soundbyte: Dramatic Sting

Raven gasps.

Ted: No shit?

Martin: As official as it gets in this day and age, anyway. She even wants to take my last name.

Raven (shocked): No way!

Martin: Yes, way. She's going to be staying with us permanently as of later this afternoon.

Larry (via intercom): Dude! You sure you want to take on that kind of responsibility?

Martin (defensive): Of course, I'm sure. What am I, an idiot? You think I'm not gonna think something like this through. Christ, I thought you guys would be happy for me.

Raven: We arrrreeee...It's just that...

Martin: What? Cause of the rumor that's been goin' around about them?

Dead air...

Martin: Didju guys think I didn't know about that? Come on... Give me some credit. And for the record, No, I don't think her and Margo are *up to something*. Funny how that rumor got started by people who've never even met them.

Larry (via intercom): I was under the impression that the

rumor came from the security team that brought them in.

Martin (annoyed): Yeah…but they were only around them for a short time. They didn't get to know them. Not like we did.

Raven is unconvinced.

Raven: All right…If you say so.

Martin sighs.

Raven: Do you think it's a good idea to separate them, though?

Martin: That was Margo's idea, believe it or not. The docs gave Sara the O.K. to leave the infirmary, but they wanna keep Margo for awhile, for further observation. She didn't want Sara to have to suffer because of her. I thought that was extremely mature of her.

Raven: Well, I definitely agree that she needs further treatment; that one.

Martin: She said that Sara needs to be around people who can care for her like she deserves instead of in this place— referring to the infirmary. We made it clear that Sara can come down and visit her sister anytime she wants, and vice versa once Margo's released.

Larry (via intercom): I think I'm actually proud of you.

Martin: Thanks.

Raven: I'll put on a smile, but I'm still a little concerned.

Martin: Well, then I guess I have to win you over, too.

Raven laughs.

Raven: I guess so.

Martin: All right...Let's move on...(to audience): So, in response to all the requests to replay some your favorite memories from our recent games, I've dug out a few to choose from. (to Raven): Wanna hear what they are?

Raven: I wanna know who, exactly is making these requests?

Martin: You'll have to ask Larry.

Larry (via intercom): We used to get calls all the time, but now it's mostly the security guys, some people from Dr. Hammond's compound, and a few other residents here who shall remain nameless.

Raven (annoyed): Why should we do anything for the people who don't have the balls to admit that they listen?

Martin: Nah...I get it. This place is like a powder keg. So many different personalities crammed together in three buildings. You're living right next door to someone whose politics are diametrically opposed to your own. The country was far more segregated than we think before 9/6. Now that's all gone.

Raven: All the more reason why they should show their support. It'll let the naysayers know that you're not the devil, and what we're doing here is actually a good thing.

Martin: Maybe I *AM* the Devil.

Soundbyte (From *PROBLEM CHILD, Jack Warden as Big Ben Healy*): It's the *DEVIL*!

Soundbyte (From *THE DEVIL'S REJECTS, Bill Mosley as Otis B. Driftwood*): I am the Devil, and I'm here to do the Devil's work.

Martin: I'm only kidding, of course...So let's get to the games. I'm gonna throw out some names and then we'll take a vote. Okay. Here goes. First up is from "I Blanked a Zombie"

Raven: I thought we were done with the perverted stuff?

Martin: Relax. It's not the one you're thinking.

Raven: The one? Weren't there several different variations of people acting out deviant sexual behavior with the dead?

Martin: Yes. But it's none of those. I promise. Remember the one where the guy claimed to have trained a zombie?

Ted: Ohhhh. That was a good one.

Raven: That's the one where the guy gets bitten at the end of the video?

Martin: Yep. He's got the thing performing all sorts of menial tasks, then at the end, he unchains it and it takes a chunk right outta his shoulder.

Ted: He was so proud of himself, too, until he got bit.

Martin: It's sad, really. The guy actually thought he was onto something. I wouldn't suggest it but for the dude's reaction. Remember?

Larry (via intercom): It was awesome the way he shifted on the fly and suddenly it became like a video journal of what it's like to turn.

Martin: Yeah. I remember being really impressed by the kid's maturity. (pause) So, there's that one. Next, I've got "The Zombie Beauty Pageant."

Raven: Meh…

Ted: That was a good one, too, but I second Raven's response.

Larry (via intercom): I thought it was hilarious.

Martin: Next up we've got, "Real or Fake: Zombie Edition."

Raven: The one with the women with the exposed implants? No, thank you.

Ted: Next.

Larry (via intercom): I'm still going with "I Trained a Zombie."

Martin: Next, we've got, "Celebrity Lookalikes: Zombie Edition."

Raven: Now, *that* was funny.

Ted: Yeah. That was a good one.

Larry (via intercom): Yup. So far, for me, it's between "I Trained a Zombie" and "Celebrity Lookalikes: Zombie Edition."

Martin: And last, but not least...My favorite of the bunch... "Dead or Ted."

Laughter.

Raven (laughing): I vote for that one.

Ted: Fuck you guys!

Raven: We can't help it that you come across subdued and unaffected. It's not like it's news to you.

Martin: Subdued and unaffected? The guy's like a fucking zombie. In fact, Ted's had the zombie persona locked down even before there were zombies. He's the original zombie.

Laughter.

Raven (laughing): The patient zero.

Ted (annoyed): NEXT!

Martin: That was the last one.

Raven: I say "Yes," to "Dead or Ted."

Ted: You're such a bitch.

Martin: Lar…

Larry (via intercom): "Dead or Ted's" good. Sorry Ted. But, I'm still going with "I Trained a Zombie."

Ted: Fuck you, too, Larry.

Martin: Whoa! Calm down, Ted. It's just a g—Oh…we have a caller. Hello caller. You're on the air.

Caller: Alex from Maple Shade

Alex is breathing heavily.

Alex: Martin. This is Alex. Alex from the stablehouse in Bucks County…

Raven: You called last week.

Martin: That's right. With the mother who was bitten…Glad to hear you're still with us, Alex.

Alex: I need your help.

Martin: What is it? What's the matter?

Alex: It's my mom. I can't find her.

A quiet moment as Martin, Raven, and Ted trade knowing glances. Martin is reluctant…

Alex: Hello?

Martin: I'm still here, Alex. (pause) Look. Maybe it's best that you let your mother go. She wouldn't want you to see her walking around like that. You know? You've gotta—

Alex: No. You don't understand. She never turned.

Raven: Wha?

Martin: Come again?

Alex: I said, she was bitten and she never turned.

Martin: Wait a minute! How is that possible?

Alex: I don't know. We waited, but the wound just started to heal like normal.

Martin: Holy shit! If this is true, then…Ho-lee *Shit*!

Alex: I swear it's true.

Raven: Whadda you mean, you can't find her, Alex?!

Alex (welling up): She tried to kill herself when we thought she was gonna change. She said she couldn't take knowing that she could possibly try and hurt me. She begged me to help her do it, but I didn't have the heart. She said I didn't love her. That if I loved her, I would do it. We kept arguing about it, and then yesterday she ran off while I was asleep.

Martin: Do you realize what this means, Alex?! You HAVE to find her! Where are you now?!

Larry (via intercom): Martin.

Martin (annoyed): Goddammit, Larry! Not now!

Larry (via intercom): We're getting bombarded with calls from Head Office.

Martin: Well, they're gonna have to wait. Alex. You there?

Alex: I'm here. Please. You've gotta help me find her.

Martin: I will, Alex. I promise. But first you have to tell me where you are.

Dead Air…

Alex: I'm in Bala Cynwyd, in a big red house on Conshohocken Road.

Raven: That's near our old studio.

Martin: What's the address, Alex?

Alex: Hold on…I'm walking to the door to check. (pause) 327 Conshohocken Road…

Martin: Okay. Alex. I want you to stay on the line as long as you can. I'm gonna see if we can get somebody to come and get you. (to Larry): Lar. See if we can get—

Larry (via intercom): Already on it.

Martin: In the meantime, we're gonna take a short break while I deal with all these calls. This could really be big, folks.

Raven: If the mother is somehow immune, would that make him immune, also. I mean, they share the same DNA.

Martin: Shit! You're right. I didn't even think about that.

AUDIO

Announcements & Ads

BSN Announcer: The following announcements and ads are provided as service of the Brand Satellite Network and the Emergency Broadcast System. The BSN and EBS accept no responsibility for any loss or damage arising in any way out of the use of, or inability to use the products or services mentioned herein.

Announcement 119
BSN Announcer: The Brand Satellite Network is currently seeking volunteers to join Dr. Hammond and his team at their Downingtown Facility. Volunteers will assist in all phases in the development of the doctor's Neurochip implant device, from acquiring subjects, to testing, to disposal, to the eventual implementation of the device. While every precaution necessary will be taken to ensure your health and safety, be aware, there is some danger involved as you will be working closely with living dead subjects on a daily basis. Interested parties should follow the contact guidelines at the end of this announcement. Come, do your part to help save humanity.

Ad 129: ANTIROT AND THE AMERICAN REBELS
Up-tempo American rock music kicks in. An equally energized rocker-type speaks over the music.

Rocker: Everybody knows that Rock and Roll will never die. They tried to kill it with Disco…

Soundbyte: A giddy Disco melody.

Rocker (Cont'd): They tried to kill it with Hip Hop…

Soundbyte: An aggressive Hip Hop beat.

Rocker (Cont'd): They tried to kill it with Grunge…

Soundbyte: Melancholy grunge chords.

Rocker (Cont'd): They tried to kill it with that watered down, pre-packaged *AMERICAN IDOL* garbage...

The music comes to a sudden stop. The rocker's enthusiasm fades with the music.

Rocker: Well, I guess that stuff did hurt it pretty bad.

The uptempo music kicks in again. The Rocker becomes energized.

Rocker: But they couldn't keep rock down, and neither can a billion stinking pusbuckets. Through our music, AnitRot and the American Rebels hopes to inspire that American Spirit in all of us, to awaken that sense of rebellion that has scored the background of social change through our great nation's history.

AnitRot and the American Rebels is available in the Philly/ Jersey area for birthdays, weddings, bar mitzvahs' or any other special event that requires a healthy dose of good old American Rock and Roll to kick start your rebellion. Remember. AntiRot and the American Rebels. Rockin' out against the undead.

CONTACT INFO
BSN Announcer: To inquire about any of the products or services mentioned herein, or to request having a cell tower erected near your settlement, or to obtain information on constructing your own satellite dish, please contact Mr. Hoffman, who will connect you with the appropriate parties. Those without access to a phone may send an unarmed representative to inquire at the Brand Compound Guard Station at the former Waterfront Luxury Apartments at 901 Penn Street between the hours of 10am and 1pm. Payment in Barter only. Weapons, Food, and Medical Supplies preferred. Please be clear and concise when presenting your inquiry to the guards. Any attempts at intimidation, or threats leveled at the guards or at any designated member of the Brand

Compound will be viewed as an act of violence and handled as such. Thank you.

END AUDIO

THE MARTIN STONE SHOW

MONDAY, APRIL 2ND, 2015 (CONT'D)

RADAR LOVE by GOLDEN EARRING plays over a black screen...

FADE IN...

Brand Compound – Reef Tower
(Formerly Waterfront Luxury Apartments)
Philadelphia, Pa

The studio (aka Apt. 3216). Raven and Ted are in Martin's booth, standing over him as he sits at the wrap-around console. They appear to be discussing something important, but we can't hear what they're saying over the music. Larry is standing at the bottom of the staircase, looking up at the loft area as if awaiting an answer to a question he'd asked previously.

The song goes on longer than usual.

Raven and Ted hurry back to their booths. On the way, Ted yells something down to Larry, who then hurries into his office/bedroom. Martin pulls his chair closer to the console and leans into the microphone. The music fades...

Martin: All right folks. We're back. Sorry for the delay, but things are a little crazy around here at the moment. You still there, Alex?

Caller: Alex from Maple Shade (Cont'd)

Alex: Yeah...

Martin: If you're just joining us, Alex called in just before the break looking for his mother, who had been bitten by a zombie eight days ago, but has not yet turned. Not only hasn't she turned, but according to Alex, the wound has begun to heal. We've set up a conference call between security, Head Office, us, and Alex, which you'll be in on—

Larry (via intercom): Head Office says they won't do it on the air.

Martin (disappointed): Really? Shit! I was all set to air the call.

Raven (to Martin): I told you.

Martin: Why not? The old man wants us to keep it positive... Well, what's more positive than this has the potential of being?

Larry (via intercom): They don't want to get people's hopes up. In case it turns out to be a hoax or something. No offense, Alex.

Alex: *I'm telling the truth! I swear! Why the hell would I lie about that?!*

Martin: Nah...They've got a point, Alex. (pause) Look at me, gettin' all excited.

Raven: I didn't want to be the first one to say it, but I'm with Head Office. I'll reserve my judgment until our doctors are able to examine the mother.

Alex: *But we're wasting time!*

Martin: I hear ya, Alex. And like Larry said, it's no offense to you. But we've gotta be absolutely certain before we make a decision that's going to put any of our people at risk. Just sit tight. The sooner we get this over with—
Oh...They're calling in now...This may take awhile folks. (pause) I'm tempted to just air the call anyway...

Raven: I wouldn't

Martin: Thaa fuck are we supposed to do during the call?

Raven: Didn't we decide on a game to run?

Martin: Good thinking. Lar…

Larry (via intercom): I say just end the show for today. I'm thinking, based on their tone when I spoke briefly with Head Office, we're gonna be dealing with this for the rest of the day. Longest game is The Zombie Beauty Pageant, at 40 minutes.

Dead air…

We hear a phone ring.

Martin: Okay. Sorry folks. We'll see you on Wednesday.

END BROADCAST

THE MARTIN STONE SHOW

WEDNESDAY, APRIL 4th, 2015

Soundbyte (From *ANIMAL HOUSE*, John Belushi as Bluto) plays over a black screen: *What?! Over? Did you say...Over? Nothing is over until we decide it is! Was it over when the... Germans bombed Pearl Harbor? Hell nooo! And it ain't over now! Cause when the going gets tough.... ...the tough get going! Who's with me! Let's GO! Come on! AHHHHHHHHH!*

The crackle of a live microphone cuts in...A rooster call turns ugly, bestial. Aggressive guitars play the Martin Stone Show Theme.

FADE IN...

Brand Compound – Reef Tower (Formerly Waterfront Luxury Apartments) Philadelphia, Pa

The studio (aka Apt. 3216). Martin, Raven, and Ted seated in their booths. As the music begins to fade...Martin leans forward and prepares to speak.

Martin (to Raven and Ted): Can you imagine if Alex hadn't called in? We'd be ready to throw in the towel. I would.

Raven: This is so awful. They could still be alive in there, though. Right?

Martin: Security has been doing fly-bys with the drone since, I think, six this morning, and still no sign of survivors. I'd say it doesn't look good for our people over there, let alone the doctor and his staff.

Raven: Why would someone do this?

Ted: I can see one nutjob wanting things to stay the way they

151

are, for whatever insane reason, he or she might've conjured up, but, I think the real question is, how do you get a group of people to follow that line of thought to the point of sabotaging something that could fix this whole thing?

Raven: Or, at the very least, put a Band Aid on it.

Martin: It's impossible to wrap your head around. It really is. (to audience): Good morning, everyone—although there's not too much good about it, as far as I can see. It seems that we've been dealt yet another major setback in what looks like an attack on Dr. Hammond's compound late yesterday afternoon. Details regarding exactly what happened are as yet unknown, however, as a result of the attack, the entire Brand Compound has been placed on Yellow Alert. The images that I'm about to put up on the flatscreen were taken earlier this morning by a Brand Inc. Surveillance Drone sent out after we lost communication with the doctor's compound yesterday at around 5pm. The images appear to show the aftermath of multiple rounds of small, and heavy artillery fire.

ON FLATSCREEN

A slideshow of still images showing the burnt out shell of Dr. Hammond's compound in Downingtown. Smoke billows from blown out windows. Vehicles smolder on the grounds. Bodies.

Raven (re: images): Ohhhhhh my God!

Ted: I think it's safe to say this wasn't zombies.

Martin: Well, whoever did it would obviously be a threat to us, too.

Larry (via intercom): Unless it came from within. That's one theory, by the way; that one or more of Hammond's guys lost it and took it out on the rest of the people. We've seen it happen before.

Martin: No offense, but I like that theory in that it doesn't put

152

us in any kind of potential harm's way. I know that sounds fucked up, but I just don't want anything to impede the research into Alex and his mother's immunity to the infection. Not to mention, I want to live.

Raven: Alleged immunity. And I thought we weren't going to dwell on the doctor's compound?

Martin: You're right, Raven. Forgive me for venting. Getting past all this is easier said than done. We'll check periodically with security for updates on the situation throughout the show. In the meantime, no more speculating. Understood? And that goes for me, too.

The image on the flatscreen is replaced by The Martin Stone Show Logo.

Raven: Understood.

Larry (via intercom): Understood.

Ted: Got it.

Martin: Good. All that shit does is rile people up—myself included. So, Raven…

Raven: Yeah…

Martin: You're still holding out on Alex and his mother, huh? Even with what we've heard about the tests results thus far? (to audience): I should mention that as of 9pm Monday evening, Alex Mull was rescued by a team led by our own Dave Straussman, aka Dave from Security, and transported back safely to the compound where he is currently undergoing tests in our infirmary.

Raven: It's hard not to get excited, but I'll wait for the official results.

Martin: I'm putting it lightly when I say that Head Office would prefer that we wait until they've completed tests before I 'go running off at the mouth about it.' And, you know what? I was actually considering holding off, but not after what happened last night. Even without that, I've just got a gut feeling about this one. And my gut feelings are generally right. How, the hell, you think I got to be The King of All Airwaves?! It certainly wasn't because of my looks.

Raven: Oh... You look fine.

Martin: Please, Raven. This is a face only a mother could love.

Soundbyte: Canned Laughter.

Martin: Now... Having watched *Animal House* with Karen recently, the great John Belushi's rallying speech as Bluto kept coming to mind as I sat there yesterday trying to put together the right words to convey the feelings of enthusiasm and, dare I say, hope, that have enlivened the compound since Alex's call, to all of you out there, who, I know are hurting, or on the verge of giving up, if you haven't already. Just to let you know that it's not over; that maybe there is a way out of this nightmare.... This was all before finding out about Dr. Hammond's compound, mind you.

Larry (via intercom): *Animal House* is one of those movies that would always make me smile when I would catch it on cable or something.

Raven: I'm not saying it's not a good movie, but there are plenty of inspiration, uplifting speeches by real, live people that you could've used. Martin Luther King's, "I Have a Dream," for instance... or JFK's "We Choose to Go to the Moon...."

Martin: Yeah... But you're missing the point, Raven.

Raven: What about the people who've never seen *Animal House*? (laughs) Especially the part about the Germans bombing Pearl Harbor... They're gonna be like, "What the hell?"

154

Laughter.

Martin: That part is great, isn't it?

Ted: It sure is.

Martin: Fucking Belushi, man…Larry edited out the part where ah…what are their names?

Ted: I think you're talking about the part where Tim Matheson leans over to Peter Riegert and says, "Germans?" in response to Belushi's comment, to which Riegert replies. "Forget it. He's rolling."

Martin laughs.

Martin: Yeah, he edited that and a few other parts out. Guess I shoulda had him leave it in, huh?

Larry (via intercom): Sorry about that.

Martin: Don't sweat it. That's beside the point. Quite frankly, my goal was to awaken that sense of nostalgia in people. Because, the fact of the matter is, in all this death and despair…most of us have forgotten or are starting to forget the way things used to be.

Raven: It's like when you hear somebody say, about a loved one after they'd died, "I can't remember what he or she looks like, anymore," which is a scary thought when you relate it to your own life. 'The way things were being the loved one, in this case.'

Martin: I'll admit having my own selfish reasons for wanting this so badly, too…

Raven: Well, yeah…I think we all have our own selfish reason. It's called not dying.

Martin: Yeah, but I'm talking about Sara. Karen and I…we've grown so close to her in the short time we've known her. Almost like she's our biological child.

Raven: In 5 days?

Martin: I know that's quick, even by post 9/6 time, but what're you gonna do? You get caught up in their cuteness and their childish frolicking and you find yourself mesmerized by their pure innocence. That's how it is for us, at least. You develop this weird protective bond, you know, where you would give up your life to defend her, and you feel the need to express that, even if it's just to yourself.

Soundbyte: Heartfelt piano music.

Raven: This is getting pretty deep.

Martin: Just let me finish, guys...The problem with all that is that, as her protector, it totally kills me to think of the world that she's going to inherit. We, at least, got to see what the world was like before all this. We spent most of our lives living in it. But *they* might never know what that's like. So, the idea of a possible future for her to dream about makes me want to do everything in my power to make that possibility a reality. I felt that way about Dr. Hammond's chip, too, to a lesser degree. (re: piano music) Allll right. Enough already, Ted. I can take a hint.

Soundbyte: Canned laughter.

Martin: In short, the transition couldn't be going any smoother with Sara. She's even made friends with some of the other children in the building.

Raven: Really?

Martin (proud): Yup. We've been letting her play with them. We figured it'd do her some good to be around kids her age.

Raven: Makes sense...

Larry (via intercom): I heard they got yelled at for playing in the kitchen.

Martin: Yeah…Kids being kids. I guess they were playing 'Hide and Seek.'

Raven: What was she doing all the way down there?

Martin: One of her new friends is the Chef's little girl.

Raven: Ohhh.

Dead air.

Martin: So…we've got a good show for you today, folks. We've got Part Three of our popular new segment; Stone Show Closest Calls. Today's entry is from Stone Show Producer Larry Del Rossi.

Soundbyte (From *YOUNG FRANKENSTEIN*, Marty Feldman as Igor): Yessss Mah-stah.

Soundbyte: Canned laughter.

Martin: We'll join Dave from Security and the rest of Team 1 as they head out in search of the second bag of Erich Ganz's stolen pharmaceuticals.

Larry (via intercom): They just left, by the way.

Martin: Ok. I was wondering if they were still going to do it in light of what happened with Dr. Hammond's compound.

Larry (via intercom): We're gonna need all the meds we can get if they find any survivors.

Martin: I see. So, we finally fitted Dave with a helmet cam, so we can be right there in the middle of the action with him.

Raven: How'd you manage that? Wasn't Head Office dead-set against the helmet cam?

Martin (coy): Were they? I wasn't aware.

Raven smiles knowingly.

Martin: We'll also talk to Dave about Monday evening's mission to rescue Alex Mull. And we'll get his take on what happened at Dr. Hammond's Compound. And, last, but not least…the always beautiful Raven catches us up on news and gossip from around the compound. (pause) Uh oh…

Raven: What?

Martin: One of your favorite callers is on line one.

Raven (suspicious): Who?

Martin (to caller): Hello Maggie.

Raven groans.

Raven (sarcastic): Yeah…My favorite.

Caller: Maggie from Lancaster

Maggie: You still haven't you learned your lesson.

Martin: This is getting old, Maggie.

Raven: Getting old?

Maggie: "But false prophets also arose among the people, just as there will be false teachers among you, who will secretly bring in destructive heresies, even denying the Master who bought them, bringing upon themselves swift destruction." Peter 2, verse 1.

Martin (to Raven): I'm always impressed by people who can retain that kind of useless information. It's like the guys who could throw out obscure baseball stats from like 50 years ago at the drop of a hat.

Raven: She's saying that Dr. Hammond was a false prophet and that's why he died.

Martin: So God killed him? We don't even know that he's dead, by the way. Unless Maggie knows something that we don't.

Maggie: The same thing will happen to the boy and his mother.

Martin: You're in an especially joyful mood this morning, Maggie.

Dead air…

Maggie: I'm still trying to figure out whether you're complicit in this blasphemy or if you truly are as naïve as your actions would suggest.

Martin: Huh?

Raven (to Maggie): Okay. I'll bite. Explain to me how any of this is *blasphemous*, as you put it.

Maggie: For the simple fact that it goes against God's plan. This boy and his mother, if they really are real, and not some characters dreamed up as some plan to win folks over, are distractions sent by the Devil himself to lure us away from the true path. But being people of science, you wouldn't know this.

Martin: Well. You know what, Maggie. If Alex and his mother are agents of the Devil, then I guess I'm a Satanist.

Maggie gasps.

Maggie (to herself): Forgive them father, for they know not what they do. Forgive them father for they know not what they do. Forgive them father for they know not what they do.

Martin: Maggie…

Maggie (to herself): Forgive them father, for they know not what they do. Forgive them father for they know not what they do.

Martin: I think she short-circuited.

Laughter.

Raven: Just hang up. She's obviously mental.

Martin: You just now figurin' that out?

Raven: No. But it seems like *you* are. You keep taking her calls.

Maggie (to herself): Forgive them father, for they know not what they do. Forgive them father for they know not what they do.

Martin (to Raven): Listen to her crazy ass. She's great. Why are you being such a buzzkill?

Raven: All that religious bullying. I just find it disgusting, and insulting to all the people who've died because they believed that God would protect them. I don't know. I just don't find it funny anymore.

Martin: Did you hear that, Maggie; what Raven said?

Maggie (to herself): Forgive them father, for they know not what they do. Forgive them father for they know not what they do.

Raven: I guess not.

Maggie stops chanting.

Dead air.

Martin: You still with us, Maggie?

Maggie: You are all gonna burn in HELL!

Martin: Yeah…I believe you told us that the last time you called in.

Maggie: Even that little whore daughter of yours.

Martin's posture suddenly inflates. He slams his hands down on the counter and nearly rises from his seat.

Martin: DON'T YOU SAY ANOTHER FUCKING WORD ABOUT HER! YOU LEAVE HER OUT OF THIS, YOU CRAZY BITCH!

Maggie: That's right. Let your true colors shine. Blasphemer!

Martin: True colors? What? That I'm a decent human being... who's concerned about his fellow man? What're you? Huh? I'll tell you what you are. You're a lonely, miserable person who can't stand other people's happiness. That's what you are.

Maggie: Blasphemer! Blasphemer! Blasphemer! Blasphe—

End call

Martin: I hung up on her ass. Crazy bitch!

Raven: Thank you. Now, I hope you've finally learned your lesson.

Martin: Now Karen's calling. (to Karen): Hey babe. What's up?

A child in the throes of a tantrum pollutes the background.

Martin: Hey! What's goin' on? Is that Sara?

Callers: Karen Stone (35) /Sara Stone (12)

Karen (exasperated): She's having another panic attack.

Martin (to himself): God-*DAM-it*! (to Karen, annoyed): I told you not to get her worked up.

Karen (defensive): I didn't. She got there all by herself.

161

Martin: What happened?

Karen: She just started going into her 'something bad's gonna happen to you and Daddy' rap and it snowballed from there. Look. I'm sorry I called during the show, babe, but she won't listen to me.

Martin: Okay. Put her on the phone.

Karen: Gimme a second.

Raven (softly, to Martin): Oh my goodness.

Martin (softly, to Raven): She gets caught up with thinking that we're in danger and it just spirals out of control.

We eavesdrop on Karen's exchange with Sara as she attempts to lure the girl to the phone. Sara's speech is affected by her precarious emotional state.

Sara: No. Get away from me!

Karen: I just want to help you, honey.

Sara: It's bad! You and Daddy'll hate me!

Karen: We could never hate you, Sara. But we can't help you if you don't tell us what it is that's so bad.

Sara: You're all gonna die and I'll be alone with HER again!

Karen: Who? You mean Margo?

Sara: I don't wanna go back to that place!

Karen: What place, honey?

Sara: [indecipherable]

Karen: Here. You wanna talk to Daddy?

Sara: [indecipherable]

Ruslting sounds.

Martin (to audience): Let's go to Larry's Closest Call while I try to calm her down.

Raven: You're not going to do it on the air?

Martin: Nah...Why? You think I should?

Raven: That's up to you.

Larry (via intercom): You would if it was any of us.

Martin: No I wouldn't. Not something like this.

Sara: Daddy?

A much calmer Sara catches Martin off-guard. She talks through heavy sobbing. Martin puts on his "Daddy Voice."

Martin: Oh...Hey, baby. How'ya doin'?

Sara: Not good, Daddy.

Martin (to audience): Back in a bit folks...

ON FLATSCREEN

VIDEO:
STONE SHOW CLOSEST CALLS #4
Larry Del Rossi – Producer

So, if you're a regular listener of the show, then you've heard me mention my neighbor, J.J.—which stands for John Jeffries, by the way—and how he had a thing for my wife, Maria. Now, J.J. was one-a these guys who would push it too far with the compliments...and he'd do it right in front of me. Then he'd give me a playful pat on the shoulder and act like I was the asshole for getting pissed at him. And he would always just happen to be outside whenever Maria left the house to go to work, or run an errand. It was like he was eavesdropping on our lives or something.

Maria would always blow me off when I would tell her how I felt. She'd say I was being insecure, which would PISS ME THE FUCK OFF. Especially since I knew she noticed it, too. I think she was playing dumb because she liked the attention. But that's a different story.

A little aside: This was right around the same time that I kept waking up in the middle of the night to the feeling that someone was in the house.

After finally making it home from the studio on 9/6, which was a story in itself, me, Maria and my 15-year-old son, Paxton hunkered down in the family room and turned the security system to Level One, which basically seals all possible entry and exit points behind reinforced steel shutters. At the time, we, like everybody else, had complete faith that the military would get control of this thing. We figured it'd be a week or two at most, and we were locked down and well-stocked, and ready to ride it out. I remember chuckling at all the times Martin busted my balls on the air about the shitload of money we spent fortifying our house in case of an emergency, and wanting so badly to tell him, "See. I told you so."

Who knew the emergency would be dead people coming back to life, though...

We played board games and watched movies to keep our spirits up while we waited for the military to save the day. We didn't want to expose Paxton to all the violence on the News, so I would occasionally sneak upstairs to my home-office to catch up on the News and to check the security cameras we had posted on each side of the house. The neighborhood was fairly overrun with deadfucks early on, but that, at least seemed to keep the looters away. At some point we heard an explosion a few blocks away and within a matter of minutes, the neighborhood was all but empty. We later found out the explosion had come from a tanker truck hauling gasoline that had crashed trying to make it through the obstacle course of cars left abandoned in the middle of the street. There were still a good number of people trying to get out of the city. I guess a lot of them got hurt in the blast. They were sitting ducks for the deadfucks.

So, anyway, it's the Tuesday after 9/6. Maria and Paxton had fallen asleep on the couch, and I was in the home-office watching the News when the doorbell rings and scares the shit outta me. I check the security camera and who do I see standing outside our front door, but J.J. He rings the doorbell over and over and starts banging on the steel shutter. "You've gotta help me! You've gotta let me in!" He's yelling. "I know you're in there!"

Now, my first instinct was to turn off the camera and pretend like I never even saw him, but that wouldn't be the right thing to do. Plus, I was worried that he'd attract the deadfucks to our house. By this time, Maria and Paxton are awake. So, I reluctantly let J.J. in. We decide to give him the downstairs study, which is located on the far right side of the house, away from everything. We stayed in the upstairs bedroom.

Things go smoothly, at first...Society's collapse seemed to mature J.J. and for a few days we all rode it out together. I would catch him staring at Maria every now and again, but I looked at it like, "Hey. Maria's a beautiful woman. Who wouldn't stare?" So, one day I'm doing a regular check of the neighborhood on the security cameras when I notice something in J.J.'s backyard. It looked like a pale arm sticking out of the dirt...and it was moving. So, I keep watching, and sure enough, I see a clearly-dead, naked woman with a plastic bag over her head slowly dig her way out from under the dirt. She's got tiny little puncture wounds all over her body and it looks like she's been dead for some time—maybe a few months. She wanders around the yard the way deadfucks do, and then she stops right in the middle and starts staring at the ground and moaning. And here's the kicker...I couldn't figure out from where, but somehow I recognized the woman.

I wait until J.J. goes back to his room and I show Maria the

Andre Duza

footage. She instantly recognizes the girl, too, but can't pin-point from where.

J.J. walks in on us watching the footage. I ask him who she is and demanded that he tell us why she was buried in his yard. He tells us that he took the woman in a few days ago and didn't realize that she had been bitten. He was forced to kill her after she turned, and then he buried her body. At the time, it sounded plausible enough, so we gave him the benefit of the doubt.

Needless to say, I couldn't sleep that night, which was nothing new, but instead of being preoccupied with what was going on outside, I was preoccupied with J.J., and the woman in his yard. So, I decide to sneak downstairs to the study to check on him. I find him fast asleep on the couch. I'm about to go back upstairs when I notice a plastic bag shoved underneath the couch. I tip-toe over and grab the thing. Inside he's got thisss…creepy stash of souvenirs of my wife. I'm talking photos of ours, a lock of hair, a couple pairs of her underwear.

I go to manhandle J.J. and find out that he's not there after all. He had used the blanket and pillows we gave him to make it look like he was lying there asleep. I run upstairs and check on Maria…

She's fast asleep in bed with Paxton. Whew!

I check the rest of the house, but no J.J. Down in the basement, I find our big oak bookcase pushed away from the wall that it normally sits up against. And get this…

The bookcase is hiding a hole in the wall that opens into a tunnel. I follow the tunnel and come out in J.J.'s basement. I search his house, but he's not there either. But then…in one of the bedrooms, I see a wall covered with Newspaper clippings about the Center City Stalker, who, if you're from Philly, you'll remember was never caught following a string of murders of young women in the area around six years ago. He's also got tons of voyeuristic photos of random women on the walls. One of them is of the naked woman in his backyard, only she's very much alive in the photo. She's standing with a little girl, who I assumed is her daughter. The girl had to've been no older than six.

Then I see that J.J.'s even got a special little corner of the room dedicated to photos of MY wife. I was so in shock that it took me a couple minutes to put it all together.

"Shit! J.J. is the Center City Stalker! And he's somewhere in my house right now!"

I turn to run back to the basement, and the next thing I know…I'm waking up lying on my back in my front lawn with my hands and feet duct-taped together and my old CD Boom Box hanging from a branch way above my head playing some Godawful death metal song on repeat with the volume cranked to ten thousand. It's funny…Well, it's funny now… That CD was a remnant from my college days when I listened to that crap. J.J. would've had to really look to find it.

So, it's around 4am when I wake up. I can tell by the color of the sky. I look around and see that the security gate at the end of the driveway is wide open. That's just fucking great. And then…

They come crawling out of the woodwork like roaches. Deadfucks. Within minutes there musta been 50 of 'em—I shit you not. I gotta tell you. I don't think I've ever been so scared. I think I may have even shit myself. Hey! I'm not ashamed to admit it. I wriggled around like a madman trying to loosen the duct-tape and/or stand to turn off the damn boom box, but the deadfucks were on me before I could manage either. I close my eyes and say my goodbyes to Maria and Paxton, and then…

Gunfire. It comes outta nowhere. Single shots spaced about ten seconds apart.

One-by-one the deadfucks closest to me go down from headshots. I hear a guy yell, "Stay down!" and then rapid fire. I bury my face in the grass. I can hear bodies being torn to shreds all around me. It stunk like singed meat.

When it's all over, a military truck drives through the gate and barrels over what's left of the deadfucks. A bunch of soldiers jump out of the back and run up to me. Just as they're helping me up, the steel shutter slides open on the upstairs bathroom, and I hear J.J.'s voice yell, "Don't let him go. He's the Center City Stalker. He tried to kill my wife and boy."

The soldiers shove me to the ground and point their guns at me.

"No. He's lying." I tell them. "It's him. HE'S the Center City Stalker" But they don't buy it.

"Ma-ther-fucker…" One guys says. "What are the odds? I saw a thing about this guy on Dateline. Likes torturing women."

I beg them to listen. I keep screaming, "This is MY house! He's got MY wife and kid in there," and it reminded me of when you're trying to explain something to someone who doesn't speak your language by simply saying the thing louder. I'm yelling for Maria both out of concern for what he's doing to her in there and to get her to say something in my defense. When she didn't respond, I thought the worse. But then, I hear her voice…

"That man out there is the Center City Stalker," she says. "He tried to hurt us, but my husband stopped him."

I knew, right away that the bastard must be using Paxton to make her say those things, but that didn't make it hurt any less to hear it. Besides, now the soldiers are itching to put a bullet in me. One of them steps forward and pushes his rifle up against my head. I thought that was the end.

Then there's a crash from the bathroom window. J.J. falls out onto the roof like he's been pushed. Something sticking out of the back of his head…It was a hammer. He crawls forward like he's struggling to hang on, and then falls flat on his face and slides down to where his upper body is dangling over the edge of the roof. I couldn't make it up if I tried.

I later found out that Maria and Paxton had worked together to outsmart J.J., who was so fucking dumb, that he really believed she had fallen for him. When he dropped his guard, Paxton clocked him from behind with the claw-end of the hammer, and Maria shoved him out the window. She still feels guilty about having to say all those things about me, and for kissing J.J., which, I guess she did to get him to turn his back to Paxton just before he got him with the hammer. It really tears her up inside sometimes, but I always tell her that she did what she had to do.

END VIDEO

Martin: You loooove the sound of your own voice. Don't you Larry? I mean…Wow!

Raven: I thought he did a good job. It kept me entertained. And this is what…the second or third time I've heard the story?

Martin: No, it was good, don't get me wrong.

Larry (via intercom, defensive): I told the story the way it happened. It was no different from the last time you heard it, Martin.

Martin (instigating): Oh, it was different.

Larry (via intercom): Gimme a fuckin' break!

Raven: I know what he means, Larry. It was more practiced than before, like you know all the important beats and you adjusted your delivery accordingly.

Larry (via intercom): I guess that's possible. I'll give you that one, Raven.

Martin: So, you agree that it was different?

Larry (via intercom): Fuck off!

Andre Duza

Soundbyte: Baby crying.

Laughter.

Larry (via intercom): Now you got Ted started.

Martin (fake scolding): Now. Now. Ted.

Ted: Sorry.

Martin: Okay. So, there you go, folks...Larry with a very compelling...and very long closest call. You're the only one left, Raven.

Raven: I've told you a million times. I don't have a closest call.

Martin: What are you; like the only person on the planet who doesn't?

Raven: Everybody knows what happened to me on 9/6. After you guys left to be with your families, I stayed at the radio station with Lovell, the front desk guy, and a few people from the law firm and the Chiropractor's Office next door until you sent Donnie to bring me here. The end. We musta been at the station for three weeks. I spent the entire time curled in a ball in the corner of my office, too scared to look out the windows, let alone leave the building. So, aside from witnessing the eventual breakdown of our group, there isn't much of a story to tell.

Martin: You said they were on the verge of killing each other before we found you.

Raven: Yeah. It was between Don, the lawyer from next door, and Lovell.

Martin: What was the fight over?

Raven: What do you think? What does every stupid fight between alpha male types boil down to?

170

Martin: Who's got the bigger dick?

Raven: Basically. I think it bothered Don that he was taking orders from a security guard.

Martin: And a black one at that.

Raven: Yeah, but Don was black, too.

Martin: Ohhhhh. I see.

Raven: It got pretty bad, but it was nothing on par with almost being eaten by deadheads, or having sex with one—sorry Ted—or being raided by scavengers or unknowingly harboring a serial killer. But if you want me to record that little bit for Closest Calls, I will.

Martin: Nah...Consider yourself lucky that you don't have one to tell.

Larry (via intercom): I agree.

Ted: Hear, hear.

Martin: All right, folks...If you were listening before Larry's Closest Call, then you heard my wife, Karen call regarding our adopted daughter Sara. Now, before anyone jumps to any conclusions concerning her mental state, I want to make it clear that she was examined thoroughly, both mentally and physically, by our medical staff here at the compound and deemed fit to live amongst the residents. What you heard was a minor tantrum. Nothing more. I was able to quickly calm her down and she is currently doing fine and going about her day with her mother. You've gotta understand... this is a girl who's spent the last two months surviving with her sister in the underground concourse. There're going to be some lasting effects.

Raven: How's the sister doing?

Martin: Margo? Good, actually. We took Sara down to see

her yesterday. She's becoming a permanent fixture at the infirmary, helping out with patients and stuff. I guess she finally opened up to the nursing staff. Apparently she wants to be a nurse, herself.

Raven: She still carrying around that doll?

Martin: You mean the stuffed animal—the rabbit? Unfortunately, yes. You should see that thing; how filthy it is. She won't let anyone touch it, not even to wash it or stitch it up for her.

Raven: Have they made a determination regarding her mental state?

Martin: I'm sure they have. Why else would they let her roam around the building with the nurses? She was restricted to her room in the infirmary the last time we were there.

Raven: I'm just askin'. What about Les? How's he doing?

Martin: They moved him to the Regatta Tower's Infirmary.

Raven: Why?!

Martin: Apparently he tried to attack Margo with a fork.

Raven: Oh my Goodness!

Martin: I know. It's sad, man. I guess losing that arm really messed him up in the head.

Raven: Yeah…He couldn't get past it. What a shame. I'm *so* sorry to hear that.

Martin: I was thinking that maybe we should try to put together some kind of get-together for him. You know; the guys in security, and whomever else in the compound he's friends with. Maybe we can—

Something steals Martin's attention in mid sentence…

Martin (disappointed): *Greeaaaat.*

Raven: What's-a-matter?

Martin: Dave's calling in…

Raven: So?

Martin: I didn't expect him to call so soon. I was planning on running the announcements before we got to him.

Raven: Big deal. Just do them after. It's not like there's gonna be anything new.

Dead air.

Martin: All right, Folks. On the phone; we're going to join our good friend Dave from Security who's currently on a mission, with the rest of Team One, to retrieve the rest of Erich Ganz's stash of stolen pharmaceuticals. Dave was also part of the team sent out to retrieve Alex Mull on Monday evening. We'll find out what that was like and we'll get his take on what happened at Dr. Hammond's Compound and exactly what's being done about it. You there, Dave?

Callers: Dave from Security / Jimmy Tran from Security (30) / Craig from City Hall (40s)

Dave: Hey, Martin.

Martin: So, tell us, what's doin' out there?

Dave (deadpan): Death, Martin. Same as always.

Jimmy Tran (in background): Smells somethin' awful.

Dave: Same as always.

Martin: Who's that, Jimmy Tran?

Dave: Yep.

Jimmy (in background): The one and only.

Martin: What's up, Jimmy?

Jimmy (in background): Whazzup, Martin?

Martin: First things first, Dave; what's the latest on Dr. Hammond's place?

Dave: Looks like it was an inside job.

Martin: How can you be sure?

Dave: Have you seen the footage from the drone?

Martin: Briefly. I'm putting it up on the flatscreen now.

The Martin Stone Show Logo fades from the flatscreen. The drone footage of Dr. Hammond's compound takes its place.

ON FLATSCREEN

A slideshow of aerial images showing the burnt out shell of Dr. Hammond's compound in Downingtown. Smoke billows from blown out windows. Vehicles smolder on the grounds. Bodies.

Dave: If you look at the main building, where the outer wall has been breached by some kind of explosive on the side, and at the back of the structure...

Martin: Yeah?

Dave: You see how the walls surrounding the blast have been blown outward? That suggests to us that the explosion came from the inside; probably some kind of IED planted by the same person or persons who rigged the vehicles and the guard tower to blow.

Martin: But why? It couldn't have been any of our people, right?

Dave: *We don't know. I doubt it was any of ours, though. Our people are carefully vetted. But you never know. Whoever did this had outside help, too. And their friends were packin' some heavy artillery.*

Martin: And you guys have no idea who that could be? I mean. I thought there weren't any more groups capable of doing something like this.

Dave: *We thought so, too.*

Martin: That's great. That's just great. I'm assuming we're amassing our forces to deal with this should—

Dave: *You'll understand if I decline to comment on that, Martin—for security reasons.*

Martin: Oh…Of course. I'm sorry.

Dave: *No worries, man.*

Raven: What about survivors? I don't see that big helicopter that the doctor came here in among the wreckage. Does that mean he got away?

Dave: *Someone did. Either that or whoever raided the place took it for their own use.*

Raven: Is there some kind of search and rescue effort being put forth?

Dave: *Again, I'm going to decline to comment.*

Dead air…

Dave: *Relax, guys.*

Martin: That's easy for you to say. We're way up here in the comfort of the Stone Show Studio while you're out in the thick of it.

Laughter.

Soundbyte: Canned laughter.

Dave: That's more like it.

Martin: Please let us know if I'm putting something out there that's going to jeopardize—

Dave: You're good, Martin. Stop worrying about it.

Martin: Okay. I'm just saying for future reference.

Dave: Noted. Now come on! We can't have you getting' all neurotic on us, Martin. We count on you to keep our heads straight during some of these missions.

Martin: Me?

Dave: It's the energy that the show generates. If that makes any sense.

Martin: It does. Thanks, man. That means a lot.

Dave: It's true.

Jimmy (in background): I'll second that.

Martin: So, how *is* the mission going?

Dave: So far so good. Simmons, Velez, Hopkins, and Wilkinson are currently in the building looking for the stash. I'm here, in the van with Jimmy and our new friend, Craig.

Martin: Who?

Dave: Craig's a former cop.

Craig: I was with the 24th Precinct before 9/6. Since then I've been working security at City Hall.

Martin: So, whose idea was it to let the Mayor go on like that?

Craig: It was his idea, to be honest. We tried to convince him not to.

Martin: Well, apparently you didn't try hard enough.

Craig: No. We did. Trust me. He was adamant that people see that the infection didn't break him. He's got this idea in his head that he's going to beat it.

Martin: Famous last words. I mean, no offense to Clay, but how many times have I heard that before? Couldn't you just knock him out or something? Don't answer that.

Raven (scolding): Martin!

Martin: I'm only joking, of course. I just...I really like Clay. I think he means a lot of things to a lot of people. Of course, most of them are dead, but that's beside the point. Seeing him like that...This symbol of strength...I think it does more to hurt our overall moral...or what's left of it.

Craig: I agree 100 percent. Clay is a good guy. One of the best human beings I know. Before all this, I woulda never even given a guy like that a chance. I think you mentioned something about it on the last show. How we used to be so segregated, but that's all gone. In some weird way this mess has brought us together. Most of us, anyway...My point is that after getting to know Clay personally, there's nothing I wouldn't do for the guy.

Raven (to Craig): What, the hell, were you doin' out in the street?

Craig: It's no secret that Clay's the glue holding our little group at City Hall together. Now that he's sick...The last week has been nothing but arguing and carryin' on. These are educated men, mind you, reduced to a bunch of knuckle-dragging, cavemen over who's gonna run things once Clay passes. They've already written him off. I couldn't take it anymore. A bunch of us have been wanting to volunteer with your people since we heard Alex's call. I know it's unlikely, but we were hoping that maybe it could lead to a cure for Clay. I'm sorry to say that I followed your guys here.

Dave (to Martin, playful): You believe this sonofabitch drew on us?

Craig: The way you guys snuck up on me like that…

Dave: Hey. YOU were the one following US.

Dead air.

Dave: Nah. It's all good.

Martin: Speaking of Alex…

Dave: You guys know more than we do at this point.

Martin: No. I'm talking about Monday evening when you guys went out to get him.

Dave: Oh. We had to pop a few pus-bags, but it was altogether uneventful—which is how you want it. Alex was right where he said he would be. We retrieved him without incident and escorted him back to the compound. He did offer some resistance when we told him that we were going to take him back to the compound before we look for his mother. He was pretty adamant that we stay out and help him look for her, but we were able to convince him otherwise.

Several chirps from Dave's walkie talkie…Heavy static follows. A male voice buried in the static. It breaks through in gaps.

Dave: They must be in the basement. (into Walkie) You guys all right down there? Over.

Male Voice (via walkie talkie): Smells like shit…otherwise smoo…as silk…Break-room up ahead about 50 feet… How's…looking…topside? Over…

178

Dave: Sittin' tight at the rendezvous point, waitin' on your slow asses. Over...

Male Voice (via walkie talkie, to Dave): Well, don't get too comfortable. We'll...back soo......

The voice is completely overcome by static.

Dave: Come again. Over...

Static.

Dave: Shit!

Martin: What's goin' on, Dave?

Dave: Nothing. It's just the walkies. They have trouble picking up the signal from the basement of the building...We expected it to happen.

Raven: But they're okay, right?

Dave: Yes.

Martin: So, where're you guys parked? Or is that too much information.

Dave: Let's just say we're somewhere near the train station.

Martin: So, you're on the other side of town. What're you, just sittin' there?

Dave: You've gotta remember, Martin...There's still a shitload of abandoned vehicles down here to blend in with.

Martin: Yeah, but how, the hell'd, you get there without the zombies seeing you?

Dave: We gave 'em the old juke.

Raven: What's an 'old juke?'

Groans from Martin, Larry, and Ted.

Dave (to Raven): Not a sports fan, huh?

Raven: Not really.

Martin: The farthest thing from it.

Raven (defensive): So. Besides…I like tennis.

Martin: That's hardly a sport.

Raven: What-*EVER…*

Dave: By juking, I mean, just sorta faking 'em out. You know? You speed up, sharp right down a side street, sharp left down another, and so on, until you reach your pre-determined destination. Then you shut everything down and hide amongst the abandoned vehicles. The pus-bags are still like five steps behind you.

Raven: Ohhhh. You gave them the slip.

Jimmy (background): Most of 'em, anyway.

Dave: Yeah. The freshly dead ones are a little faster, and smarter.

Larry (via intercom): I've seen them do it firsthand, Raven. It's pretty wild. Remember when I did that ride-along with them a few months back?

Raven: Oh yeah. I remember.

Raven laughs.

Raven (laughing): You were a nervous wreck.

Larry (via intercom): I was shitting my pants. Seems like it would be even harder to do now with as many of them as there are in the streets.

Jimmy (background): It ain't easy.

Craig: There's so many of 'em cause there's nobody left run clean up. I remember back when we were doin' 'em twice a week. I rode with a crew in Northeast Philly. Let me tell you… you gotta be pretty hardcore to do that shit.

Martin: I can imagine.

Craig: You're putting down women and kids. Sometimes you would have to pop somebody you knew. Saw a coupla guys wig out from it. One guy got so bad we had to put HIM down.

Raven (horrified): Awe, my God!

Martin: Wow! Maybe I *can't* imagine it.

Raven: I don't think anyone can unless they've been through it.

Larry (via intercom): Dave. You guys called what you did Shake n' Bake, the time I rode with you.

Dave: Juke. Slip. Shake 'n Bake. It's all good. We were doing something a little different, then.

Larry (via intercom): Yeah. You were trying to lead them away from the compound.

Dave: That's right.

Larry (via intercom): You mind if I describe it, Dave, just so these guys'll understand it from an outsider's perspective? By outsider, I mean those of us who run *AWAY* from danger instead of toward it.

Dave: Be my guest.

Larry (via intercom): What they do is they—And feel free to correct me if I'm wrong, Dave—They drive out to a fairly populated spot, somewhere out in the open, where the deadfucks can see them. Then they make as much noise as possible to attract the deadfucks' attention and get 'em all riled up. Then they sorta creep along just outta their reach—

Martin (unsettled): So you're just sitting there watching them stagger toward you?

Dave: Yep.

Martin reacts to a sudden chill.

Martin: Oh my God! You think any of us could do that?

Raven: Hell no.

Larry (via intercom): Once they've got enough of 'em corralled into one big group, they either juke em' or lead them off in the desired direction.

Martin: Sounds way too adventurous for my taste.

Raven: You and me both. I'll say it again. I don't know how you guys do it.

Dave: Somebody has to.

Martin: I'm glad there're people like you and Jimmy, and Craig, who are willing to, because I wouldn't be caught dead. You know how they say, 'The meek shall inherit the Earth?' All of us in here. We're the meek. Well…Maybe not Ted.

Ted laughs.

Martin: Aren't you afraid of being ambushed if the zombies realize you guys're there? I hear they can surround you before you know it.

Dave: Yeah…I told you that, Martin.

Martin: Oh.

Soundbyte: Canned laughter.

Dave: And most of them move so slow that in most cases you'd see them coming. Even with as many of them as there are now, there're still pretty spread out, so you could actually move around on foot if you had to. And if you do get caught up, you give 'em a good shove and nine times out of 10 they fall right over.

Raven: Yeah...if there's one or two of them.

Dave: It's not like in the movies where they can just disembowel you with their hands...

Jimmy (background): Or bite through clothing.

Dave: Exactly. So, as long as you keep your cool, you still stand a chance of surviving even in a small crowd of fresh ones. But ya kinda have to do this everyday to reach that level of calm.

Martin: So, it's like a Zen thing?

Dave: Something like that.

Jimmy (background): And even then you get rattled sometimes.

Martin: Don't knock the movies, by the way. The good ones got more right than they did wrong.

Raven (to Dave): Maybe guys like you, Jimmy, and Craig would stand a chance, but what about the average person?

Craig: Those folks aren't around anymore, unfortunately.

Raven: *We're* still around...

Dave: That's because you guys were smart enough to link up with a good group. Common sense is a survival tool, too. Maybe the most important one.

Martin: I think it's more like we were lucky.

Raven: That's what I was about to say—

Over the phone we here automatic gunfire in the distance.

Martin (alarmed): What was that?

Ted: Sounded like gunfire.

Raven (re: gunfire): Oh my.

Martin (nervous): Gunfire?

Dave (to Jimmy, re: gunfire): I'd say AR 15.

Jimmy (background, to Dave):…or an AK maybe. Sounded like it came from the river, behind the train station. (pause) Huh? Hey! Look at that! The deadfucks…They're all heading toward the sound.

Craig:…like somebody rang a dinner bell.

Dave: Yeah…Let's just hope it's not our guys down there. (into walkie talkie) Hey Simmons…We got gunfire down by the river. That's not you guys, is it? Over…

Static…

Dave (into walkie talkie): Straussman to Simmons. Come in! Over…

Static…

Dave: Shit!

Martin: Is everything all right, Dave?

Dave (to Martin): We heard some shooting down by the river. Might be our guys. Can't reach 'em on the walkie to be sure.

Craig: Hopefully it's just because of the basement.

Dave: Yeah…But I'm not waiting around to find out.

Martin: Yeah…We heard it, too. You're not going out there?

Dave: Have to...What if the rest of the team's in trouble?

Jimmy (to Dave): I'm coming with you.

Craig: Me, too.

Dave (to Jimmy): Nah, Jimmy. I know you're a good shot, but you're also the best driver we've got. We need you ready, behind-the-wheel n case it gets too hot down there.

Craig (to Jimmy): Don't worry. I got his back.

Jimmy: Make sure that you do. (to Dave): You watch you're ass. And no heroics.

Martin: Hey. Wait a minute, guys! You sure this is such a good idea?

Craig (to Dave): It's a straight shot up Market to the bridge. And they're pretty focused on whatever it is that got their attention, so as long as we're careful…We can use the cars for cover.

Martin sighs in defeat.

Martin: Just be careful, guys.

Dave: Always, Martin.

We hear movement inside the van as Dave and Craig prepare to make a run for the bridge. Their voices are suddenly muffled as if by masks of some kind.

Dave (to Craig): You ready?

Craig: Ready.

Dave: All right. On three...

Raven suddenly remembers...

Raven: The helmet cam....

Martin: That's right! Dave. Turn on your helmet cam.

The van door slides open and lets in faint street sounds.

HELMET CAM 1 (DAVE'S POV)
A swatch of urban decay illuminates the inside of cargo van. A bulky dwarf (Craig) dressed for survival crouches in the doorway next to Dave. His face is hidden beneath a paintball mask and goggles with a skull painted over them. A maskless, sienna-colored Asian man (Jimmy Tran) sits in the driver's seat, watching.

Dave: You got a visual, Martin?

Martin (re: screen) Holy shit! Craig. You're a midget!

Raven: That's little person, Martin.

Martin: Yeah. That's what I said.

Craig: Dwarf. If you wanna get technical.

Raven: My apologies, Craig.

Craig: Don't sweat it. I've been called far worse.

Dave: No offense, Martin...But I can't do this with you guys in my ear. I'll keep the camera on, but—

Martin: No. No. Of course. I wouldn't wanna put you guys at risk like that.

Raven: Yeah...Whatever we've got to say can wait.

Martin (unsure): We'll still be able to see and hear you through the video, though?

Dave: I'm assuming...

Martin: Right Lar?

Larry (via intercom): Right. But he won't be able to hear us.

Martin: Got it.

Raven: It wasn't that difficult a concept to grasp, Martin.

Dave: All right guys. I'm hanging up the phone now.

Raven: Be careful you two.

Martin: Yes. Please?

End call

HELMET CAM 1 (DAVE'S POV) (CONT'D)
Craig crouches in the doorway of the van. Jimmy Tran behind the wheel, watching. A dead cityscape on the horizon. We occasionally glimpse Dave's hand or arm enter, and then exit the frame.

Dave (to Craig): You ready?

Craig: Ready.

Dave: Okay. On three…

Craig nods.

Dave: One. Two. THREE...

Craig exits the van first, then Dave, who slides the door shut behind him. The image shakes violently, at first. Craig runs point as they move stealthy down a small corridor of loading docks and out onto a large, four-laned boulevard—Market Street.

Downtown Philadelphia is a ghost town. Death and destruction everywhere. Bodies in the streets in various stages of decomposition. Scattered refuse. Blood. Abandoned vehicles stuck in gridlock as far as the eye can see. The street leads to a bridge up ahead.

They reach the gridlock. Keeping to a low crouch-run, they move from vehicle-to-vehicle. Along the way we glimpse a bug-eyed visage staring back at us in the vehicles' windows. It's the reflection of Dave's gas mask.

We see that some of the vehicles are occupied by the bodies of the former owners. The hint of degraded vocal chords attempting to communicate nonsensical half-thoughts, fractured memories, and a general sense of confusion in the distance.

Martin (speaking softly, to Raven): Mah-rone! Are those... people in those cars?

Raven: Looks like it.

Martin: They must've been sitting there long after everybody else abandoned their vehicles, right? What's the logic behind that?

Raven: It goes back to my point about denial. People couldn't accept what was happening. They just couldn't wrap their minds around the idea of the dead coming back to life, so they froze.

Larry (via intercom): I think it was just that the alternative— getting out of the car—looked so fucking hopeless that sitting there probably seemed like your best option.

Martin: Poor bastards probably thought the police were gonna come rescue them. Awful.

HELMET CAM 1 (DAVE'S POV) (CONT'D)
Craig and Dave are still on the move, closer to the bridge. In the gaps between cars we see a mass of legs belonging

to upright corpses lumbering forward in unison on the left sidewalk. Craig and Dave move to avoid a few stragglers that lurch through the gridlock. The air fills with a collective moan. Passionate growls and retarded vocal tonnages leap out from the divas in the group. A thousand feet shuffling and stumble-stopping.

Gunshots up ahead...They are much louder than before. Healthy voices follow...belonging to the living. We hear urgency in their tones, however, we can't make out what they're saying.

Martin (to Raven, re: gunfire): Didju hear that?

Raven: I heard it.

Martin: Oh man! This is making me nervous.

Raven: Me too...Now SHHHHHH!

HELMET CAM 1 (DAVE'S POV) (CONT'D)
Up on the bridge, Dave is crouched behind the fender of an SUV. Craig squats with his back against the passenger-side door of a late model Mustang up ahead. He makes a series of hand gestures at Dave.

Dave (re: hand signals): Wha? I wasn't in the military, dude!

Craig (muffled): I said, 'hold tight. I'm gonna check out that bus over there.'

Craig points.

Dave peeks over the fender and sees...A city bus. Abandoned. Blood smeared on several of the windows. Front and middle doors closed.

The living dead congregate on the sidewalk between the outer lane of cars and the bridge railing. Some are leaning over and reaching at something in the Schuylkill River, 60 feet below. Several of them fall or are pushed over the railing in the melee.

Voices from below...

Male Voice: Woo Hoo! C'mon! C'mon! You can make it!

Female Voice: Just keep comin! Don't stop and don't look down! No matter what!

Craig (to Dave, re: bus): We can see down to the river from the windows.

Dave: Ok. I'll cover you.

Craig creeps between the SUV and the Mustang and makes his way up to the bus. He squeezes through the front doors and disappears inside. Through the bus windows, we watch Craig move from front to rear, checking each seat on the way. Afterward, he gives Dave a 'thumbs up.'

Dave makes his way to over to the bus. Craig slowly opens the front door, careful not to make a sound. Dave slips inside and Craig immediately closes the door.

They converge in the middle aisle. Dave is crouching on one knee. Craig is in a squat with his hands on his knees. The bus lists from the mass of zombies squeezed between it and the bridge railing. The backs of their heads darken the bottom of the windows on the left side of the bus.

We see a pile of devoured corpses huddled in the back of the bus. There are children among them.

Makeshift bedding on a number of the seats in the middle of the bus looks fairly new.

Raven gasps at the pile of bodies.

Martin (whispering): Oh ho ho MAN!

HELMET CAM 1 (DAVE'S POV) (CONT'D)
Inside of bus…

Dave (re: bodies in back): Looks like they got themselves trapped.

Craig (re: bedding): Looks somebody's been living here since.

Dave: You'd think they woulda gotten rid of the bodies, huh?

Craig: Nothing surprises me anymore, brother.

Dave: Amen to that!

Dave and Craig head over to a pair of seats on the left side. Dave crouches on the floor between two seats and slowly rises until his eyes break the surface of heads and shoulders on the other side of the window. Craig climbs up onto a seat and does the same.

A layer of death coats the surface of the Schuylkill River like a fleshy pool-tarp that extends to the river bank on both sides. Bodies of the dead and the living dead overlap, limbs clumsily interlaced. Some of them are moving, thrashing at air or simply undulating facedown in the water. Vehicle husks afloat on their backs or nose down/ass up, punch holes in the fleshy tarp.

Further south we see another bridge topped with dead automotive gridlock and zombies worked into a frenzy over the 42-foot Yacht cutting a path through the fleshy tarp on its way toward Market Street. More specifically, they are reaching for the three warm bodies moving about the deck of the yacht.

Standing at the back of the boat, there is an olive-skinned man and a ginger waif. Both appear to be in their 20s. They are dressed in rags and armed to the hilt. They are facing the east bank where another young man, tall, thin, with a floppy hairdo stands looking all kinds of nervous.

Andre Duza

At the front of the boat, a slightly older man, armed like the others, appears in the doorway leading to the vessel's cabin and begins rifling through the dashboard compartments. He stuffs anything usable into an army green satchel strapped across his chest.

Olive-Skin (to Floppy hair): Would you just go already!

Floppy-hair: Shut, the fuck, up and gimme a minute! I gotta visualize this!

Ginger waif: Dude! You just visualized the rest of us do it! What, the hell's, the problem?

Older man: Tell that shithead to hurry up. We've called enough attention to ourselves as it is.

On the bus, Dave and Craig speak quietly about the people on the yacht.

Dave: Scavengers?

Craig: Scavengers wouldn't be this stupid. More likely they're on the run. Probably from some nearby settlement that they left on bad terms.

On the left bank of the river, Floppy-hair takes off running. The fleshy tarp comes alive as he steps from body to body, his feet barely touching each floating corpse before thrusting off and to the next. Navigating on the fly, Floppy-hair moves with an ugly stride, retarded by soft, squishy surfaces shifting underfoot. He dives forward onto the hood of a partially submerged Volkswagen, Beetle. He belly flops onto the hood and immediately begins to slide off. Reaching frantically, his hands find purchase around the lower lip of hollowed windshield frame. His feet scramble to find traction on the slippery, curved hood. Finally he gets his knees underneath him and begins gulping air.

Ginger waif: Tha fuck are you doing?! Keep going!

192

Floppy-hair: Get off my back!

Suddenly, from inside the Volkswagen, a living dead man lunges through the broken window frame. Floppy hair thrusts himself backward, away from the thrashing, flailing thing, with its long, rotten teeth and its soggy, bloated face, and falls onto the fleshy tarp with a deadened splash. The loose weave of carrion separates and Floppy-hair disappears beneath the surface of the filthy, toxic water.

Olive-skin: Oh shit!

Floppy-hair surfaces, gasping for air, and struggling to stay afloat against an ambush of limbs suddenly enlivened by his presence. He shoves away thrusting, bloated faces baring teeth and predatory frowns. Loose skin slides away from bone of one of them revealing a smiling skull-face interlaced with decomposing muscle and sinew. The dead man in the VW clambers out through the broken windshield and slides down the car's rounded hood toward the water.

A shot rings out and the living dead man's head is yanked to the side spraying brain matter and bits of bone marinated in blood. He collapses, lifeless to the hood, and slides, head-first into the water.

Ginger waif stands, with a rifle raised, on the deck of the yacht, smoke billowing from the tip of the barrel.

Ginger waif (to Floppy hair): Get back to the car!

Floppy-hair (struggling): I can't! Too many of them!

Floppy-hair grows tired. Coughing and spitting water, he submerges and comes up fighting. Each time he stays under a little longer. Several shots ring out, and one-by-one the ravenous, floating living dead are dispatched by Ginger waif's rifle. But Floppy-hair is becoming too fatigued to stay afloat. We hear the yacht's engine roar to life.

Olive-skin (to Older man): Hey! What are you doing?!

Older man: Forget him! He's done!

Ginger waif: Fuck you! We're not leaving hi—

The older man guns the throttle and the yacht pushes forward. Olive Skin and Ginger waif are thrown off-balance. They grab hold of the nearest rooted object to keep from falling.

Struggling to stay afloat amidst a barrage of grabbing hands, Floppy hair calls out to the retreating yacht...

Floppy hair: No! Wait! Where are you going?!

He is eventually dragged underwater.

On the yacht, Ginger waif hurries clumsily to the front of the vessel to confront the older man.

Ginger waif (to Older man): What the fuck, man! You gone crazy er somethi—

The older man snatches a pistol from his belt and aims it at the Ginger waif's head. She stops cold.

There's a brief exchange, but we can't make out what they are saying. And then...Ginger waif lunges at the older man. He pulls the trigger and shoots the young woman in the head, killing her instantly.

Olive skin: Noooooo!

The older man turns the gun on Olive-skin, who throws his hands up in surrender.

Older man (to Olive-skin): You got something to say?!

Olive skin shakes his head, "No."

The older man lowers the gun and takes the wheel of the yacht. The engine roars and the sleek vessel pushes forward against a swell of chunky carrion broth. The living dead on the Market Street Bridge become more aggressive as the yacht comes closer, and then…

A hissing sound emenates from somewhere overhead.

On the bus, Dave and Craig share a curious stare.

Dave: You hear that?

Craig: Yeah…

They look up just as a phallic blur enters the top of the frame traveling downward at an arc, and explodes upon contact with the yacht. The sound is deafening. It strains the camera's speakers. The air fills with splintered wood, metal, body parts, and filthy, toxic water.

Dave: Holy Shit!

Craig: Take cover!

Dave and Craig dive for cover as the debris from the blast blows out some of the bus' windows.

We are looking at the back of the seat in front of Dave. Craig is lying in that seat. Blood splatter decorates the top of the seat from debris hitting the wall of living dead standing on the other side of the window. The blast has energized them, or maybe it's the fact that their food has been taken away. We can hear the yacht, in flames down in the river.

Dave (to Craig): You okay?

Craig (off-camera): Yeah.

Dave looks up and sees the broken window. Blood spatter decorates the window frame, and the ceiling of the bus as well. Suddenly…

A voice comes over Dave's walkie talkie…

Jimmy Tran (via walkie talkie): Psssht! Dave! What the fuck is goin' on! You guys all right?! Over!

Another voice comes through as Dave fumbles to lower the volume on his walkie talkie…

Simmons (via walkie talkie): Psssht! Tell me that wasn't an explosion I just heard. Over.

Dave finally manages to adjust the volume. Afterward, he lays there, frozen. Aside from the cackling flames on the river, it has become eerily quiet outside of the bus. And then…

Dead fingers curl around the bottom of the window frame. A rotten-faced old man peers in the window. Or maybe it's a woman. Death has wiped the thing of gender recognition. Dave remains still, but the gender-neutral zombie eventually sees him. Its eyes light up.

Dave: Shit! They made us!

Suddenly the window is full of rotten faces jockeying for position. They begin reaching inside, and attempting to climb in.

A skull-face pops up from the seat in front of Dave. It's Craig. He moves out into the aisle and aims his weapon at the crowded window. Dave does the same.

Craig (to Dave): Go! Now! I'll cover you!

Dave nods, and in an instant, he is moving rapidly toward the front of the bus. Through the windshield, we see a regimen of zombies moving around the front, toward the door. Shots ring out behind us. Dave opens the door and picks off the first wave. He turns to Craig who's picking off trespassers as they attempt to climb in.

Dave (to Craig): Come on!

Craig runs toward Dave. Dave turns and heads out the door.

He picks off a few more on the way out.

The two men make a hasty retreat through the gridlocked traffic on the Market Street Bridge, a battalion of eager zombies in tow. Dave and Craig make quick work of the stragglers who lumber independent of the main hoard, with well-placed headshots.

A voice comes over Dave's walkie talkie.

Jimmy Tran (via walkie talkie): What's happening out there?! You need me to come and get you guys?!

Dave (into walkie talkie): We're okay! The explosion wasn't us! We're on our way, now, but we've got company! Over.

Simmons (via walkie talkie): You were supposed to wait in the van! Over…

Dave (into walkie talkie): We heard shooting! Couldn't reach you guys on the walkie! Thought you might be in trouble! Over.

END VIDEO

The studio (aka Apt. 3216). Heavy static interference warps the sound and picture. Beneath the interference we can see Martin, Raven, and Ted staring at the blank flatscreen monitor waiting, on pins and needles, for the live video feed of Dave and Craig to return.

Martin springs to his feet.

Martin: What the fuck?!

Ted: Z'gotta be the satellite.

Heavy static.

Larry (via intercom): It is.

Martin: Well. Do something! Get it back! Get Dave on the phone! Something!

Raven: I hope they're all right?

Larry: (via intercom): Hold on…The phone lines are blowin' up, Martin. I was so into the video that I didn't notice.

Heavy static.

Larry (via intercom): Wait-a-minute. These are all internal—from the infirmary. Listening to the voicemails now. (pause) Some kinda outbreak in the building. Food poisoning or stomach virus.

Martin (scared): Virus?

Raven: Oh my God!

END BROADCAST

THE MARTIN STONE SHOW

THURSDAY, APRIL 5TH, 2015

Over a black screen we hear the combined din of 100 conversations taking place at once.

FADE IN...

Brand Compound – Reef Tower (Formerly Waterfront Luxury Apartments) Philadelphia, Pa

VIDEO

Ballroom A. Seventy plus residents of the Reef Tower are seated in folding chairs facing a podium at the front of the room. Others are standing in the aisles, talking. More people slowly file in and take seats. Security officer armed with M16s and gravitas hold up the walls on the outskirts of the crowd and answer questions from worrywarts.

Martin speaks softly over the footage.

Martin (off-camera): You are watching live feed from Ballroom A here at the Reef Tower where, in approximately 30 minutes, an emergency meeting will be held to discuss the sudden outbreak of a devastating illness that, as of last count, has stricken 172 of the building's 260 residents and resulted in 12 deaths. Symptoms of the mysterious illness include: Nausea. Vomitting. Diarrhea. Severe stomach cramping. Hair loss. Loss of reflexes. Convulsions. Headaches. Numbness. Dementia. And psychosis. Doctors still don't know what, exactly we are dealing with here, however it is thought to have been transmitted through the building's food supply. Whether it was accidental or a deliberate act remains to be seen.

The image cuts to...

The Studio (aka Apt. 3216). Martin, Raven, and Ted seated in their booths. The live feed from Conference Hall A on the flatscreen.

Martin (Cont'd): To my fellow residents of the Reef Tower. I know you're scared. But no matter how bad it gets, we have to be resolute in our fight to survive and overcome this latest obstacle that we are faced with just like we have overcome everything that we as a people have been faced with up to this point. We cannot. I repeat CAN NOT give in to fear and paranoia.

Dead air...

Martin: For those of you left hanging after the abrupt end of yesterday's show, I should mention that Dave from Security, Jimmy Tran, and the rest of Team 1 made it safely back to the compound following the unexpected turn of events during their mission. In a rather heartless move, in my opinion, Craig Welling, the former cop from City Hall who also made it back with the rest of the Team, was turned away at the front gates by security and not allowed to enter.

Raven: I'm afraid to say, I agree with Head Office on this one. As heartless as it may seem. We're on Orange Alert, remember? That's nobody in or out of the building.

Martin: They coulda made an exception. You saw him out there with Dave. I think he proved his usefulness. And the guy was a cop. That's not a valuable skill?

Raven: All they said was that the compound is currently in crisis mode, and can't afford the resources to properly vet any prospective residents. He's welcome to come back when the alert has been lifted.

Martin: Who knows when that's gonna be?

Larry (via intercom): Not to be a Debbie Downer or anything... But I see this getting waaay worse before it gets better...IF it gets better...And I'm not just talking about the people who are sick. Have any of you guys been down to any of the common areas in the past 24 hours.

Martin: You know I rarely leave my apartment?

Ted: Nope.

Raven: No. Why?

Larry (via intercom): For one thing, the rumor mill is definitely in full swing. People are saying that Sara and Margo are somehow behind everybody getting sick.

Martin: I'm not surprised. They'd had it in for the both of them from the start. Did I tell you that some of the parents in the building wouldn't let their kids play with Sara?

Raven: No.

Martin: Yep. Can you believe that?

Raven: Actually, I can.

Larry (via intercom): I've got two calls holding, Martin. On Line One is Maggie from Lancaster—

Martin: *Nooo*…That's the last thing I need.

Larry (via intercom): I figured as much.

Martin: Why would you even take her call?

Larry (via intercom): Because if I didn't, you'd bust my balls for that, too.

Martin (annoyed): Who's on Line Two.

Larry (via intercom): Dave's on Line Two.

Dead air.

Larry (via intercom, defensive): What?

Martin (pointing at flatscreen): You see what's going on downstairs? Why would you even think there'd be any question as to which call I'd rather take outta those two.

Martin: Hey. I was just covering my ass, is all.

Martin: Just put Dave through.

Larry (via intercom): That's all you had to say.

Martin shakes his head at Larry's remark, and then takes a deep, composing breath.

Martin: Dave? You there?

Caller: Dave from Security

Dave: Yeah, Martin…

Martin: You sure we're not interrupting you with everything that's going on?

Dave: We've got things under control…for the moment.

Martin: Where're you; the infirmary?

Dave: Yep. Just stepped out into the hall to talk to you.

Raven (concerned): For the moment?

Dave: I'm not gonna lie to you guys, it's pretty bad down here. The bodies are piling up faster than we can incinerate them. We got 48 residents and five of our guys listed in serious to critical condition. Everybody's scared shitless.

Raven gasps.

Martin (shocked): More died since the last count?

Dave: Four more.

Martin: Holy Shit, man!

Dave (annoyed): Between the panicking patients, the lack of space to put them in, the overworked medical staff, and the loved ones of the deceased wanting answers, it's a wonder we haven't had a riot down here yet.

Raven: I hear they had to expand the infirmary to the entire third floor to accommodate all the people.

Dave: And it's still not enough room.

Martin: Any word on a cause?

Dead air…

Martin: Dave?

Dave: I think I'd better let the old man address that one at the meeting.

Larry (via intercom): Any truth to the rumor that it was done deliberately?

Dave: Again…I'd prefer to let the old man address it at the meeting.

Raven: Can't you, at least, give us a hint?

Dave: Sorry, Raven. I will say that we do have a plan in motion to deal with the problem.

An ambush of raised voices from the flatscreen.

ON FLATSCREEN

VIDEO
Ballroom. An argument erupts between two male residents as people sit waiting for the meeting to start.

Male resident #1: How DARE you accuse me of something like that!

Male resident #2: Well, if the shoe fits!

Without warning, heated words escalate to blows. People scream and run away from the flailing combatants.

Anonymous: Somebody do something!

Martin: Look at those idiots.

Raven: This is how it always starts...

Martin: What's that?

Raven: The breakdown of a settlement.

VIDEO (CONT'D)
The fight goes to the ground. Some of the other male residents hurry over and pull the men apart. Seconds later, two security guards move in and take over.

Security guard #1: What the hell! We've got enough problems here without the two of you carrying on like a bunch-a-fucking adolescents!

The other residents grumble approval. A couple people clap. Suddenly...

The crowd's attention turns to the door as a nurse enters the room pushing a metal cart with squeaky wheels. A tray full of medicine vials and syringes lined up in neat rows on top of the cart. We hear a swell of whispered conversation from the curious residents. And then...a collective gasp when a young girl follows the nurse into the room pulling a large picnic cooler on wheels behind her. The girl has a stern face partially hidden by a veil of mousy brown hair, eyes set too far apart, and an overall maturity that contradicts her slight, pubescent frame. A tattered, mud-caked stuffed rabbit doll lay atop the cooler.

Raven: Is that the older sister?

Martin: Yep. That's Margo. And that thing on the cooler is her creepy stuffed rabbit.

Raven: I see…Look at how they're watching her?

Martin (concerned): Maybe you should be up there, Dave, in case somebody tries something?

Dave: I'm more worried about what could happen down here.

VIDEO (CONT'D)
The security guard orders the two men to sit down. Their fight is old news to the crowd of residents, forgotten in favor of the nurse and her young assistant, who make their way to the front of the room under an ambush of suspicious eyes.

Martin: What about Alex? Is he okay?

Dave: He's fine. We have him in protective custody. I'm not gonna say where.

Martin: Fair enough. As long as he's okay. With Dr. Hammond gone, that guy's our last hope.

Dave: By the way, Martin. Thanks for what you said about Craig earlier.

Martin: Oh. Of course. Turning Craig away like that was the wrong thing to do.

Raven: I still disagree. Let me rephrase that. Maybe it *was* the wrong thing to do, morally, however it was the right thing to do given the situation.

Dave (annoyed): Look, Raven. I know, first-hand, what can happen when people are not properly vetted. But, like Martin said, "they could've made an exception." I vouched for the guy. Jimmy Tran vouched for him. The rest of the guys didn't really get to talk to him much on the ride back to the compound, but they trust mine and Jimmy's judgment enough to have our backs on it. So, you've got five members of Team One telling you that the guy is good people. But I guess that wasn't good enough.

Martin: Have you heard from him?

Dave: Unfortunately, no. But Craig's a survivor. He'll be all right. My guess is that he'll go back to his crew at City Hall, at least for now. That's what I would do.

Martin (to Dave): So, those people on the yacht yesterday...

Raven: They looked like kids.

Dave: Yeah. They were young—maybe early 20s. Except for the one driving the boat...

Martin: He seemed like the leader to me.

Dave: Looked that way.

Martin: Still no idea who they were or where they came from, huh?

Dave: That's what we're trying to figure out.

Martin: I'm guessing there's no way they survived that blast.

Ted: Are you kidding?

Raven: Oh. I wouldn't think so.

Dave: That's a negative, Martin.

Martin: And that explosion wasn't you guys, Dave?

Dave: What? The RPG? No. That wasn't us. We're in the dark on that one, too.

Martin (thinking aloud): The hell is going on out there? There's so few of us left. We should be working together, not killing each other…

Dave: I hear ya, man. Listen. I gotta get back inside. I just wanted to reach out to help clear up some of the confusion.

Martin: All right. Keep us posted, Dave.

Dave: I will.

Raven: Bye, Dave.

Larry (via intercom): Dave! Wait!

Dialtone…

End Call

Larry (via intercom): Dammit!

Martin: What's the problem?!

Larry (via intercom): I wanted Dave to hear something.

Martin: Hear what?

Larry (via intercom): A guy just called not even a minute ago, who says he has info about the people on the yacht yesterday.

Martin: No shit? Why didn't you put him through while Dave was on?

Larry (via intercom): I was trying to make sure the guy was legit. I didn't know Dave was gonna to hang up so soon. You want me to get him back on the line?

Martin: No. I don't want to bother him.

Larry (via intercom): What do you wanna do?

Dead air…

Martin: Let's talk to the guy.

Larry (via intercom): Okay. His name is Gabriel. Apparently he's with the people who fired the RPG. It's a pretty bad connection, by the way.

Martin: Thanks. You're on the air, Gabriel.

Caller: Gabriel "Gabe" from Harrisburg (30s)

We are ambushed by static interference. It continues throughout the call.

Gabriel: Am I on the air? Is this the Martin Stone Show?

Raven (re: static): Oh my!

Martin: You are, and it is…I can barely hear you through the static, Gabriel.

Gabriel: It's Gabe. First of all, I want to say that we are NOT murderers.

Martin: Ooo-kay…Why would you assume—

Gabriel:—I just wanna get that straight from the start. We're from a settlement in Harrisburg. Good, decent people. Those assholes you saw on the yacht yesterday. They played us for fools. We're down to 12 members from 45 just two months ago thanks to those four.

Raven: Who were they?

Gabriel: We found them during a supply run. They were near death—or so we thought. We took them in, nursed them back to health, and they repaid us by sabotaging our medical supplies—what little bit we had. Stuff we needed. People died as a result.

Martin: Were these people addicts?

Gabriel: That was our first thought, too, when the medicine went missing, or that they stole it with the intent to use it to barter for food or supplies or weapons. But instead the bastards threw it in a barrel and burned it.

Raven: Did you actually see them burn the stuff?

Gabriel: Yeah. They made sure of that.

Martin: What, the hell, kind of sense does that make?

Gabriel: They broke pretty quickly once we took them into custody; told us that they were with a religious group who call themselves The Left Hand of God. The Left Hand's sole purpose is to ensure that God's plan of the Biblical End of Days is carried out. They use decoys to infiltrate settlements and destroy them from the inside out by using suicide bombers, or turning members against each other or tampering with the medicine or food supply. They're led by an old woman named Mother Margaret.

Martin: Margaret? Where's this group based?

Gabriel: We're not sure. Somewhere in—

A swell in the static overwhelms Gabriel's voice.

Martin (re: static): You've gotta be kidding me! Gabriel! Gabriel!

Dialtone.

End call

Martin: SHIT!

Dead air...

Raven (to Martin): What's on your mind?

Martin: I just had a crazy thought.

Raven: Yeah?

Martin: Their sole purpose is to ensure that God's plan is carried out. Who does that sound like?

Raven thinks for a moment

Martin: They're led by an old woman named Margaret...

Raven gasps.

Ted: Maggie from Lancaster!

Martin: Bingo!

Larry (via intercom): And guess who's still holding on Line One?

Martin: Put her through!

Caller: Maggie (aka Mother Margaret) from Lancaster

Martin: Hello Maggie. I'm guessing you've been listening to the show.

Maggie (calm): I have.

Martin: And am I correct in my assumption that you are, in fact, this Mother Margaret character that the previous caller spoke of?

Maggie: You are.

Martin: You sneaky bitch! I knew you were mental, but this takes the cake!

Maggie: That's right. Let the filth flow from your sinful gullet. It'll only hasten your fall into the pit of Hell.

Raven: You know, Maggie...you talk all high and mighty, like you're somehow saving humanity in the name of God, when really all you are is a scared, weak-minded murderer.

Maggie: And you are the Devil's whore! So I guess we're even!

Raven (exacerbated): Oh. *Fuuuck* you!

Martin: So, now I'm the Devil? If that were the case then why, the fuck, would I care if I went to Hell? I'd essentially be going home, right? Get your ideology straight.

Maggie: Your faith in science is admirable, Martin, but horribly misplaced. Your doctor friend shared your beliefs and look where he and his people are now.

Martin (shocked): Dr. Hammond? You were behind that, too?

Raven: It certainly makes sense knowing what we know now.

Martin: I swear to you. When this is over I'm gonna—

Maggie:—when this is over you will all be dead. Mark my words! In 24 hours you people will know the folly of your ways just as the doctor and his people did, and just as everyone else did who dared defy God's plan. And when that happens, the Left Hand will rejoice the demise of the great Devil, Martin Stone and his motley band of sinners.

Dialtone

End Call

Martin: The bitch hung up!

Dead air…

Martin: All right. I'm gonna go out on a limb here and say what I think we're all thinking; Maggie and her cult is behind what's been going on here at the Reef. Tell me I'm crazy for thinking it.

Dead air…

Martin: Fuck…*FUUUCK!*

Raven: If it's true that Maggie's behind this, then wouldn't that mean—

We hear muffled voices coming from the hallway outside of the studio. It sounds like a woman and a man arguing.

Female Voice (off-camera): Let…Go of me! I need to speak to my husband!

Male Voice: (off-camera): Ma'am Please!

Martin recognizes the voice and springs to his feet.

At that same moment, Larry comes running out of his office, his head whipping from Martin, to the door.

Larry: You hear that?!

Martin (concerned): Yeah…Sounded like Karen; right?!

Larry: Yeah. I thought so, too.

Female Voice (off-camera): I said, LET ME GO!

We hear the sound of a tussle on the other side of the door.

Male Voice (off-camera): Stop! I can't let you go in there!

A loud thud against the door...Martin runs out from behind his booth and hurries down the steps. Larry runs up to the door and opens it. He jumps out of the way as Karen Stone stumbles into the room dragging a harried security officer in tow. She is in hysterics, her make-up smeared from crying. She spots Martin coming down the steps and reaches out to him.

Security Officer (to Martin and Larry): I'm sorry, guys.

Karen (to Martin): You have to help me find her!

Martin (to security officer): Let go of her!

The officer releases Karen. Martin hurries over to console her. Karen collapses in Martin's arms and cries into his shoulder. Martin glares at the security officer.

Security Officer: Hey. I was just doing my job.

Martin pulls Karen away and holds her at arm's length. Fear in his eyes…

Martin (to Karen): What is it? Are you sick? Please don't tell me you're—

Karen: I'm fine.

Martin exhales in relief. His posture deflates.

Karen: It's Sara! She ran away!

Martin: Ran away?

Karen: She's somewhere in the building! But I don't know where!

Martin: Why did she run away? Did something happen?

Karen hesitates.

Martin: What?! Just tell me!

Karen (ashamed): I slapped her.

Martin lets go of Karen and runs his hand through his hair.

Martin (angry): Jeee-zus Christ, Karen! Why, the hell, would you do that?! Huh?! You know how fragile that poor girl is! You know what she's been through! That's the last thing you—

Karen: Because of what she told me! That's why!

Martin and Larry share a knowing glance.

Martin (reluctant): What did she tell you?

Karen looks around the room and shakes her head, "No."

Karen: Not here. Not on the air.

Martin looks up at Raven and Ted standing outside of their booths at the top of the stairs.

Martin (to Raven): Can you take over? I'll be right Back.

Raven is in shock and doesn't respond.

Martin: RAVEN!

She snaps out of it and runs around and into her booth.

A male voice, full of rage, leaps out of the flatscreen and startles everyone. Their eyes follow the voice to the screen.

ON FLATSCREEN

VIDEO
Ballroom. The crowd has broken into two lopsided factions. Some are hiding behind their chairs while the majority is on the move, screaming as they push nervously toward the front of the room and away from the angry, one-armed gunmen who has just burst through the doors at the back.

Gunman: OUTTA MY WAY! MOVE!

The man is bald and wearing a security officer's uniform. His left arm is but a stump ending at mid-bicep. In his right arm, he waves a handgun at the crowd.

Martin (re: gunman): Shit! It's Les!

Raven: What's he doing?!

Martin: He's lost it!

VIDEO (CONT'D)
The other officer's reluctantly train their guns on their former colleague.

Security Officers (various): FREEZE! DON'T MOVE! DON'T DO IT, LES!

Les finds Margo standing near the podium clutching her stuffed rabbit like a deer in headlights. He points his gun at her and starts walking toward her. Margo cowers behind her arms.

Les (to other officers): She's the one you should be pointing your guns at! SHE did this! Her and her little sister! They poisoned the food! I tried to tell you people, but nobody listened! Now look at you!

The nurse pulls Margo into her embrace and turns her back to Les to protect the girl.

Security Officers (various): Put the gun down, Les! Stop approaching the girl! Stand down, Les, or we will be forced to shoot!

But Les ignores them. One of the officers runs over and stands in front of the nurse and Margo and raises his hands in surrender. Les stops.

Security Officer #1: Come on, Les. You don't wanna do this, man.

Another officer is attempting to sneak around behind Les. The others keep their guns on him.

Les (to officer #1): Outta my way, Goddammit! I don't want to hurt you, but, at this point, I will shoot right through your ass to get to that bitch!

Anonymous: Stop it! She's only a child!

Anonymous #2: But what if he's right?

Les: I AM right, Goddammit! (to Margo): Tell 'em! Tell 'em the truth about you and your sister! Tell 'em what you did to the food or I swear to God I will—

Officer #2 tackles Les from behind. The gun flies out of his hand. The others strap their rifles across their chests as they run over to assist. Officer #1 drops his rifle and joins his colleagues.

The officers struggle to subdue Les, who continues to resist them.

Officer #2 pleads with him to stop.

Officer #2: Stop it, Les! Stop fighting us! We're on your side, dammit!

Les: Noooo! You don't understand! They're gonna kill us all! You have to stop them!

Gunshots…

Bullets tear into the huddle of security officers killing two of them instantly. The others dive for cover.

We see Margo in a practiced stance, holding the M16 that the officer left on the ground, her face devoid of emotion. The stuffed rabbit is seated on the floor at her feet as if it sat there on its own to watch. Margo turns the gun on Les as he backs away from her on his ass, and squeezes the trigger.

Les throws his good arm up at the last minute. His hand disappears in a red mist. A mangled stump remains at his wrist. A pressurized spout pours from the stump. A steady flow spills over flayed skin and down his forearm. Realization takes shape, but never fully materializes as the assail of bullets moves on to his torso, making him dance and then

216

body-slamming his lifeless torso.

But Margo isn't satisfied. She squeezes the trigger again.

Afterward, Margo turns the gun on the crowd. A collective "No!" leaps at her as she opens fire and waves the gun back and forth to cover the entire room.

Margo: SINNNNERRSSSSSS DIE!!!!!!!!

Bullets find their marks without prejudice. The panicked screaming dies down as the death, near-death, and wishes-they-were-dead-toll rises. People, dead on their feet, crash into chairs and each other on their final descent to the cold, hard floor. The egregious letting of blood makes quick-moving feet hydroplane. Margo picks off a few more as they try to find their footing on the slippery coating.

A single bullet punches Margo in the shoulder and knocks her off- balance. She is stunned, in disbelief. The gun falls to the floor as she can no longer hold it.

A second bullet opens a garish wound in the girl's throat. Margo's eyes shoot wide open. She reaches for her throat and goes down choking on her own blood.

Bodies everywhere. Some are still moving, barely. The lucky folks come out of their hiding places. The remaining security officers surround Margo as she lay on her back, choking and gasping for air. Clenching her teeth at the pain in her throat, she looks up at them with wide, pleading eyes. Her hardened exterior is gone, replaced by the face of a terrified 17-year-old girl.

The guards look equally terrified that they've been forced to shoot a child. A voice from the crowd…

Anonymous: Somebody get a doctor!

Heads whip in search of the nurse. They find her body on the floor riddled with bullet-holes and twisted into a painful pose.

Security Officer (re: Margo, indifferent): Don't bother. She's not gonna make it.

As she lay there struggling to breathe, Margo motions for something off to the side…It's her stuffed rabbit. One of the officers grabs the thing and reluctantly hands it to her.

Margo cradles the stuffed animal in her arms. She sticks her hand into the hole in the thing's side and fishes for something. She finds it and pulls it out—some kind of cylinder with wires sticking out. She holds the thing up for the officers to see and manages a smile. One of the officers leans in for a closer look, and then…

Security Officer: BOMB!

The device explodes before anyone can react…

The screen fills with static

END VIDEO

Martin (shocked): HOLY—! They killed her!

Karen: OH *GOD*! We have to find Sara before security does!

Martin and Karen head for the door. On the way he yells over his shoulder.

Martin: End the show! We gotta find Sara!

END BROADCAST

The crackle of a live microphone…Raven speaks over a black screen, desperation in her voice.

Raven (off-camera): To anyone in the building who can hear this. We need your help. Our people have been stuck in Elevator A between the 25th and 24th floors for over an hour now. I know it's a lot to ask considering what's happening all over the building, but if you are anywhere in the vicinity of those floors, I'm begging you to help.

SECURITY CAM
ELEVATOR A
The lights flicker on and off. Occasionally the darkness persists for more than a few seconds. The camera is pointed down at an angle. Martin Stone stands in front of the camera, glaring impatiently into the lens. Karen Stone is seated on the floor with her face buried between her knees. Larry Del Rossi paces in the background while the same security officer who failed to stop Karen from barging into the studio earlier kneels in front of the soot-cover wall of the elevator shaft on the other side of the pried-open elevator doors. With the side of his face pressed against the wall, the officer attempts to peer through the tiny sliver between it and the elevator, searching for a way out. .

Martin complains to the others.

Martin: Where the hell is Raven?! She said she'd be right back.

Raven (off-camera, breathing heavily): I'm here, Martin!

Karen lifts her head at the sound of Raven's voice. Larry stops pacing and turns toward the camera.

Larry (under his breath): It's about fucking time.

Martin: What the hell, Raven! What was that; 30 minutes?!

Karen: At least…

219

Raven: I'm sorry! I was helping Maria and Alicia with the kids.

Larry perks up at the mention of his wife's name.

Larry: How is she? How's Paxton?

Raven (off-camera): They're fine. They're downstairs at Ted's place with Alicia and Tara. So, you haven't heard from Ted, yet?

Martin: No. Why?

Raven (off-camera, hesitant): We couldn't get anyone to help, so, he went down to try and get you guys out himself. But that was about half an hour ago.

Martin: Whaddayou mean; nobody would help? Didn't you tell them who it was?

Raven: No. I was afraid that might make some people less likely to help.

Martin (thinking): You're probably right. (to himself): Shoulda known not to take this fucking thing. FUCK!

Raven: The dead…They're so many of them now, Martin. And they're spreading throughout the building. Most people tried to escape through the front doors, but Head Office ordered them locked. No one in or out of the building. People were trapped in the lobby. That increased the dead's numbers pretty quickly. Then they started making their way up the stairs.

Karen (confused): Locked the doors?! But they can't do that!

She looks over at Martin, who seems to understand the situation.

Karen (to Martin): They can't do that!

Martin leans over toward the security officer…

220

Martin: Hey! What's going on? Why aren't they letting people out?

The officer ignores him.

Martin: Hey!

The elevator jerks...and then drops rapidly for several floors. It comes to a dead stop. The camera shakes. The image onscreen is briefly warped by the violent impact. The occupants are violently flung into walls. The officer's head smacks the ceiling and is forced to the side by the weight of his body, like a pinched-off garden hose.

Heavy bar interference...

The lights flicker on and off. The image finally settles on four bodies sprawled out on the floor. Martin and Karen are huddled close together, Larry and the security officer lying nearby. The officer is facedown. Blood pools around his head. Raven calls out to them through the camera. Fearing the worse, she struggles to hold it together.

Raven (off-camera, scared): Martin! Larry! Karen! Wake up! (to herself): Oh my God...

The elevator doors are still pried apart. The soot-covered wall claims most of the space beyond the pried-open doors, however, the backs of a pair of sealed doors is visible as well. It appears that the elevator has overshot one of the floors by several feet leaving only the bottom half of the doors visible.

Martin's head bobs. His eyes flutter open. He frowns at the pain in his head, and follows the ethereal voice up to the camera...

Raven (off-camera): Martin! Oh, thank God!

Martin starts to push himself up to a seated position, his head ringing from equal parts trauma, and the flickering lights. He looks around while massaging a sore spot on his head.

Martin (confused): Wha…happened?

Raven: The elevator just…dropped. (welling up) I thought you were dead.

Martin: What floor are we on?

Raven: It looks like the elevator's stuck just below the 12th floor. (pause) You fell 15 floors, Martin.

Martin appears to ponder the distance between floors. His arm brushes up against something soft and warm. He freezes. A moment later the fluster leaves him and he remembers his wife. He rolls over, grabs her by the shoulders, and shakes her gently.

Martin: Babe! Babe! Wake up!

When that doesn't work Martin slaps Karen across the face. She awakes in full panic.

Martin pulls her close and embraces her.

Martin: It's okay, babe. We're okay.

Karen struggles momentarily, and then…acceptance. She jumps and lets out a mousy shriek when the lights flicker off and back on.

Behind them, Larry slowly regains consciousness. He is in pain, but undamaged. He sees the security officer lying face-down in a pool of blood and thrusts himself away from the horrifying sight.

He sits there in a daze. Realization sets in and Larry crawls back over to the officer and places two fingers against the man's neck.

Martin takes Karen's face in his hands.

Martin (speaking softly): Are you hurt?

Karen takes a moment to assess her condition.

Karen: I don't think so. What happened? What's happening?

Martin: The elevator fell. We're lucky to be alive.

Martin points at the 12th-floor doors.

Martin: Look. We can get out, now.

Karen looks over at the 12th-floor doors. The hint of hope materializes on her face.

Karen: We have to find Sara.

Martin: I know. We will. Mark my words.

Larry: How long we been out, Raven?

Raven: About 10 minutes.

Karen turns toward Larry's voice and shrieks when she sees the officer's body.

Karen (to Larry, re: security officer): Is he…?

Larry nods, "Yes."

Larry: Which means that we need to get outta here, ASAP.

Karen: Oh my God!

Martin and Karen back away simultaneously. Larry slides the officer's handgun from its holster at the man's waist and joins Martin and Karen on the other side of the elevator. Holding the gun with intent, he glares momentarily at the dead man and then turns to the 12th-floor doors.

As Larry hurries up to the doors...

Larry (to Martin): C'mon! Help me get these open?

Andre Duza

Martin walks up to his side.

Larry digs his fingers into the crease where the 12th-floor doors meet. Martin does the same on the other side…

Raven (off-camera): Wait! It's not safe! The dead…They're everywhere.

The lights flicker…Martin, Karen, and Larry standing there nursing stupefied expressions…

Karen breaks down in Martin's arms.

Karen (crying): Sara's out there with them! She must be SO afraid!

Larry: Well, we can't stay in here! This guy's gonna wake up any second!

Raven: Hold on. I'm trying to bring up the camera in the 12th-floor stairwell on your computer, Larry.

Larry: It's the same way you found the Elevator Cam.

Raven: Ted's the one who found it.

Larry: Okay. You see the tag that says, "Multi-view?"

Raven: Yeah. I see it.

Larry: Click on it.

The screen divides into three smaller windows, each depicting security camera footage from various locations throughout the Reef Tower. The cameras have all been programmed to pan from right to left automatically. Window three is the only one with sound.

SECURITY CAM
WINDOW 1: BALLROOM
A thin fog has settled in the air. Destruction fans out from the

spot where Margo lay dying before the blast; the blast radius indicated by the 10 plus-foot circle of charred carpet and pulverized floor underneath. Blood. Bullet holes in the walls and floor. Bodies on the floor, half-eaten, each with their own regimen of zombies hunched over them in a feeding frenzy. Victims of headshots lay twice-dead nearby.

SECURITY CAM
WINDOW 2: INFIRMARY

Zombies lumber about, flowing in and out of the room, awkwardly navigating overturned beds, and medical carts lying on their sides. Medical equipment, and broken glass, and papers scattered on the floor. Footprints in smeared blood. Bodies leaking from head wounds.

SECURITY CAM
WINDOW 3: ELEVATOR A (MAIN)

Martin, Karen and Larry standing by the pried open doors, eager to exit the confined space. The lights flicker on and off.

Raven: Okay…I'm there.

Larry: Which window are we in?

Raven: Three.

Larry: Okay. In the search bar on the right side of the screen, type in Windows 1 and 2: 12th-Floor Hallway North & West, and 12th Floor Stairwell…You'll only want sound in the main window, which should still be the elevator.

Raven: It is.

Larry: Okay. The easiest way to keep up with us when we're on the move is to keep checking the box marked "Main Window" in the scroll-down column as we go.

Raven: Got it.

Seconds later the images in Windows One, Two and Three cut to…

SECURITY CAM
WINDOW 1: 12th FLR. HALLWAYS NORTH & WEST
We are looking down diagonally at of the tops of Elevator Bank from the camera's position high on the wall in the crease where the two hallways intersect in an L-shape.

A long hallway lined with doors recessed into fancy archways stretches away from the elevator bank—north. A maintenance cart full of supplies outside one of the doors. A covered vent near the floor toward the rear. A glass wall at the far end looks out at the Camden, New Jersey skyline across the Delaware River.

The intersecting hallway to the right (west) is nearly identical to the north hallway, but for an exit sign that hangs over the stairwell door in the middle. A large, antique armoire has been shoved up against the door to prevent it from opening.

SECURITY CAM
WINDOW 2: 12th FLR. STAIRWELL
A small cluster of zombies congregate on the 12th-floor landing. Some pound and scratch the door while others just stand there looking lost and confused. More zombies stumble up the descending and ascending staircases to the left and right respectively.

Raven: Okay. Got them all up onscreen.

Larry: Whaddayou see?

Raven: The 12th floor looks clear.

SECURITY CAM
WINDOW 3: ELEVATOR A (MAIN)
Martin and Larry standing in front of the 12th-floor doors, ready to pull them apart. Karen clinging to Martin's back. The lights flicker.

Raven (off-camera): But there are deadheads in the stairwell, right outside the door; maybe about 20 or 30 of them. You might be stuck on 12.

Martin: Well, we can hide in one of the residences. (thinking) I think Nick Parker lives on 12. You know, the mechanic? He'd let us in.

Larry: He was at the meeting. I remember seeing him on the video.

Martin: Shiit!

Raven (off-camera): Doesn't mean he's dead, though. The people, who could, ran back to their residences when it started. That's what led the deadheads up the stairwell. So, I guess it's worth a try.

Martin and Larry work together to pull the 12th-floor doors apart. It takes a while, but they eventually budge. Afterward, Martin interlaces his fingers and lowers his hands providing a foothold for Karen to use to climb out. Larry moves closer to her to assist.

Karen steps into the foothold and starts to climb through the opening. She is halfway through when the lights flicker off for several seconds. When they return, the re-animated security officer is standing behind Larry. The officer is several shades whiter than before. A venous pattern decorates one side of his face like some sort of grotesque tribal tattoo. His lips are curled into a snarl. His eyes are fat with wanting.

Raven (off-screen): LOOK OUT!

Martin (to Larry): BEHIND YOU!

Larry turns around just as the living dead officer lunges at him. He raises the gun and fires at the officer until it clicks empty. The bullets punch the man in the torso and shove him backward, but he is still standing.

Martin: YOU'RE SUPPOSED TO SHOOT 'EM IN THE HEAD!

As Larry throws the empty gun at the officer...

Larry: I KNOW THAT!

It misses by a mile.

The officer lunges again, his mouth stretched wide open. Saliva pours down his chin like clear syrup. Larry charges the officer and slams the living dead man up against the wall. Leaning with all of his weight, he uses his forearm to pin the officer there.

Martin works frantically to push Karen out of the elevator. Once Karen is out, Martin turns to help Larry.

Larry (to Martin): I got 'em! Just go!

Martin: What about you?!

Larry: I'll be fine! Just hurry!

Martin climbs out of the elevator as fast as he can. Afterward, he turns and reaches out to Larry.

Martin: Come on! I'll pull you out.

Larry uses his leg to kick the officer's legs out from under him. He throws the man to the ground, hurries over, and climbs through the opening. The officer recovers faster than expected. He lunges and grabs hold of Larry's ankle and tries to pull him back into the elevator. Larry panics and starts kicking wildly, but the dead man is stuck like glue.

SECURITY CAM
WINDOW 1: 12ᵗʰ FLR. HALLWAYS NORTH & WEST
Way at the back of the hall, the ventilation cover in the wall pops off and a figure emerges from the inside. It's Ted Morrison.

Watching from the security camera, Raven is the first to see him.

Raven (off-camera, pleasantly surprised): Ted!

Ted jumps to his feet and runs toward the elevators. He grabs a mop from the maintenance cart along the way.

Karen screams and jumps out of the way. Martin is too preoccupied with pulling Larry out to notice.

SECURITY CAM
WINDOW 3: ELEVATOR A (MAIN)
The lights flicker…Larry struggles against the living dead officer's grip as the man tries to pull him in. The dead man cranks his head back and opens his mouth in preparation for a sizable bite.

The long, wooden, mop-handle pierces the frame. The tip lodges in the dead officer's mouth causing him to choke. He grabs the stick in both hands and is pushed back into the rear wall and held there.

SECURITY CAM
WINDOW 1: 12th FLR. HALLWAYS NORTH & WEST (MAIN)
Larry climbs out of the elevator and past Ted who is on one knee, leaning forward and using his bodyweight to hold the officer against the elevator wall. Martin and Karen are watching from the background. Their heads occasionally whip toward the pounding and scratching at the stairwell door.

Larry (to Ted): Where, the hell, have you been?!

Ted: I got pinned down a few floors up! Made my way down through the ventilation system!

SECURITY CAM
WINDOW 3: ELEVATOR A
The mop stick breaks and Ted falls forward and into the elevator. The living dead officer lunges for him, but Ted is able to keep the man away with his feet. He gives a good kick, knocking the officer back. Ted jumps to his feet and turns toward the doors when the elevator jerks, and then drops like a lead balloon.

We hear Martin, Karen, and Larry cry out from the hallway just as the elevator falls. Ted stumbles into the wall. The living dead man is on him before he can right himself. They struggle with each other as the elevator plummets, picking up speed with each foot. They eventually become weightless and begin to float. In the midst of their struggle, neither of them seems to notice. Seconds later, their intertwined bodies are yanked violently downward, and then...

Raven: Ted! Noooooooooo!

Static in Window Three.

SECURITY CAM
WINDOW 1: 12th FLR. HALLWAYS NORTH & WEST (MAIN)
Martin and Larry are frozen in disbelief near the pried-open elevator doors. Karen in a heap further down the north hallway with her hands held over her ears, eyes squeezed shut.

We hear Raven breaks down in tears.

Martin (incredulous): Ted's gone?

Larry doesn't respond

The ruckus has caught the attention of the zombies in the stairwell. We can hear it in their voices, and in the intensity of the pounding and clawing at the stairwell door. We see the armoire begin to move as their combined weight pushes the door open slightly. From where they are, Martin, Karen and Larry can't see down the west hallway, but they can hear the noise loud and clear.

Martin (re: door): What do we do?

Larry looks around. He spots the vent that Ted came through just a few minutes ago and points to it.

Larry: There!

Larry runs up to the vent, gets down on his knees and looks inside.

230

Karen takes a look at the vent. Her eyes fill with terror. She shakes her head from side-to-side as if crawling through the vent is a cardinal sin.

Karen (terrified): I can't go in there! I can't! You know how claustrophobic I am!

Martin: Baby, we have no other choice!

As Larry starts to crawl into the vent…

Larry (to Martin and Karen): Come on!

Karen becomes hysterical.

Karen: No! I'll die if I go in there! There has to be another way!

Martin (angry, scared): GODDAMMIT! WE'LL BOTH DIE IF YOU STAY OUT HERE, CAUSE THERE'S NO WAY THAT I'M GONNA LEAVE YOU. YOU WANT BOTH OUR DEATHS ON YOUR HANDS!

Karen: Just leave me here, then! Just go!

Martin rubbernecks for an alternative escape route, and comes up empty.

Larry leans out of the vent. He is anxious to go, but hesitant to leave Martin and Karen behind.

Larry (to Karen): What? So, you'd rather be eaten alive?!

Martin waves Larry off.

Martin (to Larry): Get outta here, Larry! I'll deal with this!

He grabs Karen by the shoulders.

Martin: I need you to calm down and listen to me. Okay!

Karen continues to cry.

Martin: OKAY!

Karen shakes her head, "Yes."

The armoire's clawed feet slice into the carpet, tearing through fibers as the stairwell door is pushed open a little wider with each collective shove.

Martin: Do you hear that?!

Martin points his head toward the stairwell door and the intense guttural tonnages coming from behind it.

Martin: That's the sound of dead people, Karen. Zombies. And if we don't leave through that vent right now, they're gonna come in here and—

The armoire topples and makes a loud crash. The stairwell door swings open with impunity and spills a dozen zombies into the west hallway.

Larry gets up and takes off running toward the elevators.

Martin: What the hell are you doing?!

As Larry runs toward the elevators…

Larry: Just stay outta sight!

The zombies slowly, awkwardly pick themselves up and make their way toward the bend. Their eyes grow wide when Larry crosses their paths…

Martin: Larry. No!

…and leaps through the elevator doorway and out of our view.

We hear Larry's voice coming from the elevator shaft.

Larry (off-camera): Come on, you stupid fuckers! Come and get me!

Zombies wretch toward Larry's voice with renewed verve. They reach eagerly, salivating at the prospect of a warm, living meal. The first few to arrive are shoved forward. They topple into the elevator shaft and out of view. Several more follow, reaching as they fall into the dark abyss.

Down the hall, Martin grabs Karen and pushes her into one of the doorways of one of the apartments. He instructs her to press her back against the door and appear as flat as possible. Martin squeezes in next to her and does the same.

Larry continues to taunt the zombies…

Larry (off-camera): That's right! Keep comin'!

…and they continue to take the bait. The mindless, shoving procession into the elevator shaft claims two-dozen zombies before one of them—an older man wearing pajamas—stops at the edge and appears to ponder his situation.

Larry (off-camera): Come on! What are you waiting for?!

The old zombie seems to sense that something is wrong as his dead eyes volley from the dark expanse beyond the elevator doors to where we assume Larry must be clinging to the dangling elevator cable.

More zombies stumble up behind the old zombie. They shove him with their bodies, nearly causing him to fall, but the old man maintains his balance and then shoves back at them, grunting angrily. The procession from the opened stairwell door has slowed to a few stragglers.

Larry (off-camera): Come on! Goddammit! I can't hang here forever.

Without warning, Martin bolts from the doorway…

Karen: Martin! Wait! What-r-u…

…and charges toward the crowd of zombies standing before

233

the elevator shaft. He lets out a primal growl. A few of the zombies turn toward the sound just as Martin rams them with his forearm and continues to shove forward, sending them toppling into the elevator shaft.

His head whipping toward the stairwell door and back, Martin squats down and reaches into the elevator shaft with both hands...

Martin (to Larry): Hurry! Swing this way and I'll catch you!

Martin grabs hold of Larry as he swings into view hugging a thick, greasy cable that has left a linear stain on his shirt. Larry let's go of the cable and for a moment, he and Martin embrace. Karen comes running up from the background.

Larry runs up to Elevator B and starts pressing the "Up."

Martin: What, the hell, are you doing?

As Larry backs away from the elevator and waits.

Larry: I've gotta get to Maria and Paxton.

Martin: You're seriously gonna get on another elevator after what just happened?

Larry: What choice do we have? We can't take the stairs!

Karen (to Larry, hysterical): What about Sara?! You have to help us find her?!

Larry: I'm sorry, Karen.

Karen: You're just gonna leave us!

Martin to Karen): No one's leaving anybody. Now look... We're no good to Sara if we're dead. The first thing we have to do is survive! Sara's a tough kid. Remember how long she survived out there is the shit before we found her? She'll be all right.

Raven's voice comes from the camera's speaker and startles them.

Raven (off-camera): There're more coming up the stairs, but it's pretty clear between the 12th and 14th floors. If you hurry, you can…

Larry: But, what if the doors are barricaded like this one was? Then we're fucked.

Larry presses the "Up," button again, and backs away.

Martin runs to the stairwell door and looks out. He pulls his head back in seconds later, his face broadcasting urgency.

Martin: They're at the bottom of the stairs! We can probably make it to the next floor up!

As Larry dances impatiently, waiting for the elevator.

Larry: Go if you want to. But I'm not getting myself trapped in the stairwell.

Karen (re: elevator): It's not gonna get here in time!

Larry: I have to try.

Martin starts to peer into the stairwell again…

Martin: Shit!

…but snatches his head back before taking a good look.

We hear a swell in the zombie's carnal growling.

Martin: They saw me! They're halfway up. We have to go, NOW!

Martin reaches out to Karen summoning her to him outside the stairwell doorway. Karen runs up next to him.

The zombies are close enough that we hear specific voices within the chorus of guttural moans and growls.

In the background, we see an apartment door open on the left side of the north hallway. A man's head peeks out, and then tip toes out into the hallway looking curiously toward the elevator bank.

Martin takes Karen by the hand. He turns to Larry.

Martin: Be careful, man.

…and motions for the stairwell when the elevator dings.

Martin freezes and whips his head toward the elevator…In the quiet moments before the elevator doors open, we hear raised voices coming from the inside…

Larry: You hear that? Hey Raven. Check the camera in Elevator B.

Raven (off-camera): I'm looking at it right now. It's a blank screen. Camera must not be working.

The elevator doors glide apart and people run out screaming; too many people, it appears, to have fit into the tiny box. They react with terror at the sight of Larry, standing there, dumbfounded. One man raises a handgun and starts firing wild shots at him.

Larry throws his arms over his head and ducks. The bullets smack the wall above him.

Martin calls out in Larry's defense…

Martin (to man with gun): Wait! He's alive!

The man stops firing and drops his hands. People continue to push their way out of the elevator. They appear to be running from something. We see several children among them. Karen calls out to one of them; a little girl, approximately 12-years-

old, being dragged by the arm.

Karen: Sara!

Sara hears the voice and turns around. As she's being pulled away…

Sara: Mommy.

Karen starts to run over to her but stops when she sees the two remaining occupants of the elevator.

Inside the elevator, Dave Straussman uses his M16 to pin an aggressive zombie against the rear wall. He yells over his shoulder at the people who have just exited.

Dave: All clear?!

Anonymous voices (various): Clear!

Dave shoves the zombie into the back wall of the elevator, runs out into the hall, and shoots the zombie in the head with his M16.

Martin: RUN!

The crowd follows Martin's voice to the stairwell door just as a swell of eager zombies push through and stumble after them, arms outstretch, finger curled into claws.

As Dave waves the crowd away from the stairwell doors...

Dave: GO! GO! GO!

The crowd takes off running around the bend and down the North hallway. Martin is right behind them, Karen in tow. Larry flanks them on the right. They spot a man running into his apartment further down the hall.

Dave (re: man running into apartment): Hey! You! Stop!

Andre Duza

The man tries to slam the door, but Dave runs over and wedges his foot between it and the doorframe. The scared resident attempts to stomp and kick Dave's foot, but more people, including Martin, arrive to help him.

Raven (off-camera): Martin! Wait! The cameras can't see you in there!

But Martin is too preoccupied with getting into the residence. A small crowd has gathered around the door. They force the door open and disappear inside.

Raven (off-camera): Martin!

The first tier of zombies round the bend just as the door slams shut. They turn toward the sound, in unison, like a flock of migrating finches, and stare with dumbstruck curiosity. Stumbling drunkenly, they make their way toward apartment 1205 and start pounding and clawing the door.

Raven (off-camera, to audience): Stay with us people. As it stands, Martin and Karen have found Sara. They are currently out of camera range, holed up, along with a small group of survivors, including Dave Straussman, in suite 1205. Please stay tuned while I try to contact with them.

The living dead mob continues to grow in the north hallway. A disjointed line forms from the stairwell door to Apartment 1205.

Raven: (off-camera, to herself): Oh...There's so many. (to zombies): HEY! YOU ALL! GET AWAY FROM THAT DOOR! THERE'S NOTHING FOR YOU IN THERE!

Heads turn lazily toward her voice. Their eyes light up.

Raven: THAT'S RIGHT! OVER HERE! COME AND GET IT, YOU BASTARDS!

It starts small, with just a few zombies breaking from the hackneyed formation and shambling up to the camera. More

238

follow until the entire crowd congregates underneath the camera, pushing and shoving for a prime spot. The camera is mounted well out of their reach, yet they try to grab it.

The phone rings and startles Raven. She lets it ring several times before answering.

Raven (off-camera, hesitant): Hello?

Martin (via phone): Raven. It's Martin. We're okay. We're in suite 1205.

We can hear voices in the background of Martin's call.

Raven: I know. I've been trying to lure the deadheads away from the door. There're so many of them out there. People we know. It's like 9/6 all over again. This is so awful. I can't—

Martin: Listen. I want you to switch the live video feed to Dave's Helmet Cam.

Raven: But—

Martin: You can do it from Larry's computer. It's simple. Just go to his desktop and click on the camera icon labeled Helmet Cam 1: Dave from Security. I'll hold while you do it.

Raven: Okay.

Several seconds pass, and then…

We are ambushed by the sound of several conversations overlapping, people speaking in jovial tones and laughing heartily. Music in the background. It sounds like a party.

Martin (via cell phone): What is that; those voices?

Raven: I still had a clip from the party you threw for my birthday last year on my phone. I got it up to the mic. I needed something to keep their attention. Now, hold on while I switch to the helmet cam.

The image cuts back to single-screen view…

HELMET CAM 1 (DAVE'S POV)
Dave is standing behind a kitchen counter looking out into the vast living room stocked with high-brow art and expensive antiquities. A jumble of heavy furniture pushed up against the front door. A wall of tempered glass stretching from floor to ceiling makes up the back wall of the apartment. Along with the occupant of Apartment 1205, a rail thin sophisticate with a pole up his ass, there are 16 people; a diverse amalgam of residents. Couples. Families with young children. Several individuals. A small group of men and women armed with baseball bats and golf clubs form a loose barrier around the children, while a matronly woman attempts to keep their young minds distracted from current events. A dark-haired young man with sharp features is seated on a chair within the protective barrier. We get the impression that he is seated there against his will.

The rail thin occupant stands at the windows, looking out. Others stand nearby doing the same. The general mood is grim. Many people wallow in shock.

We see Martin talking on a cell phone in a corner of the room. Karen is perched in a squat nearby, consoling a stone-faced Sara as some of the other folks glare at the girl in disgust.

We hear the video clip from Raven's phone in the background. Save for Martin, who is speaking to her over the phone, the people holed up in Apartment 1205 cannot hear Raven or the clip.

Raven (off-camera, to Martin): Okay. Feed from the helmet cam is up.

Martin looks over and gives a thumbs-up to Dave while holding the phone to his ear. Raven continues to talk to Martin.

Raven (off-camera): Looks pretty intense in there.

Martin: See the young guy sitting with the kids? Looks all pissed off?

240

Raven: Yeah…

Martin: That's Alex Mull.

Raven: Reeeally…

A woman wearing Yoga pants and an over-sized T-shirt stands by the window looking out at the neighboring building.

Yoga pants: What are they doing?! They're just standing there?! Why don't they do anything to help?! Why? Why? WHY?!

The woman is quickly scolded with a collective "Shhhh!" from the others. She collapses into the arms of a well-built hipster standing next to her. Presumably they are a couple. We recognize the hipster as the man who accidentally shot at Larry when the group exited the elevator earlier.

Raven (off-camera): What's going on?

Martin: I don't know.

The rail thin man becomes suddenly animated.

Rail thin (excited): Hey! It's Mr. Brand! They're taking him away! Maybe they'll come back for us next!

Dave moves over to the window and looks out…

Dave (to Rail thin, disappointed): Don't get your hopes up.

Rail thin (to Dave): What is THAT supposed to mean?
Dave hesitates.

Through the window we glimpse the Regatta Tower sitting some 100 feet away. The residents are standing at their windows, entire families, in some cases, watching the unraveling of the Reef Tower. We can see horror in some of their faces.

Dave looks down...we see the well-manicured courtyard between the two towers. Morgan Brand is being led away from the Reef Tower by two security officers.

Rail thin (to Dave): Well? What's that supposed to mean?

Dave looks around the room. He has become the center of attention.

Dave (to Rail thin): It means, they've left us to die in here.

A rumble of dissatisfaction from the crowd. A woman cries out in hysteria; a voluptuous blond with straw hair fashioned into a bun.

Group (to voluptuous): SHHHHHH!

The children are briefly alarmed by the raised voices, but the matronly woman is able to calm them down.

Rail thin: Mr. Brand wouldn't do that. He's a GOOD man. He's gotta have some kinda plan to evacuate us.

A rumble of accord from the crowd...

Raven (off-camera, scared): Oh my God!

Martin (to Raven): What???

Raven (off-camera): I hear something outside the door. I think they're up here.

The image cuts to...

SECURITY CAM
32nd FLR. HALLWAYS NORTH & WEST
There are fewer apartments up here. Otherwise the layout and décor is identical to the 12th floor. A sign marked "studio" hangs over a door on the far right side. We see a handful of zombies clawing, and scratching and pounding on the studio door. A few more enter from the opened stairwell door and

head toward the others.

Raven (off-camera): They're at the door! What am I gonna do?!

Martin (worried): Try not to panic. They shouldn't be able to get through, but barricade the door, just in case. We'll be up to get—

We hear raised voices in the background of Martin's call.

Martin (re: raised voices): HEY!

Commotion on the other end of the line.

The image cuts to...

HELMET CAM 1 (DAVE'S POV)
Dave runs over toward an altercation between Karen and the woman in yoga pants. Sara hides behind Karen's leg. The well-built hipster and one other man struggle to hold Yoga pants back. The activity frightens the other children.

Karen (to yoga pants): You stay away from her! She's just a child!

Yoga pants: She's old enough to know how to poison the food supply. And don't give me that, 'she was brainwashed shit!' She knows what she did was wrong! (to Sara): Don't you, you little BITCH?!

Karen: Don't you dare talk to her that way!

Martin hurries over to Karen and tries to pull her away. She gets her arm free and hurls a wild punch at yoga pants, hitting the woman in the face. The blow knocks the woman on her ass.

Dave jumps between the two women...

Dave: Enough!

Karen's posture deflates. The men help a dazed Yoga pants

to her feet. She snatches her arms away from them and glares at Karen while massaging her sore jaw.

Dave (to group): Now, we've gone over this before! The girl is coming with us! I don't care what she's done! Anybody who's got a problem with that can take it up with me!

No one responds.

Dave gives Sara a comforting pat on the head and then squats down to her level.

Dave: I'm not going to let anyone hurt you, honey. All right?

Sara nods and smiles timidly.

Martin is standing behind the girl. He lifts the cell phone to his ear.

Martin (to Raven): Did you catch all that? Humanity at its best…

No answer…

Martin: Raven? You there?

Still no answer…

Martin: RAVEN!

Anonymous voices shush Martin. He stands there with the phone to his ear, crestfallen.

Dave stands up.

Dave (to Martin): What's the matter?

Martin: Raven's not answering.

Suddenly…

Raven (off-camera): Martin!

Relief washes over Martin's face.

Martin: What the hell?! I thought that maybe...

Raven: I'm fine. I'm trying to reinforce the door. Be right back...

Martin: Raven...Raven...

Martin exhales, frustrated. Larry walks up beside him.

Larry (to Martin): Everything okay upstairs?

Martin (hesitates): Yeah...(to Dave, quietly): Listen...What you said earlier about the old man leaving us in here to die... Why would you say something like that? Mr. Brand has always been good to us.

Dave (shaking head): You've obviously been drinking the Kool Aid like everybody else. Morgan Brand is an opportunist, first and foremost. He doesn't give a fuck about you unless you can help him push his agenda, which, I'm afraid to say has more to do with power than that humanitarian bullshit he's been shoveling down your throats.

Rail thin: Then why, the hell, are YOU still here, if he's such a bad guy?

A few people voice their approval of Rail thin's comment.

Dave: It's called survival, people. It ain't like any of us had a lotta options.

Rail thin (re: Alex Mull): I thought the boy there was supposed to be some kind of 'miracle' who was gonna lead us to a cure for this mess? Why would they leave HIM behind?

Dave: They wanted me to hand Alex over to them when this all started, but I refused. That's why they turned on me. It doesn't matter, anyway. They've got enough samples of his DNA to develop a vaccine without him. They just didn't want anybody else to have access to it.

A noise from the door steals the group's attention. It sounds like a hand sliding down on the other side, and a beleaguered voice barely moaning into the door.

The group trades knowing glances. A sudden pounding on the door gives them a jolt. More hands join in the pounding attack.

Anonymous woman: Oh God! They know we're in here! They're coming for us!

Sara buries her face in Karen's leg and begins to cry. The other children become upset.

Dave throws his hands up.

Dave: Everybody calm down! We start falling apart and we're never gonna make it outta here!

A begrudging silence falls upon the group. They listen as the voices at the door become louder, more agitated. The pounding and clawing becomes more aggressive.

Suddenly…An alarm sounds…It wails like an air raid siren. The group recoils from the horrible noise. People throw their hands over their ears to block it out.

As the alarm sounds…A pleasant female voice comes over the intercom system.

Pleasant Female Voice: STERILIZATION PROTOCOL HAS BEEN ACTIVATED. YOU HAVE 15 MINUTES TO EVACUATE THE PREMISES BEFORE SPRAYING COMMENCES.

The group stares up at the ceiling listening to the serene voice.

Raven (to Martin): You hearing that?

Martin holds the phone to his ear.

Martin (into phone): Raven! You okay?

Raven: Yeah. What's going on?

Martin: I don't know. But it can't be good.

Dave (to himself): Holy Shit! He's actually gonna do it!

Martin (to Raven): Sit tight. I think Dave knows something.

Martin lowers the phone and moves closer to Dave.

Martin (to Dave): Do what?

Dave pulls Martin and Larry off to the side, away from the others.

Dave (to Martin and Larry): The old man. He ah…He had the sprinkler systems in both buildings retrofitted to spray hydrofluoric acid in case of an outbreak like this.

We hear Raven gasp.

Martin (shocked): What?!

Larry: My family!!!!

Dave: Keep your voices down!

In the background…people wonder aloud about the announcement and worry about the noise at the door. Their eyes dart between the door and Dave. The people guarding the terrified children seem especially concerned. One of them, a short, clean-cut man with muscular forearms, steps forward.

Clean-cut (to Dave): Hey! Shouldn't we be worried about the announcement?

Without looking away, Dave holds his hand up to the man...
Dave: *Give us a second, huh!*

The clean-cut man looks annoyed. The announcement repeats.

Pleasant Female Voice: *STERILIZATION PROTOCOL HAS BEEN ACTIVATED. YOU HAVE 15 MINUTES TO EVACUATE THE PREMISES BEFORE SPRAYING COMMENCES.*

Dave *(to Martin)*: *We were told that it would only be used once the building was completely evacuated of the living. (to himself): That motherFUCKER!*

Martin *(scared)*: *So, what now?!*

Dave *(to Martin)*: *We have to go. Now!*

Martin: *Go where?! They locked us in, remember? Can't we hide in the closets or under the furniture or something?*

Dave shakes his head "No."

Dave: *If the acid doesn't get you, the fumes will. (pause) The window outside in the hall. We can jump from there.*

Martin: *Into the river??? But we're 12 floors up. And what about the zombies? They're not just gonna stand there and watch us.*

Larry: *What about my family?!*

Martin: *And Raven, too...They're all still upstairs.*
Dave: *I know. That's why Larry and I are gonna go get them.*

Martin: *I'm going with you.*

Dave: *No. Your place is with your family. Plus, I need you to make sure things run smoothly while we go get the others.*

Martin: *But—*

Dave: But nothing! Now, just do it! Please? We don't have time to argue.

Martin reluctantly accepts.

Larry (to Dave): How're we gonna get up there?

Dave: The elevator. Unless you've got a better idea.

Larry: Not at the moment. (re: M16) How many bullets you got left in that thing?

Dave: Not many.

Larry: What about the guy who almost shot me out by the elevators?

Dave: Empty. And he couldn't have hit you with that gun if you were standing still.

Larry is disappointed.

Dave: Don't worry. We'll manage.

The wailing alarm…The uneasy crowd…The pounding and clawing at the door.

The clean cut man takes a few steps closer to Dave.

Clean cut: Are you gonna tell us what's going on?!

Rail thin: Yeah. Are we safe in here?!
Many in the group share the men's concerns.

Dave walks out into the middle of the room and clears his throat in preparation to address the group.

Dave (to group): All right. I need everyone's attention. The announcement you just heard is proof that Morgan Brand doesn't give two shits about you. Right now, the residents of the Regatta Tower are probably hearing some kind of announcement about how we are all infected.

Anonymous woman: But that's not true!

Dave: Exactly.

Clean cut (impatient): What does it mean; Sterilization Protocol?

Dave: It means that in 15 minutes the overhead sprinklers will rain down hydrofluoric acid on everything and everyone left in this building. Dead or alive.

As the group struggles to fathom yet another life-threatening turn of events...

Dave: Our only way out is through the window in the hall.

Gasps.

Clean cut: You want us to jump into the river from way up here?! Why, the hell, didn't you tell us that when we were down in the infirmary?! Huh?! We got kids here, for Christ Sakes! There's no way they'll—

Dave: You can come up to the 32nd floor with Me and Larry, and try it from there.

Clean cut: I thought we were all gonna go to the roof to wait for the rescue.

Dave: That was before I realized that they were leaving us for dead! And before the announcement you just heard.

Anonymous woman: So, there's no rescue?

Dave: I'm afraid not.

Rail thin: How are we supposed to get past all those zombies out there?!

Dave: I'm gonna go out first and act as a decoy. Now, once I get them into the stairwell, you'll all have to move quickly! No hesitation! Get it out of your mind how high up it is! It's either jump or die! It's that simple! I'm sorry to put it so bluntly, but that's just the way it is! Everybody got that?!

Some people nod.

Dave (to Martin): Remember! Women and children first!

Martin nods.

Dave (to Larry): You ready.

Larry: I'm ready.

The group prepares to move. The matronly woman rounds up the children and gives them a pep talk. Dave looks around the room. He spots a wooden end-table next to one of the couches. He clears the table in one swipe of his arm, turns it over, and breaks off one of its legs.

Rail thin (re: coffee table): Hey!

Dave ignores the man and flips the table-leg in his hand and tests its weight as a bludgeoning object.

As Martin walks over to Karen and Sara…He lifts the phone to his ear and starts to speak into it, but he is cut off…

Raven: I heard what Dave said. Listen! He doesn't have to go out there! I can lure the dead into the stairwell with the cameras!
Martin: Good idea!

Martin hurries over to Dave, excited to pass on the news.

Martin (to Dave): You don't have to run decoy. Raven can lure the zombies into the stairwell with the cameras.

Dave thinks it over…and then reaches out to Martin.

Dave (to Martin): Give me the phone.

Martin hands Dave the phone. Dave takes it and holds it up to his ear.

Dave (into phone): How bad is it up there?

Raven (off-camera): I'd say there're about a dozen of them.

Dave: What about on 31? That's where Larry and Ted's families are, right?

Raven (off-camera): Yeah. Apartment 3106. Hang on…

The image cuts to…

SECURITY CAM
31st FLR. HALLWAYS NORTH & WEST
A hallway lined with doors. A large window at the back. Not a zombie in sight.

Raven (off-camera): No. Nothing on 31.

The image cuts to…

HELMET CAM 1 (DAVE'S POV)
Apartment 1205. Martin awkwardly supervises the group as they prepare to leave. Dave holds the cell phone to his ear. Larry stands next to him.

Dave (to Raven): Good. I need you to contact them. Tell them to be ready, and to listen for the elevator. We'll come get you after.
Raven (off-camera): Okay.

Dave: I'm gonna stay on the line from here out. Let me know when you've got the zombies in the stairwell. We'll be waiting by the door.

Raven (off-camera): Will do.

The image cuts to…

SECURITY CAM
12ᵗʰ FLR. HALLWAY NORTH & WEST
Most of the zombies are concentrated under the camera where Raven's party clip continues to play on a loop. They have given up trying to reach the voices, and instead just stand there staring up at the camera. Others crowd the door of Apartment 1205.

The clip goes silent. We hear a rustling sound. Seconds later, Raven calls out to the zombies crowded around the door of Apartment 1205.

Raven (off-camera): HEY! SHITHEADS! OVER HERE!

They lurch toward the sound of her voice. The zombies beneath the camera reach for it with renewed vigor.

Raven (off-camera): Thaaat's right! Keep comin'! Come to mama!

As she waits for the zombie's by the door to join the rest of the crowd beneath the camera...the pleasant female voice blares from the intercom.

Pleasant Female Voice: STERILIZATION PROTOCOL HAS BEEN ACTIVATED. YOU HAVE 10 MINUTES TO EVACUATE THE PREMISES BEFORE SPRAYING COMMENCES.

The image cuts to...

SECURITY CAM
12ᵗʰ FLR. STAIRWELL
We hear movement from below and above, however the immediate vicinity is free of zombies. Bits of tattered clothing on the floor. Footprints in blood. Bloody handprints smeared along the walls. The stairwell door hangs open. We see a few feet into the west hallway, enough to see the overturned armoire lying on its back.

Raven calls out to the zombies in the hallway.

253

Raven (off-camera): HEY! WHAT'RE YOU DOING?! I SAID I WAS OVER HERE! COME ON! COME AND GET ME YOU UGLY BASTARDS!

Raven repeats the taunt until we see several pairs of legs stagger into view. The zombies push through the doorway and move with retarded zeal toward the camera mounted high in the corner of the stairwell wall. The crowd quickly grows. Dozens more shambling corpses travel up from the lower floors and down from the floors above. Space on the landing becomes scarce, but they are undeterred. The undulating, pulsating mass of living carrion continues to grow. Those at the back are shoved down the stairs and over the railing.

The image cuts to…

SECURITY CAM
13th FLR. STAIRWELL
The stairwell is in a similar state to the 12th floor. There are zombies here, but they are fairly spread out and heading down toward the sound of Raven's voice.

Raven (off-camera): NO DUMMIES! I'M UP HERE! COME ON! COME AND GET ME!

The zombies stop in unison, and turn their heads toward the camera. Their bodies follow. Raven repeats the taunt until the stairs and landing are crowded with zombies. A silent pause and then…We hear Raven's birthday clip pour from the speakers once again.

Raven (off-camera): Okay Dave! Go! Now!

The image cuts to…

HELMET CAM 1 (DAVE'S POV)
Dave moves quietly down the north hallway wielding a torch fashioned from a coffee-table leg in one hand and the cell phone in the other. Larry is a few steps behind him, an unlit Molotov cocktail fashioned from wine bottles in each hand. They hurry toward the elevators and stop just before the

254

intersection of the north and west hallways. Dave glides over to the wall and peeks around the corner at the stairwell doorway. Larry comes up behind him and waits for the "all clear."

The 12th floor stairwell is overrun with zombies flowing upward toward the jubilant voices coming from the surveillance camera mounted high on the 13th floor landing.

Dave sprints up to the door and starts to close it. This attracts the attention of the zombies passing by the doorway at that exact moment. They change direction and glare at him. Heightened aggression enlivens their affected bodies. It causes a domino affect that reaches up and down the stairs. Within seconds every zombie in sight is aware of Dave standing there.

He thrusts the torch at them as they move to attack. They recoil in unison, pushing backward, away from the cackling flames. They fall into each other as Dave moves forward, waving the torch back and forth. Some topple over the railing.

Dave turns and runs out of the stairwell. Larry runs up to meet him and holds the bottles out to Dave, who lights the cloth dangling from the tips and yells…

Dave: GO!

Larry hurls the bottles at the horde of confused zombies, one after the other. They burst against their sodden bodies and engulf several of them in flames. The zombies whip and thrash. The pitch and intensity of their indecipherable vocal mutterings becomes heightened.

Dave slams the stairwell door. Larry joins him and together they lift the armoire and push it up against the door. We hear the zombie's intensified groans on the other side.

Dave (to Larry, breathing heavily): Okay! You hold the elevator! I'll get the others!

Larry runs up to Elevator B and presses the "Up," button

several times in rapid succession.

Dave hurries down the hall toward Apartment 1205. We hear the elevator ding behind him.

Dave (to group): EVERYBODY OUT INTO THE HALL! NOW!

The door opens and people run screaming from inside. The children are shielded by a barrier of adults led by the matronly woman. Linked by the hands, they form a human chain.

Dave runs up next to Martin as he guides the armed men to break the window at the end of the hall. Down the hall, the zombies begin pounding on the stairwell door. Larry is standing half-inside Elevator B, holding the door open with his body.

Larry (to Dave): Hurry up!

The armed men hit the window until it breaks. It takes longer than expected. Afterward, Dave runs up to the broken window and leans out. We see that the group must clear a five-foot deck that separates the building from the calm, dirty waters of the Delaware River.

He leans back in and turns to the group.

Dave (to group): You're gonna need to take a running start to clear the deck!

Many, in the group, are frightened to tears by the possibility of falling to their deaths.

Dave: Let's go, people! I want all of the capable men to take a child!

The group hesitates.

Dave: GO! GO! GO!

The clean-cut man runs over and scoops up a 10-year-old

boy in his arms. Holding the 10-year-old against his chest, the boy's legs wrapped around the man's ribs, he backs halfway down the hall, settles into an upright runner's stance, and takes off running. The boy cries out and buries his face in the man's shoulder. The Clean-cut man lets out a primal holler as he leaps from the window with the child in his arms. A few of the women scream.

People run up to the window and look out.

The pounding on the stairwell door intensifies. It sounds like the zombies are making progress.

Larry (to Dave): COME ON, DAVE! WE GOTTA GO!

The people looking out of the window cheer seconds later.

People (various): They made it!

Martin hurries over to Dave as a second man scoops up a child and prepares to jump.

Martin (to Dave): Just go! I got this!

Dave hesitates, and then he gives Martin an affectionate pat on the shoulder and runs toward Elevator B. Larry stands halfway inside the elevator waving Dave forward. The zombies finally force the stairwell door open. Several badly burned arms reach into the hallway. The armoire falls over just as Dave runs into the elevator. Larry darts inside after him and rapidly presses the button for the 31ˢᵗ Floor.

We can hear the zombies lurch and crawl toward the elevator as the doors begin to close. Dave yells out to the remaining group down the hall as the next person prepares to jump. We see Martin working to move things along.

Dave (to group): Hurry! They're coming!

The elevator doors close. The chaos in the 12ᵗʰ Floor Hallway North and West is replaced by PUTTIN' ON THE RITZ, by

257

Taco wafting from a speaker in the ceiling of the elevator. The wailing alarm provides background noise.

Dave and Larry stand with their backs against the rear wall. Dave is breathing heavily. Suddenly, the pleasant female voice interrupts the song.

Pleasant Female Voice: STERILIZATION PROTOCOL HAS BEEN ACTIVATED. YOU HAVE FIVE MINUTES TO EVACUATE THE PREMISES BEFORE SPRAYING COMMENCES.

Larry (re: announcement): Five minutes?! Shit!

Dave: We'll make it!

Dave pulls the cell phone from his hip pocket and holds it up to his ear.

Dave (into phone): Raven. You there?

Raven (off-camera): I'm here, Dave. Maria, Alicia, and the kids are waiting for you.

Dave: Good. We're on our way up. Stay on the line. Okay?

Raven: Okay.

Dave slides the phone back into his pocket and lifts the M16 over his shoulder. Holding the gun in front of him, he removes the magazine, checks it (it's nearly empty), and then pops it back in.

Larry stares straight ahead, his body swollen with anticipation, chest heaving. The look in his eyes says, "Bring it on! I'm ready for anything!"

Dave (to Larry): Listen. I know you're all amped up about saving your family, but you've gotta try not to let your emotions make your decisions for you when we get there. I know that's easier said than done, but—

WZMB

Larry (preoccupied):—I got it.

The elevator dings. Larry takes off running without warning when the doors slide open.

Dave: Larry! Wait!

But he keeps running toward an apartment near the back of hallway.

Larry: Maria! Paxton!

Dave (to Larry): Keep your voice down!

Larry: Maria! Paxton!

An apartment door swings open. Maria Del Rossi (Caucasian, 35) comes out running. She sprints toward her husband with tears in her eyes. Paxton Del Rossi (Caucasian, 15 and Tara Morrison (Caucasian, 16) run out holding hands. Alicia Morrison (Caucasian, 39) is right behind them.

Larry, Maria, and Paxton embrace in the middle of the hallway. Alicia and Tara stop beside them.

Alicia: Where's Ted?

Larry looks over at her but doesn't respond.

Dave: Let's go!

They hurry toward the elevators and run inside. Dave is the last one in. He presses the button marked "Penthouse Suites," and stands back. Larry and Maria embrace again as the elevator doors close and the elevator jerks, and then slowly ascends. PUTTIN' ON THE RITZ by Taco still pours from the overhead.

Alicia (to Dave & Larry): Where is Ted?!

They are hesitant to tell her. Alicia jumps in Dave's face.

259

Alicia: Where is my husband, Goddammit?!

Dave (hesitant): He didn't make it.

Tara Morrison slides down the wall in tears.

Alicia: Whaddayou mean, he didn't make it?! Where is he?! Where's Ted?!

No response.

Dave: I'm sorry, Alicia, but—

The elevator dings. The doors slide open. Dave shoves Alicia away and swings his gun around toward the opening doors.

Zombies standing in awkward poses stare back at them from the hallway, their attentions suddenly diverted by the elevator's dinging arrival. Over the zombie's shoulders, we can see the studio sign above a door near the back of the hallway. For a few tense seconds, the zombies are locked in a stand-off with Dave and the others. The lead zombies move to approach.

Dave (to group): GET BEHIND ME!

Dave lowers his aim and opens fire on the zombies' legs. They fall hard and sloppy as the bullets tear into their brittle appendages. This, however, does nothing to stop their determination as they continue to move forward on their stomachs.

Dave: RUN OVER THEM! GO FOR THE STUDIO! GO! GO! GO!

The group runs screaming from the elevator. They step and jump over the reaching zombies.

Dave yells at the phone in his pocket as he runs from the elevator.

Dave: RAVEN! COME ON!

The group runs toward the studio…Tara stops running and casts a worried expression at the elevators.

Tara: MOM! NO!

Dave looks back and sees…Alicia Morrison is still inside the elevator. She pushes a button and waits for the doors to close.

Dave: ALICIA! WHAT THE HELL ARE YOU—

The elevator doors close before he can finish. At that same moment, the stairwell door flies open. More zombies enter the hallway and give chase. They trip over the zombies crawling on the floor. They clumsily regain their footing and continue after the group.

Dave takes off running toward the studio. We see Raven standing in the doorway beneath the studio sign. Larry stands next to her. Maria and Paxton run up to them and disappear inside. Frozen in shock, Tara just stands there, in the middle of the hallway, as the zombies approach.

Larry: TARA! RUN!

Dave reaches Tara just as a crawling zombie grabs her ankle. He wraps his arm around her tiny waist and lifts her off the ground, snatching her ankle away from the zombie. She flies into a panic and fights against Dave's embrace.

Dave: Stop it! Tara! We don't have time for—

Larry runs toward them…Using all of his strength, Dave tosses Tara in Larry's direction. She lands five feet away. The impact knocks her dizzy. Larry runs up to Tara and drags her, by the arm, toward the studio.

Dave turns and immediately starts firing at the putrefied faces that surround him, as they reach and claw at his legs and torso, and lunge at him with mouths opened wide. Some are dispatched by headshots while others are simply knocked backward.

Dave (to group): THE WINDOW!

Pleasant Female Voice: STERILIZATION PROTOCOL HAS BEEN ACTIVATED. YOU HAVE ONE MINUTE TO EVACUATE THE PREMISES BEFORE SPRAYING COMMENCES.

Dave's gun clicks empty. Without missing a beat, he turns it over and uses it as a bludgeon. He backs away swinging.

Larry takes a golf club from one of the men in the group. Together, they run up to the window at the back of the hall and start hitting it with their golf clubs until it shatters.

As Dave continues to swing his gun…

Dave (to group): HURRY! I'LL BE RIGHT BEHIND YOU!

Tara is standing in the studio doorway with others in the group.

Tara: I'M NOT LEAVING WITHOUT MOM?!

Larry grabs her by the arm and tries to pull her toward the window, but she resists.
As Dave continues to swing the gun, his arms growing tired…

Dave (to Larry): JUST GO! I'LL DEAL WITH HER!

Paxton Del Rossi is the first to jump, followed by his mother, Maria. Larry waits by the window, watching to see if they made it. Raven jumps next. Larry watches her descent, from the window. Afterward, he runs over to help Dave.

Dave (to Larry): I SAID, GO! I CAN HANDLE THIS!

But Larry ignores him and starts swinging his golf club at the zombie's heads.

The elevator dings. The zombies freeze and turn toward the sound. Dave uses the distraction to gain some distance from the undead horde, Larry moving in tandem. They watch the elevator doors slide open...

We can see through the doors, that there is movement inside. It's Martin Stone. He is struggling with a charred zombie attached, by the mouth, to his forearm. Behind him, Alicia Morrison sits slumped against the back wall of the elevator, dead. Blood drains from a large bite taken out of her neck.

Over by the window, Tara cries out at the sight of her mother's lifeless body...

Tara: *NOOOO!*

...and collapses to her knees

Larry: *THIS WAY, MARTIN!*

Martin stumbles out of the elevator with the zombie attached. More zombies move toward him. The others turn their attention back to Dave and Larry, who are not where they stood only seconds ago. The dimwitted things are momentarily confused by this until they look up and find the two men standing ten feet away.

Martin manages to shove the charred zombie away, but more are on him faster than he can react.

Larry (to Dave): *WE HAVE TO HELP HIM!*

Pleasant Female Voice: *STERILIZATION PROTOCOL HAS BEEN ACTIVATED. YOU HAVE 10 SECONDS TO EVACUATE THE PREMISES BEFORE SPRAYING COMMENCES. 10...9...8...*

Dave: *I got 'em! You get her outta here!*

Larry nods and hurries over to Tara. He grabs her by the shoulders and attempts to lift her, but she goes limp in his grasp.

Pleasant Female Voice: *7...6...5...*

Andre Duza

Dave uses the butt of his M16 to beat a path to Martin, who is bitten several more times before Dave can reach him.

We see the elevator doors slide together in the background, Alicia Morrison slumped against the back wall, dead. Her eyes fly open seconds before the doors meet.

Martin is doubled over, dizzy, nearly unconscious, from loss of blood, and tired from fighting with the zombies. Dave tries to move him, but Martin is too weak to reciprocate.

Dave: I need you to dig deep, Martin! Ignore the pain!

Martin: It's over. I'm already dead.

Pleasant Female Voice: 5…4…3…

Dave looks up at the sprinklers, and then over at Larry, who is having similar trouble with Tara.

Dave (to Larry): GET UP AGAINST THE APARTMENT DOORS AND MAKE YOURSELF AS FLAT AS POSSIBLE!

Pleasant Female Voice: 2…1…STERILIZATION PROTOCOL COMMENCING.

Dave grabs Martin by the collar and pulls him over to one of the doors. He pushes his back against it, and runs over to the door across the hall and does the same.

Liquid hisses from the sprinklers. Smoke instantly rises from everything it touches; the walls, the floor, the zombies, both dead and undead.

Larry is still trying to coax Tara into one of the doorways when the toxic liquid rains down on him, smoke rising on contact. He cries out in pain and throws his arms up over his head. He does a frantic dance and then runs up to the nearest door and presses his back against it.

Tara screams and dances around in a similar frantic style as the acid burns her arms and scalp. She runs over to the door next to Larry, who slides to the side to make room for her.

The zombies react with fractured wonderment to the acid as it begins to melt their skin.

The rising smoke settles into a fog that blankets the entire hallway. Blinded by the fog, and by their melting skin, the remaining zombies wander and crawl searching for Dave, and Martin, and staggering toward the sound of Tara's crying. Larry clamps his hand over her mouth to no avail.

Though they are spared the brunt of it's sizzling touch, Dave, Martin, Larry, and Tara aren't completely safe, as the toxic rain dampens their clothed legs and feet and begin to eat through the fabric.

Dave: WE'RE DEAD IF WE STAY HERE! WE'VE GOTTA MAKE A BREAK FOR THE WINDOW! LARRY! YOU AND TARA FIRST!

The zombies hone in on Dave's voice, but they are still hampered by the fog, and by their melting flesh.

Dave watches as Larry says a few words to Tara. He takes her by the hand and together, they push off of the door and thrust forward. Larry groans at the acid's sizzling, scalding touch. Tara screams. Smoke rises from their shoulders and heads as they run for the window and jump out holding hands. A few zombies follow them out.

Dave begans to cough from the toxic fumes. He looks over at Martin who is coughing as well. We can barely see him through the smoke. Weakened, and tired from the loss of blood, Martin is having trouble standing. Smoke rises from his arms, shoulders, and feet as he leans, drunkenly forward, threatening to fall.

Dave: MARTIN!

But Martin is too woozy.

Dave: MARTIN!

Martin looks up and squints to see through the stinging fog.

*Dave: WE HAVE TO GO NOW! ON THREE! OKAY?! ONE…
TWO…THREE!*

*Dave explodes forward with his arm held over his head.
Grunting at the pain, he sprints over to Martin, who has
barely moved, and drags him toward the window. The frame
shakes and jumps, but we can still see the window rapidly
approaching. They reach the window and jump out.*

*As Dave falls…We can see and hear people in the water
below. We can also see that a few of the jumpers from the
12th floor weren't able to clear the walkway. Alex Mull is one of
them. His body lay broken on the walkway. The voices below
become louder as we rapidly descend. We are just about to
hit the water.*

STATIC…..

THE MARTIN STONE SHOW

TUESDAY, JUNE 12ND, 2015
The crackle of a live microphone...

FADE IN...

Mount Weather
Emergency Operations Facility
Bluemont, Virginia

Raven Tremble and Larry Del Rossi are seated at an L-shaped console in a military radio station. The minimalist décor consists of the Homeland Security Seal and a framed photo of President Barack Obama.

Raven Tremble: Good morning everyone and welcome to the Martin Stone Show. Why are we still calling ourselves the Martin Stone Show? Because that's what Martin would have wanted.

Larry: We need to come up with some theme music for you.

Raven: I don't want to go that far. You know how hard it was for me to agree to do this in the first place. I just feel...

Raven chokes up.

Larry: I know. I feel the same way. But, like you said...it's what he would've wanted. It's what Ted would've wanted, too.

Raven (endearing, between sobs): I can just hear them both making fun of me for all my crying on air.

Larry: I think they'd be touched.

Raven clears her throat and takes a deep breath.

Raven: Okay...In keeping with our recent theme of "The

more things change, the more they stay the same..." I'd like to apologize for our abrupt departure yesterday, which we're being told was due to yet another power outage here at the compound.

Larry: They're saying that we may have lost everything since we started back up.

Raven sighs, disappointed.

Raven: Well...yesterday was the last time I'm reliving the story of how we got here, so if you missed it—

Larry: It's not like there's anyone listening. Not outside the compound anyway...

Raven: You sound like Martin.

Larry: Yeah...But it's even truer now than before. We haven't had one call from outside the compound in the three weeks we've been on the air here.

Dead air.

Larry: You know, you never actually finished the story.

Raven: Where'd I stop?

Larry: We had just jumped out the window into the Delaware.

Dead air.

Larry: You okay?

Raven (welling up): I will be in a minute...(pause) You know, I was actually relieved when we were cut off.

Larry: Yeah...you were pretty choked up. We both were.

Raven: And I just said about all my crying on air. (pause) I don't know if I can go back to that place again, mentally.

Larry: I could run a few of the "Day in the life of…" interviews with base personnel?

Raven: No. Let's save that for later. I'll just do the abridged version.

Larry: Up to you.

Raven: Okay. So…Only nine of us survived the jump into the Delaware River. Some weren't able to reach the water, some drowned, and some…(pause) They started shooting at us from the compound. That's when they got Dave, and a few others. One can only assume that they thought we were infected. They would've gotten us all, but then they just stopped firing. Of course, we know now that, at that very moment, the shit had just hit the fan in the Regatta Tower, thanks to another one of Mother Margaret's decoys.

Larry: He was posing as security officer. They say he released some kind of toxic chemical in the ventilation system. The people, who survived that, then had an infestation on their hands. I guess the guy was supposed to do it in conjunction with Margo's flip-out in the ballroom, but somehow he got interrupted.

Raven: I'm ashamed to say that I felt a moment of satisfaction when I first heard that.

Larry: Me, too. For more than a moment…How could you not after what happened?

Raven: But it wasn't the residents' fault. They were duped just like we were. There were families in there, with children.

Raven makes an exasperated sound…

Raven: See what I mean about reliving this shit!

Dead air.

Larry: Want me to finish?

Raven: No. I can do it. (pause) After all that, we drifted for a few hours on a piece wood that had broken loose from one of the docks on the Philly waterfront. Funny, that I don't remember any of that part. I must've been in shock.

Larry: I remember. And, you were. You were like, in a waking coma or something, just staring off into space with this blank look. You wouldn't respond to anyone. I mean, you wouldn't even look at us.

Raven: I don't remember anything until Craig and his crew from City Hall found us. You remember Craig. After being turned away from the Brand Compound, he made his way back to City Hall. They had been listening to that last broadcast, and tracked us as we drifted down the Delaware. They fished us out just outside of Dover. (pause) I was still pretty out-of-it, at that point, so I don't know who's idea it was to make our way here.

Larry: It was pretty much a group decision. We knew it was unlikely that they'd let us in without some kind of incentive, so, a couple of the guys went back to the Brand Compound a few days later to retrieve Alex Mull's body. They said that the entire place was overrun with deadfucks. We were lucky to have made it out when we did.

Raven: If you've been listening, over the past three weeks, then you know that Dr. Hammond is here as well, along with a small group who survived the attack on his compound. I guess he's still pursuing his chip implant idea, but the main focus has been on developing a vaccine from Alex's DNA.

Larry: They're saying that they need more donors who share his peculiar immunity. They gave up hope of finding his mother.

Raven: And now it's up to us to help find those donors. Not an easy task, one would think.

Larry: There's gotta be others out there like Alex and his mom.

Raven: I'm sure there are. At least there *were*. Just because you can survive a bite doesn't mean a bullet or a knife or a million other things couldn't kill you.

Larry: You can't think like that, though. What would Martin say?

Raven: I *knooow*. 'Positive thinking, Raven.' (pause) Regarding Martin; we never found his body after he jumped. We initially thought that he hadn't cleared the walkway, but there was no sign of his body there, either. The assumption is that he was knocked unconscious by the fall and simply drowned. But there's no way to be sure.

Dead air.

Raven: I guess I can say that I finally got my closest call.

Larry: Martin would be proud.

Raven: He would be. Wouldn't he?

Dead air.

Larry: We're getting a call from security.

Raven: Put it through...(pause) Hey, Dave.

Caller: Dave from Security

Dave: Hey guys...

Larry: Hey Dave. How're you feeling?

Dave: Still not 100 percent. But almost...The docs are saying that I should have full use of my right arm again. They were firing on us with a minigun back at the Brand. I'm lucky to have an arm and shoulder left.

Raven: Happy to hear it, Dave. It wouldn't be the same without you around.

Larry: Here. Here. So, how's the new gig?

Dave: *I'm learning that us 'civilian' security guys don't get as many 'perks' as the military crew, but other than that it's pretty much the same as before.*

Raven: I was saying earlier about how 'the more things change, the more they stay the same.'

Dave: *How bout that…So, listen. Did you get the video clip yet, Larry?*

Larry: What clip?

Dave: *I just spoke to the guys in Communications. They said they sent it to you 10-minutes ago.*

Larry: Lemme check.

Raven: What video, Dave?

Dave: *You have to see it to believe it.*

Larry: Here it is. (to Dave): The one labeled Mother Margaret?

Dave: *That's it.*

Raven: Really? I'd rather not listen to that murderous bitch spout her—

Dave: *You'll want to see this, Raven. Trust me.*

Dead air.

Raven: Okay, Larry. Play the video.

Dave: *I'm on duty right now, so I can't talk. I just wanted to make sure you guys saw the video.*

Larry: Okay, Dave. Talk to you later.

Raven: See ya.

Dialtone

End Call

VIDEO
An older black woman with a long face that eschews warmth for authority, eyes that radiate lunatic devotion, and hair resembling a ceremonial headdress, sits behind a desk in a non-descript room, facing the camera. She is Mother Margaret aka Maggie from Lancaster. We get the impression that all of her speeches are made from this room, at this very desk.

Margaret: There is still more work to do, my children. As long as there are sinners out there defying the Lord's plan there will be work to be done. They'll call us murderers, terrorists. But I ask you; who are the ones prolonging this life of pain and misery and death that waits for us when we open our eyes every morning? THEY ARE! Who are the ones keeping us from the paradise that is HIS holy kingdom? THEY ARE! Who are the ones—

A gunshot rings out. Margaret's head explodes into several pieces. The force of the blast shoves her body right out of the frame.

Raven gasps.

Larry: Holy Shit! What just happened?!

VIDEO (CONT'D)
The desktop is covered with blood. A few specks dot the lens of the camera and run down, slightly obstructing our view. We hear someone sobbing off-camera. The sobbing grows louder until a thin man with bad posture steps into the frame. Although we can only see him from his shoulders to his waist, we assume from his clothing and posture, that he is an older man. The old man stands there, sobbing. A familiar voice, rife with emotion…

273

ILoveMyWife *(trembling, between sobs): I love my wife. I love her so. Please forgive me for what I've done, but she wouldn't listen to reason.*

The old man starts to cry uncontrollably. We catch a quick glimpse of his profile as he crouches down and out of the frame. He looks like a typical grandfather; white hair against leathery, chocolate skin folded into noble creases. We can still hear his voice as he crouches over his wife's corpse.

ILoveMyWife *(crying): I love my wife. I love her. I love my wife.*

The screen goes black.

END VIDEO

Raven and Larry are rendered speechless by the clip. The phone rings as they sit there wallowing in "what the fuck." It rings several times before the sound reaches either of them.

Larry (re: call): Oh shit! This is coming from outside the compound!

Raven (excited): Put it through. (pause): Hello caller, you're on the air.

Caller: ?????????

The call is filled with static. A male voice breaks through. We can't decipher what he's saying through the static. But then…A few seconds of clarity.

Caller: Raven! It's Martin!

ANDRE DUZA is an actor, stuntman, and a leading member of the Bizarro movement in contemporary literary fiction. His writing has been described as horrific, bizarre, smart, funny, and fast-paced, with lush, finely-detailed prose. He is fond of collaborating with artists to create macabre illustrations for his books.

Andre's novels include DEAD BITCH ARMY, JESUS FREAKS, NECRO SEX MACHINE, TECHNICOLOR TERRORISTS and his graphic novel, HOLLOW-EYED MARY. He is the co-author of SON OF A BITCH co-written with Wrath James White, and the comic book OUTER LIGHT, co-written with television writer/producer Morgan Gendel.

Andre has also contributed to such collections and anthologies as BOOK OF LISTS: HORROR, THE BIZARRO STARTER KIT, UNDEAD, UNDEAD: FLESH FEAST, and THE MAGAZINE OF BIZARRO FICTION.

Andre is also a Certified Fitness Trainer and a Kung Fu Instructor. He lives in Philadelphia with his wife and four children.

deadite press

"Header" Edward Lee - In the dark backwoods, where law enforcement doesn't dare tread, there exists a special type of revenge. Something so awful that it is only whispered about. Something so terrible that few believe it is real. Stewart Cummings is a government agent whose life is going to Hell. His wife is ill and to pay for her medication he turns to bootlegging. But things will get much worse when bodies begin showing up in his sleepy small town. Victims of an act known only as "a Header."

"Red Sky" Nate Southard - When a bank job goes horrifically wrong, career criminal Danny Black leads his crew from El Paso into the deserts of New Mexico in a desperate bid for escape. Danny soon finds himself with no choice but to hole up in an abandoned factory, the former home of Red Sky Manufacturing. Danny and his crew aren't the only living things in Red Sky, though. Something waits in the abandoned factory's shadows, something horrible and violent. Something hungry. And when the sun drops, it will feast.

"Zombies and Shit" Carlton Mellick III - Twenty people wake to find themselves in a boarded-up building in the middle of the zombie wasteland. They soon discover they have been chosen as contestants on a popular reality show called Zombie Survival. Each contestant is given a backpack of supplies and a unique weapon. Their goal: be the first to make it through the zombie-plagued city to the pick-up zone alive. But because there's only one seat available on the helicopter, the contestants not only have to fight against the hordes of the living dead, they must also fight each other.

"Muerte Con Carne" Shane McKenzie - Human flesh tacos, hardcore wrestling, and angry cannibal Mexicans, Welcome to the Border! Felix and Marta came to Mexico to film a documentary on illegal immigration. When Marta suddenly goes missing, Felix must find his lost love in the small border town. A dangerous place housing corrupt cops, borderline maniacs, and something much more worse than drug gangs, something to do with a strange Mexican food cart...

www.ingramcontent.com/pod-product-compliance
Lightning Source LLC
Chambersburg PA
CBHW051145030726
47504CB00004B/1053